Walter Besant

All in a garden fair

The simple Story of three boys and a girl - Vol. III

Walter Besant

All in a garden fair
The simple Story of three boys and a girl - Vol. III

ISBN/EAN: 9783337082659

Printed in Europe, USA, Canada, Australia, Japan

Cover: Foto ©Andreas Hilbeck / pixelio.de

More available books at **www.hansebooks.com**

ALL IN A GARDEN FAIR

The Simple Story of Three Boys and a Girl

BY

WALTER BESANT

AUTHOR OF 'ALL SORTS AND CONDITIONS OF MEN' 'THE REVOLT OF MAN'
'THE CAPTAINS' ROOM' ETC.

IN THREE VOLUMES

VOL. III.

London

CHATTO & WINDUS, PICCADILLY

1883

CONTENTS

OF

THE THIRD VOLUME.

PART III.—THE REWARD OF THE MAN.

THE REWARD OF THE MAN

CHAPTER I.

A WOMAN'S REASONS.

I WISH to tell, in my own words, how I chose between the three men who had done me the greatest honour that a man can confer upon a woman—the offer of his love and service. It is, I know, just as true that no greater honour can happen to a man than the confidence and love of a woman. And yet—to me—because I am a woman, I suppose, it does not seem quite so great a thing. My father, in the gallant and old-fashioned way with which he always talks of women, reminding one of old books, powdered wigs, patches, and hoop petticoats, says, that the highest distinction and glory for a man is to have it recorded that he was loved by many women. I suppose, however, that any

man would be more than contented with the
love of one, if he loved her in return.

At the age of eighteen I was told by these
three young men that they were in love with
me. I was myself too young at the time to
comprehend all that this meant. Perhaps, too,
my lovers were themselves too young and too
ignorant of the world to understand the importance of what they offered. If my mother
had been living she would have taught me that
these young men proposed to give me nothing
less than their whole lives, with the fruits of all
the work they would ever do. Can any man
offer more? But my father did not teach me
this: he spoke a little about the favour of my
smiles and the great happiness which awaited
the one whom I should accept—things which, I
dare say, turned my head—and then he said no
more about the matter, but carefully avoided it,
until the time was close at hand, when the
decision had to be made. I do not say that I
never thought about it: there was not a single
day, to tell the truth, in which I did not have

it on my mind. But always, until near the
end, as of a thing far off, which need not disturb
my mind.

No one must think that I made, consciously
at least, any difference between two of the boys.
As for the third, I knew very well, even at the
beginning, what answer I should have for him.
But I speak of the two in whose delightful
society I had spent always, in all seasons and
in all weathers, some part of every day. Yes;
every day; for on half-holidays, if it was fine,
we walked or ran in the Forest; and if it was
wet they came to the Cottage and we read or
played; and in the evenings they came to talk
French; and on Sunday afternoons they came
to talk or to walk. Every day I saw them;
they were my brothers; I could not love one
more or one less; both were kind and thoughtful; both were as dear to me as one human
soul can be to another. I have made my decision, now, and made one contented, I hope, for
life—yea, and for the after-life as well, through
all the ages, when we shall together, and side

by side, grow more and more in the spiritual life. Yet, still, when I think of the other my heart goes out to him, and I wish that he, too, were with us in the house, as in the old times. I could never refrain or cease from loving both these boys.

Their own homes were not happy. Their parents were dreadfully poor. I do think that there is nothing worse for a boy than the continual pressure of grinding poverty. I have seen Will clench his hands as he spoke of the shifts to which he was put in order to make a decent appearance **at** school. I have seen Allen weep with bitterness for the same cause. Allen, at least, had the satisfaction of knowing that his own poverty was due to no fault of his father, unless it be a fault to trust an old friend, your partner. Poor Will had not that consolation; he knew that his father had ruined himself and thrown away a fortune in the pursuit of mad-brained schemes; it was difficult for him, remembering his father's folly, to keep the fifth commandment in spirit as well as in letter.

We, to be sure, were poor enough, but then we had the French thrift, and so we seemed richer. At all events, we lived contented with quite simple things, and did not repine at what we could not prevent. Mr. Massey, on the other hand, continually lamented the ill-fortune which had robbed him of the vast wealth he looked to make, grumbled daily over the plainness of his food, and spent his evenings in examining the papers relating to each scheme and its failure. Allen's mother, for her part, could never recover from the shock of her husband's dreadful death, brooded over his calamities, and lost no opportunity of exhorting her son to wipe out the disgrace of his father's misfortunes by making money for himself. Poor woman! She was brought up to consider poverty a sin, and failure as the greatest offence against her fellow-creatures and himself that a man can commit. So poor Allen's boyhood was made wretched, save for the happiness which he enjoyed with my father and myself. And so, in this way, from the very first, the boy was led to conceive a deadly hatred of the City and all that belongs to money and money making.

Never any boy, I should think, was so fond of books as Allen. He read all that he could lay his hands upon, in French and English. When he first went into the City he used to save half, out of the shilling which was meant for dinner, in order to buy books. He read all that we had, all he could borrow from everybody in the village; though I suspected nothing at the time, it seems to me now to have been quite certain from the beginning that he must become a man of letters, and I can never sufficiently thank my father for finding this out and for training him in literature and style, and afterwards in Art, and in the knowledge of actual life, which fitted him for the work he was to do. Of course I knew very well that Allen could never, never take up the active political life of which my father dreamed.

When first he read us his verses I thought that I had never heard anything so bad as they were. But my father saw promise, and encouraged him and led him on step by step to love letters and books more and more. He waited till he was past twenty-one before he could follow the profession of letters, and then he tore himself from the City and plunged into the new world of print and ink with a heart full of courage.

When he refused the appointment in China and told his mother of his resolution, she first implored him to accept the post and then upbraided him, and when she could not alter his purpose she came to my father and begged him to use his influence. When he refused, and assured her that her son was taking the best step to insure his happiness and success, she flew into the most violent passion that I had ever seen. I would not repeat words used in wrath by an angry woman. My father listened without changing his countenance or losing his politeness, though she reproached him for his poverty, for his country, for his profession, for having led Allen away from the business of his life, and even for making him think of love when he ought to have been thinking of money, and for throwing his penniless and designing daughter in the boy's way.

When she went away, with white cheeks and quivering lips, my father shuddered.

'Against the words of an angry woman,' he said, 'there is no reply but silence. Do not cry, Claire, my child. Play music for the peace of our souls. Poor woman! Yet she must have been beautiful once. It is only the happy woman who remains beautiful.'

A few days later I met her in the village; she begged to be forgiven, saying, humbly, that all her hopes had been for her boy to follow in the footsteps of his father, and by his own success to make that disgrace to be forgotten. I told her that, as for the anger, it was forgotten already; and as to the disgrace of which she spoke, that was long since forgotten and only the pity of it left, because everybody knew how good and honourable a man was her husband. She shook her head and said I was a girl and did not know all. Then I told her what we hoped of Allen, and how bright and clever he was, and what great prizes in reputation as well as in money await those who write beautiful things in prose and verse. But this she could not understand.

Allen did not come back to us for six months, but he wrote telling of the bad luck which his poems encountered everywhere, and the unanimous opinion of publishers about their merits. When, at last, he came, it was to tell us that he had actually got work of a humble kind, yet better than nothing.

And soon after this he told me of his new friends, to whom he owed all the success which he has since obtained. I was very curious about them. There was his friend, Mr. Lawrence Ouvry, who was so wise and knew everything, and especially everything about literature, whose father and mother and all his relations had been poets, editors, novelists. How strange to hear of such a family! And then there was Miss Gertrude Holt, the best and kindest of ladies. It seemed as if our boy was actually

on the road to success when he was invited to
'At Homes' crowded with literary people, and
it looked like real success when Isabel recited
his poems before them all. Then came his
first paper in the magazine, which gave him a
chance, and this was success! Yet still we were
not satisfied; it was not for papers of criticism
that Allen entered the profession of letters;
nor was it until his first tale appeared that we
knew for certain that he was in the right line at
last—the line for which his genius was fitted.

He was always the same Allen to me, yet
he changed—oh! how much he changed. We
lost our eager boy, ignorant of the world, full
of enthusiasms and rages, his large eyes aflame
with hope or indignation—he was gone. Gertrude—let me call her at once by her name—
and Isabel, between them, changed him. They
calmed him; they made him fitted for work by
praising some of his enthusiasms and cultivating
others; they introduced him into society; they
led him on, developed him, kept him from trying impossible things, and advised him wisely.

It was what most he wanted, the society of ladies who could advise him and give the kind of sympathy which helps a young man. Nothing could be greater than his gratitude. His letters were full of his friends. He was always making excuses to be with them ; he was always trying to do something for them ; and when he called upon me it was, after he had told me of his own affairs, to talk about Gertrude and Isabel.

'Claire,' he would say, 'we must make up a plot to bring them here. I want you to know them, you will like them as well as I do, and better, if that is possible. Of course, everybody falls in love with Gertrude at once, but you must know both of them.'

I promised I would do what I could to help him in bringing them to the Forest.

Isabel, I could understand, encouraged and pushed him on, while Gertrude kept him back. Now I knew that Gertrude was an old lady, and I always, until I saw her, thought that Isabel was old too, but not so old. This was, perhaps,

the reason—though I would fain think otherwise
—why I was not in the least jealous of either of
them.   It is true that I thought little about the
decision before me, but yet—when a man has
said that he is in love with you—to hear him
praise continually another girl might make any
woman jealous.

Isabel encouraged him to work, pointing
out how this man or that man, without half
his abilities, was pushing his way into notice.
Gertrude encouraged him to wait, urging him
to give nothing but his best, and letting him
understand that his work, as yet, was immature.
It was delightful to think that he was so carefully looked after.   When I heard that Isabel
recited his poems I ought to have known that
she was young ; a sense of incongruity came over
me as I read his letter—one would not like to
think of elderly ladies reciting ; yet actresses,
I suppose, like other women, become old.

As for Will, he, too, wrote to me once a
month—long and beautiful letters, telling me
everything that he thought I should like best

to hear and that would interest me : all about the strange people of China, and the colony of English, Germans, and Americans among whom he lived, so that I seemed to know them all. Then he told me—if this would interest me— what he read, and what his thoughts were upon all kinds of things—nothing, I am sure, improves a man more than to go away and be made to do responsible work by himself. And of the parties that went on, how he had learnt to dance and to ride, and of the dinners and picnics— why, what a life of pleasure and excitement he was leading compared with what he had left behind ! And he used to send me presents, such as silk, and things in carved wood of strange fragrance, and chests of choice tea, all with a chivalrous resolution not to say or do anything which might perchance prejudice Allen, which made Will keep praising him and prophesying greatness for him, as if he would rather—though I knew he never really wished—that I would accept Allen than himself. I thought a great deal of Will, almost as much as I did of Allen.

And oh ! it is so great a pleasure to think of a man as strong, self-reliant, and full of good principles. I pictured to myself the tall, handsome lad becoming a tall and handsome man, stronger than most, braver than any, honest as the day. It would be a cruel thing to wound that noble heart.

I am sorry to say that, when these two went away and Olinthus remained for awhile, he endeavoured to take advantage of his position and presumed to talk to me about abridging the period of waiting. This was ungenerous in him, and when he found that I thought so he desisted and presently went to London, where he took chambers and lived alone. I saw him very little after this for some time. His sisters did not, in those days, call upon me, and, I think, were greatly displeased that their brother's affections were bestowed ' beneath him.' To be sure I was only a teacher of French—and of everything else—in a girls' school. I had never thought of being called upon or recognised by the ladies in the village. In time one lives down even the sense of social inferiority. My father, for his part, never felt that he could possibly be considered as socially inferior to any one, especially in a village full of bankrupt bourgeois.

Presently we heard, to our great surprise, that Olinthus was making a great fortune. It seemed quite true. He actually became suddenly clever, he who had been always thought so stupid.

He even came himself to tell me so, puffing and swelling his cheeks like a turkey.

'It is really true, Claire,' he said. 'Where is your clever Allen? Starving in a garret. Where is Will Massey? Clerk in a silk house. Where am I? In West-End chambers. I've got a cab and a tiger; I drive into the City every day; I've got a club; I buy the best cigars and drink the best champagne. When I choose to say the word there is the best society in London open to me.'

'We are very glad to hear it,' I said.

'What has done this?' he asked grandly.

‘ Reading books ?   Riding on bicycles ?   Walking about the streets ?   Brains, Claire.   Brains. Remember that.’

I believe that when he visited his mother and sisters plainness of speech was used as regards the daughters of French masters, and he was given to understand that young men in his position should look higher—very much higher.   But he had always been a headstrong boy, and opposition only made him more obstinate.   Besides—yes—I am sure that Olinthus was always fond of me, after his fashion.

I did not quite know, then, how he was growing so rich.   I was told, but one does not easily understand these things, that it was by buying with nothing and selling for a great deal, or by buying what did not exist and selling what there was none of; which seems absurd. Perhaps it was by pretending to buy of one man and making somebody else believe he was selling ; and this, too, seems a strange way of making money.   However that may be, he was greatly envied, and Sir Charles, with tears in his eyes, prayed that he might live to see a failure which promised to be greater even than Mr. Colliber's.

It was somewhat less than a year after the boys went away that our good fortune came to us.

I suppose it is ridiculous to confess the thing, but, in truth, we did not at first understand how such an enormous income could possibly be spent. I know by this time that the income is not large at all, compared with what English people generally call large; yet to us it was a great and splendid fortune, and our eyes were dazzled.

Remember that all we had in the world to live upon was the cottage, which was our own, and some thirty or forty pounds a year, which I believe was mine, and had come to me from my mother. Then my father received seventy five pounds a year from the school, and I had twenty-five. Altogether a hundred and forty pounds a year. We lived with the greatest simplicity. My father had no expensive tastes at all. Our garden provided us with fruit, vegetables, and flowers. I made my own dresses and trimmed my own hats. I should have made my own boots, too, if I had known how to get inside them in order to sew on the soles. It is dreadful to think so much about such things as boots; and I wore out an immense quantity.

Fancy, if you can, the change from a hundred and forty pounds a year, which means calculation by pence, to twelve hundred pounds a year, which means calculation by sovereigns!

The magnitude of the thing once over, we began to feel how, in a hundred different ways, we might expand our mode of living without changing the simplicity to which we were accustomed. We first resigned our work at the school—I am ashamed to think of the happiness with which I looked forward to doing no more work for money—then we moved into a larger house, a pretty house, too, with gables and a porch, and a great garden.

I found one room into which I moved all the dear old shabby furniture of my old room. And then we went up to London and saw all the sights which I had last seen in company with the boys; also, I was able, for the first time in my life, to buy music, books, ribbons, lace, and all the gloves and pretty things I desired. It is such a happiness to buy pretty things! I wished to publish Allen's verses for him, now that we were rich, but my father would not permit it. He would have Allen owe to himself the whole of his success, if he had any; and this my father, full of his own project, refused to consider possible. I think now that he was right. It was certainly better for Allen to acquire hardness by fighting and temporary defeat. And then all the ladies of the village, Lady Withycomb, Mrs. Massey—she was a very stately person, and always looked forward to the time when her son would find money enough to start some more of her husband's schemes again—Mrs. Gallaway, and the rest, called upon me. They came and made pretence as if I had only just come into residence, and were kind as to a stranger, and spoke of my father as an interesting foreigner whom they should study with pleasure and advantage, and of whom they had just heard for the first time. When they went away they shook hands warmly, and said they hoped that they would be able to see a great deal of us, and that we would call often. It really was delightful! My father shrugged his shoulders and asked if we were really more virtuous to-day than we had been yesterday; and I laughed. Yet I was pleased. Whether people have small minds or not, one likes being recognised. They only treated me as they treated each other. No one called on Mrs. Skantlebury because her husband had made money in the retail way, but they all called on Mrs. Massey because her husband had failed in the wholesale way.

I was especially pleased with the behaviour of Olinthus's sisters. Before the arrival of the fortune they always got out of my way if they met me, to avoid speaking. As soon as the knowledge of our accession to wealth was established they all three called together, and were most friendly, and begged that I would consider their home my own—for the sake of dear Olinthus.

When we were fully established in our new house, and had received the calls of our neighbours, my father opened a subject of considerable importance. He began one morning by remarking that in France, even in the provincial towns, ladies have their evenings, and there is society. Again, that in some parts of London, as he was credibly informed, there were clubs or societies for singing, and young people danced, and the evening was not considered as a dull three hours of preparation for a long night of bed.

'In this village, my daughter,' he said, 'I observe with regret'—he had got into the habit of speaking about himself as Sir Charles, and everybody else spoke about him, namely, as a new comer—'with great regret, that there is no society at all; no lady has an evening.

Claire, it is for you to reform this state of things.'

'What can I do?' I asked.

'You will, my child,' he said with solemnity, 'create a *salon*.'

I was to create a *salon*. Alas! where were the materials? My father left me to think over the idea. Of course, I thought about it. By this time I had heard of Gertrude's 'At Homes.' Could I not create a *salon* in the same manner? But then I should have to make my evenings pleasant, and we knew no interesting people at all.

'Can I'—it was after a sleepless night— 'can I be at home on Saturday evenings?'

'Nothing more easy,' said my father. 'In fact, you are always at home on that and on every other evening, except when we go to the pit—I beg your pardon, Claire — since our inheritance—to the dress-circle, of the theatre.'

'And could we get any one to come?'

'Nothing, again, more easy,' he replied, just

as if he had been in English society all his life.
' You will attract the elder people with a little
supper, and the younger '—he paused in order
to give point to the advice, but then he loves
an epigram so much—' with a little love.'

'The supper is easy; but who is to make
the love ? '

'That, my child, they will make for themselves.' And then he spread his hands, and
smiled as if he had said something happy.

These general maxims in which my father
delights are very well, but they do not help
much. For instance, how can the girls make
love if there are no young men? Now there
were no young men in the village at all, since
the boys went away.

Nevertheless, I thought it would be delightful to have an evening if people would come.
What could we do?

I remembered how Isabel recited Allen's
verses, and I made up a little plan for an
evening's amusement.

It was difficult, because, though everybody

came, they were awkward and not accustomed to be amused. You may very easily get quite out of the habit of being happy, if you like. I got some of the elder girls from the school, with Miss Billingsworth's permission, to act a little comedy, which the girls played with a great deal of spirit. This made everybody laugh ; I really do think that some of those poor girls had not laughed for years. Then we had some singing ; and then, though there were no young men, we cleared the room and danced, and Sir Charles said it reminded him of the famous Calico Ball he gave at the Mansion House in the year when he was Lord Mayor. Then there was a little supper, and claret-cup, and they all went away well pleased.

That was the beginning of my evenings, and in this way we introduced society into the village.

They only wanted somebody to start them. Once started we went on easily. Every week we invented something for the evening's enter-

tainment, and on every occasion we ended with
a dance.

Then my father's wise sentence proved true.
We did not find the love-making, which was
found by the girls for themselves. For they
brought young men from far-off places, such as
Chigwell, Loughton, and Buckhurst Hill. It
appeared that there are everywhere quantities,
really large numbers, of young men who are
always ardently desirous of a dance, and
respond with the greatest alacrity to the chance
of getting one every week, summer and winter.
Naturally, therefore, flirtations began, and
though the peace of the village vanished, the
anxieties and flutterings, the whisperings and
confidences, the anticipations of the evening,
and the pleasure of wearing one's best frock,
being in one's sweetest temper, and, better
still, living in that delightful sun-lit haze which
precedes an engagement—all these things together fully compensated. Besides, the peace
of the village had been only a monotonous
and sluggish calm, like the smooth surface

of a duck-pond, which the girls regretted not.

In this creation of a *salon*, in receiving and reading the letters from Will and Allen, in visits to London, where we saw all the best pieces at the theatre and all the pictures, and in reading and music, the weeks passed swiftly away. At the end of the first year we were in our new house, the richest people in the village; at the end of our second year Allen had already struck the vein by which he has won recognition, and Olinthus was at the height of his success. It was in the beginning of the third year that my father took me for the first time to France. It was a delightful time, if only the boys had been with us; but I could not at all feel as if I was French by birth. We stopped a day or two in Paris, and I saw the spot where the shop had stood which supplied the barricade with my father's poems. Oh, those unlucky poems! There had been the long period of the Second Empire since then, and another revolution; but my father folded his arms as he stood upon the sacred place, and was once more in imagination Philipon of the Barricades—Philipon, the Poet of Revolution. He is the kindest-hearted man in the world, and the most forgiving. Yet I am sure that at the moment the fierce desire of battle was upon him, and he felt that strange joy of the fight which we women read about but cannot understand.

Then we took the train and went to Orleans, and from Orleans to Tours, where we stayed, and whence we wandered about in the pleasant country of Touraine—why were the dear old provinces ever turned into departments? We saw Chambord and Chenonceux, Loches and Amboise, Chinon and Saumur, Azay le Rideau, and Blois. We went on to Poitiers and to Angoulême, where one could dream away a life on the terrace overlooking the sweet and sunny plains, and to La Rochelle, the strange old town with the stone arcades in the streets and the shields of the Huguenot gentlemen. We were three months on our holiday—the first I had ever had.   I learned, at least, to understand one reason why a Frenchman loves his country.

Then we returned, when the autumn colouring was on the Forest, and the sad, rainy English summer, which promises so much and gives so little, was over.

Allen had spent his summer at Richmond with Gertrude and Isabel, writing stories and poems, and getting daily better known; Will had done something, the nature of which I do not know, which greatly pleased his seniors; and Olinthus was simply dazzling. I forgot, because it is a little detail which really does not matter, and is not a part of the story, that several of the young men who came to my evenings made the mistake of falling in love with me, and I had the very disagreeable duty of advising them to think about it no longer. I dare say they are cured by this time; but one or two of them, I remember, gave me a great deal of trouble.

Then the autumn slowly passed away, and when Christmas came and the new year, there remained less than six months to the time when I must make my decision. It is the story of that six months which I have to tell.

CHAPTER II.

HIS FIRST BOOK.

ALLEN's first book of collected tales appeared in February of that year.

Nothing that a writer ever does seems to me quite to come up to his earliest and freshest work. · Yet one could see that his touch was becoming firmer, the grasp of his art stronger, and his powers more developed. As yet, he confined himself wisely to short studies. They were not sketches at all, but careful and finished pictures. Some of these stories were sad, some humorous, some satirical; but they were all, one felt, true. Like all true stories, they suggested things which were not in the pages. They reminded me of what Allen once said about the theatre.

' The actors on the stage, if you can forget their acting and see only the story, tell a hundred tales besides the one which they represent. The study of Mercutio is a tragedy in itself. The story of Tybalt is as touching as the story of Romeo. What of Romeo's first mistress? Do you not think that she, too, sometimes came to weep over the grave of the lover who had been faithless to her, but whom she loved still, remembering the days when he sat at her feet and played with her golden tresses? Even the nurse and the apothecary and Friar Lawrence, especially the apothecary, could tell their tale.'

And thus he sketched the story of the apothecary. He was a student, Allen said, of Salerno, the great school for medicine: he went from Salerno to Montpellier, in order to attend the lectures on anatomy of Rabelais, the great anatomist and physician: he knew Servetus, that other great physician, and had talked with him. He was a poet and an enthusiast. But he failed, somehow. It was probably through lack of common-sense, a thing which has caused many to lag behind or go out of the way: and because he was too often running after the shadow instead of picking up the substance; for instance, he used to read books on alchemy, and sought the Great Projection; he wrote poetry which nobody read; he dangled after patrons who neglected him and gave him nothing; finally, he became a lean and hungry seller of drugs and misanthropic. As for poisons, he would gladly have poisoned the whole of mankind, could he, by a potent draught, have made an end of all. He went on to sketch the end of that apothecary's career: how he hit upon a cosmetic which all the ladies of Verona rushed to buy; how he grew rich and sleek, forgot his old misanthropy, married the daughter of a wealthy merchant, burned his poetry, put his books on alchemy into the hands of the In-quisition, said nothing at all about that little transaction with Romeo, and, when he died, left money—to the disgust of his heirs—for the erection of the most beautiful tomb, all jasper, a miracle of marble, with a lovely little chapel, to be placed over the bodies of the unfortunate lovers. Thus, no one but Shakespeare knowing his history, he showed, in the end, his repentance. I always thought of this story when I read one of Allen's, because he had the art of finding materials for a human comedy where most people would see nothing at all but a squalid street with mean houses and cabbage-stalks. He was like a child who can play with two bits of stick and pretend everything. His work was a collection of all his stories. It was published in two volumes, first, though now you can get it much more cheaply in one. He sent me a copy, but I had read the contents already in the magazines. Yet I read them again.

Then Allen sent me the criticisms. How hard and unappreciative they seemed to me! but then I could read between the lines, and I saw Allen's soul in the book, and that he had put into it his noblest and best. Yet I believe they were really kind and helped the book greatly. One or two spoke slightingly of the new writer. I was indignant. The men who wrote such things were unworthy, I thought, of the name of critic.

Isabel, afterwards, told me all about the reviews and the reviewers. She knew the names of the writers, even the unsigned reviews. This one, she told me, was the work of a man born to be a critic; not an unkind or harsh critic, but a just man, though sometimes hard in his judgments. Another was the work of an unsympathetic and unimaginative writer, on whom the pearls of fancy were thrown away. Another was written by a well-known novelist, and this was the most generous of all. So it is pleasant to think that there is no envy among novelists. Another was written by a man who wrote a leading article every day of his life for a daily, and two every week for a weekly, and one article at least every month for a monthly, and one long paper every quarter for the *Quarterly,* and brought out a book or two every year, and was suspected of being a London correspondent to a colonial paper : and yet found time to read novels and to review them. What a wonderful thing is the world of letters ! Some day writers will insist on signing all their articles in newspapers and everywhere else. Then, at last, we shall see them take their right position in the world. As for the notices in half-a-dozen lines, Isabel told me that it was absurd to look at them, or to consider them, because at a guinea or two for a column, who can afford to read the half-dozen books with which they have to fill up that column ? Yet an injury may be done to a writer even in half-a-dozen lines.

'You are proud of him, then, Claire ?' said my father, as I stood with the book in my hands.

'Yes—but——'

'The drop of bitterness which is in every-thing. What is it, Claire ?'

'I should like the book better, if he had

not told us—if I thought that he loved his character.'

'The girl told him her story and went away, and he remembered her no more.'

'He makes us love her so much that we feel we ought to love her still.'

'There was an artist once,' said my father, 'who tortured a slave in order to paint the agony. Do you think he felt those pains himself?'

'No — but yet —— And he was a Wretch!'

'Many artists paint beautiful women. Do they love them all? My child, be reasonable. Our boy is an artist—only an artist,' he sighed, ' who might have been a Luther.'

Allen wrote so truthfully and so tenderly that we ought to have been satisfied. Yet— I suppose because my father had talked so much about it—it seemed to me a smaller thing to set forth the life of the people than to study it, and to learn what they want to make them happier. Yet it was a beautiful thing

that he had done. The volume, daintily
bound, stood before me in mute reproach.
When I opened it, the pages reproached
me still more. It was Allen himself who
seemed to say, ' Claire! did you believe that I
could do this—even when you encouraged me
most? Are you not proud of me? Did you
think your old playfellow would ever write so
well? If I move your heart and compel your
tears, and force you to love these puppets of
my brain as if they were living creatures—
more, because if they were living, you, with
your small imagination, would see only common
working girls and working men, and you
would not love them at all ;—if I have this
mastery, will you still look for more, and waste
regrets upon an idle dream ? ' It was un-
grateful: and yet the thought possessed me
that there was something nobler in my father's
dream. It is very good to write of men and
women truthfully, and with love and com-
passion ; but, perhaps, better to work for them.
One thinks more of the poor soldiers who rush

into the fight than of the piper who keeps up their spirits.

'I have not yet,' said Allen, 'sent my mother a copy. Gertrude is going to take one. Will you, too, dear Claire, be with my mother when Gertrude calls? I cannot tell you how much I want you to know Gertrude and to love her.'

The house occupied by Mrs. Engledew was one of the smallest in the village; a house of white boards with a porch covered over with honeysuckle and jessamine. There was a flower-garden in front, yet with few flowers. Outside, the house was clean and trim as becomes the house of a widow lady; within, its silence and sadness fell into one's heart. You wished to whisper—to laugh would have been wicked—the very furniture seemed to have caught the sadness of the poor woman, who had no hope left at all, since her son had left the City. I used to take her all the things that Allen wrote—but she read none of them. As for his papers on French literature, they might please some, she said, but she did not want to know about foreigners; and when the stories began and I tried to interest her in them, she said that there was quite enough misery in the world without inventing more; and as for making people laugh, Allen was not brought up to become a Tomfool at a fair, but to make money in a proper and becoming manner in the City. It was wonderful that a woman could be so fixed in her ideas.

I think that when she was young she must have been beautiful; one afternoon in summer when I called I found her sleeping in her chair —her head lay back and the reflection of the sunlight fell upon her cheeks from the open window. I stood looking at the face on which I had never seen sunshine before, and I understood how the thin cheek and wasted features might have looked when, four-and-twenty years before, she was a young a beautiful bride. Four-and-twenty years ago! and for three-and-twenty of them she had been a widow, with the dreadful recollection of a ruined husband, bidding her go home, kissing her for the last time and then . . . . then . . . . the suicide. And after that the long struggle with poverty, made tolerable only by her hopes—poor woman!—of the boy who would redeem the family honour.

I went to see her on the day of the visit, thinking I would prepare her mind. I told her how Allen's tales were now collected into a volume, which was so well received that it seemed as if his future was assured.

She heard me coldly. She seemed to take no kind of interest in the subject.

'As for the boy's future,' she said, 'that cannot be assured by writing books. I am glad to hear that he is not starving. It is not the life for which he was brought up, and I can never think of it without disappointment.'

'Oh!' I said; 'try to think of it with pride.'

'No. I cannot. I looked to see him winning good opinions in the City; he came of a business family; all his relations have always been in the City, none of them ever ran away to sea, or—or anything. Why should he want to be anything different? If he was in a line which leads to money I should not mind so much. But he is not.'

I told her, next, of the ladies who had been kind to Allen, and were coming to see her and bring her the book that very afternoon.

'They must come, I suppose, if they like,' she replied ungraciously, and then went on as if defending herself, 'I do not blame you, Claire; I blame nobody any more; not even your father, who encouraged Allen most. Because he is a foreigner, and cannot know the mischief he was doing when he filled the boy's head with nonsense.'

While we talked there was the sound of carriage wheels, and our visitors came. They were two ladies; one of them—I knew her at once—must be Gertrude; an old lady with white hair and the kindest face imaginable. With her was a young lady—who could the

young lady be?   Then I suddenly remembered
that Allen had never told me what Isabel was
like.   Could Isabel be young?   Could this be
Isabel?   It must be—it could be no other;
and instantly I felt the truth.   This beautiful
girl, with the indefinable *cachet* of London,
beautifully dressed, was the reader of Allen's
poems; she it was who rowed with him, walked
with him, talked with him, encouraged him;
of whom he spoke and thought continually.
Should I not be more than woman if a pang of
jealousy had not caught my heart and held it
still for a moment?

The elder lady—Gertrude—it was who
spoke :

'I am a friend of your son's, Mrs. Engledew '—the widow bowed stiffly—'I am a great
friend of his.   I love him as if he were my
own son.   Is that a sufficient excuse for my
calling upon you ? '

She held out her hand, which Mrs. Engledew took coldly.

'My son,' she said, 'has made many friends

in his new profession whom I do not know. Will you take a chair?'

We sat down, the widow in her arm-chair beside the fire. Do you know how, in very quiet houses, the fire is always dull, never goes out, never flames or cracks or burns cheerfully? That was the kind of fire that Mrs. Engledew always had. I sat behind her. The two ladies sat on the opposite side, and I became conscious that the younger one was looking more curiously at me than at Mrs. Engledew.

'You do not know my name, perhaps?'

'Claire—Miss Philipon—this young lady— has told me you were coming.'

'Thank you, Miss Philipon,' said Gertrude. 'I made Allen's acquaintance nearly two years ago. He is so bright and clever, so certain of distinction, that it has been the greatest joy to me, I assure you, to know him.' She paused, and looked for some word or smile of response, but there was none. 'I have never before known a young man with so much promise.'

'Oh,' I said, taking the widow's hand, 'does it not make you proud to hear this?'

'When my son,' she replied, 'was in the City, he showed so much promise that they offered him a post of the greatest responsibility in China. This would have led to a partnership in one of the best Houses. Yes, he is a boy of great promise, which makes my disappointment the worse.'

'But, my dear lady,' Gertrude continued, 'it must be pride and thankfulness, not disappointment, that you should feel. He may become—he *shall* become—one of the best writers of his age. You could not pray for a better son.'

'He should have become one of the leading merchants in London; a grave and serious man, with a character. Not a play actor, to make the people laugh and cry.'

Gertrude sighed.

'I have brought you his book; we have had it bound for you. See! Allen has written in it:—"For my mother. The first copy of my first book."' Mrs. Engledew received it passively. 'We brought it ourselves, in order to tell you, what he cannot, how good and clever it is, and how much it is already praised.'

'I do not read what is called light literature,' the mother said. 'I am no longer young. I think of my soul and my husband in heaven, where I wish to join him. I have no desire to laugh. There are sorrows enough of my own to cry over. Tell Allen, if you please, that I thank him for his book. Claire has tried to read me some of his things, but they do not interest me. The boy's business in life was in Silk, not in story telling; he had excellent chances in Silk; he has thrown them away in order to write stories. He will never make any money now. Do not ask me to read his foolish books.'

'My dear lady,' Gertrude pleaded, 'it is not, believe me, a question of money. Yet your son will make an income which will enable him to live comfortably. Do not doubt it.'

'I think of what he has thrown away,' said his mother.

'Think rather of what your son has gained. Oh! Mrs. Engledew'—she leaned forward and took both of the cold reluctant hands—'such a writer as your son will be is a gift of God; he teaches while he touches the springs of tears and laughter; he shows the world what it is, and makes us discontented with ourselves. Can you doubt that it is better to be such a teacher than only one who buys and sells?'

I felt myself guilty while this enthusiast for literature pleaded Allen's cause. Yes; it was not only a story that he would tell, but lessons, exhortations, example, admonitions that each reader might draw from his page. Only a story-teller! Only an artist! Why, how ignorant was I even in thought, to underrate the power of Art!

Mrs. Engledew replied, unmoved by this appeal, that as for teaching, there were school-masters for the young and clergymen for the grown up. Allen was neither a schoolmaster nor a clergyman.

'But your son will be loved by everybody,' said Gertrude.

'His father did not want to be loved by everybody, nor his grandfather, who was also in Silk. They desired to do their duty, have the approval of their conscience, to increase their credit and their balance, and to find safe investments. What more should a man desire? As for people's love, I do not see why a serious man should care whether he is loved or not.'

This was very discouraging, and presently, after a few more vain attempts to make the poor frozen woman understand, Gertrude rose.

'You will not read Allen's book, perhaps,' she said. 'Yet it will remain here for you to look at. It will remind you that he is a man now who has done something already, and will do a great deal more. You will begin to feel differently about his work.'

'Never,' said the mother, bitterly. 'His work is not his father's work. His friends are not his father's friends. If he gets talked about in all the papers, which you call getting honour, I shall feel no pride in him; not any. I should have been proud of him had he never been mentioned in any paper at all, but had risen in the City and become a partner in his House. But now—never!'

So Gertrude said no more, but left her. I went with them.

'My dear,' she said outside, 'Allen told me you would be here. I know all about you—you are Claire. Claire,' she repeated, taking both my hands in hers, 'take us to your house. Let us call upon you. Allen has told you about us, I know. Isabel wants to know you as much as I do.'

It *was* Isabel, then. But, of course, I knew it could be no other. And how stupid I was! How could I have gone on thinking that Isabel was not young? My little jealousy had nearly vanished by that time, and I could think to myself how good and true she looked, and worthy to be loved by such a man as Allen; while, as for myself—oh! it was only schoolboy and schoolgirl. Of course, Allen could never think of me beside this girl, whom I knew already so well, because he had told me so much. We shook hands and became friends at once—and if one was unworthy and jealous, she felt ashamed of her meanness, when the other two were thinking, not of themselves at all, but of the boy whom all three loved. They came with me, and I showed them all the treasures of the bygone time, of which they wanted to know so much. There were the photographs of the two boys when they were fourteen. 'Oh, look!' said Isabel, at Allen's great eager eyes'—and when they were eighteen and when they were twenty-one, just before they went away. There were Allen's first verses—I gave some to Gertrude. There were Will's drawings; there were the books we used to read in, the Lamartine and Chateaubriand, the Montaigne, the old Plutarch, in Amyot's French, Béranger, one or two of Victor Hugo's novels, Molière, and Racine, Boileau, and our English Milton, Shakespeare, and Pope.

There was Allen's own copy of Keats, which he gave me when he went away, because he loved it so much. Then there were the presents which Will had sent me from China, and the drawings of the people and the places which he made for me, and his letters. I showed them all the things belonging to the boys, kept with the shabby old furniture of the dear old room.

'When the summer comes,' I said, 'I will show you the Forest. Come with Allen. We will walk where we used to play together under the trees and among the hawthorns. I have no heart to go there by myself.'

'My dear,' said Gertrude, 'it is a truly beautiful thing for a girl to have the love of two such men. I say so who never had the love of one.'

Her eyes glistened. One could not choose but kiss her.

'It is an idyl,' she said. 'It is like Paul and Virginia, but Virginia remains behind.'

'And it is Paul who goes away into a far country,' said Isabel; and afterwards I wondered if she quite knew what her words might mean.

CHAPTER III.

I suppose that it must have been early in this year that Mr. Massey and Mr. Skantlebury yielded to temptation, and went up to town to make money in the easy way which Olinthus had adopted. Mr. Colliber had been gone nearly two years; he began to go regularly to London about the time when Olinthus had entered upon his career of greatness. First he went in the morning and returned at night; then he went on Monday morning and returned on Friday evening. The little party which met daily on the Green was then reduced to three. Now Sir Charles alone was left. My father, for his part, seldom joined a parliament which talked of things whereof he was profoundly ignorant.

One morning in March I was crossing the Green and passed Sir Charles, who looked so lonely that I stopped to talk with him. Where, I asked him, were his friends?

'They are gone to town,' he replied gloomily. 'They are gone to make their fortunes.—Ho!'

I begged him to explain.

'Colliber,' he said, 'has left us a long time. I don't know where he is, and Massey tells me that he isn't seen about the City. But he is doing something, Colliber is. He is pulling strings in a corner, I expect, and raking in the money. I knew he would go back to it. Men like him can't keep away. Then, you see, none of us except Massey, who doesn't care, like to be seen much in the City; so that Colliber keeps in the background. There are always, my dear young lady, disagreeable people in the world who won't take the right view of—of the pluck and enterprise which led to their losing money. I was myself, you know, so full of enterprise that I lost an immense sum of money—other people's money it was chiefly.'

'Yes, Sir Charles.' I was afraid he would go on to dilate on the glory of his failure.

'So,' he went on, 'none of us can very well walk about the City. Now Colliber's case is worse than mine, because he, too, let in so many —I mean lost so much more money. He is pulling the strings—I know he is pulling the strings somewhere. He is up to devilry. There was always something unnatural in a man who failed for so much and took so little pride in it. But as for Massey and Skantlebury, especially Skantlebury, I *must* say——'

Nothing in the language means more than this little phrase, 'I must say,' unless, perhaps, it is the corresponding expression, 'I do think.' It is, in itself, an interjection, meaning quantities of things.

'What have they done, then?'

'They have gone off, my dear young lady, actually gone off, at their time of life, to speculate in Stocks. Massey has got nothing at all to lose, because what little there is was settled on his wife. Skantlebury has got about twelve thousand pounds. He says that when he has doubled it he will rest content. Ho, ho! And they've gone—being as ignorant as mice about the ways of Capel Court—they've gone in a mean and sneakin' manner to young Gallaway.'

'Gone to Olinthus?'

'They've gone to young Gallaway. There's a man for you! For that matter, Claire, I hope he is for you. Bless you, my dear! I know all about the three lovers. Will Massey is the best set up, but he is in China. Young Engledew may be clever with books, but he is only a literary scrub after all; and his stories, which I have tried to read, are, I must say, desperately low. Whereas, with Olinthus Gallaway, you will be a happy woman if money can make you happy. And a good-looking young fellow, too, though a little coarse in the gills, from too much champagne. You will cure him of that, my dear, and any other faults he may now possess. He has champagne for lunch and champagne for dinner; and on Sundays, I am told, he does not go to church, which is wrong, but has champagne for breakfast. Well, youth must sow wild oats; and he makes a splendid income; and no one, not even Colliber in his best days, ever had such a head for finance. With him, my dear, you will be happy.'

'Thank you, Sir Charles. And about Mr. Massey?'

'What Massey has done is this. He talked it over with Skantlebury, and they made up a little plot together. First one was to call on young Gallaway, and then the other. They would communicate to each other their information, and so double their gains. I didn't think Skantlebury had it in him. Well, they went up. First Massey went. Gallaway told him he had five minutes and no more, pulled out his watch and kept looking at it. Massey said that he was come as an old friend to ask a favour. " I never grant favours," said Gallaway

"To me you will," said Massey. "Why, I've known you since you were a boy. Come, Olinthus—I still say Olinthus for old times' sake, you know, but one ought to say Mr. Gallaway, or Lord Gallaway, or Duke Gallaway —hang it! to such a fellow as you. You know Massey's manner. If he'd got a hundred thousand to his name he couldn't be more so. Well, he bluffed young Gallaway out of a straight tip. He did, indeed. Gallaway just turned red—I don't know why—and whispered, " Will you promise not to tell Mr. Colliber? Sell Egyptians." '

' And did Mr. Massey sell Egyptians ? '

' He did. He told Skantlebury; they both sold Egyptians. And Egyptians turned up trumps. Very well then. It is Skantlebury's turn next. He goes humble—you know his way—and asked the favour, if so small a man as himself may ask a favour of Mr. Gallaway, who has always been as generous as he is brilliant. And it would be the making of him, it would. And so on. Well, he gets his favour, too. Oddly, too, on the same promise not to tell Colliber. Why shouldn't he tell Colliber? Professional jealousy, I say. Colliber was in the same line, and greatly distinguished himself, but not a patch on Gallaway.'

'Did Skantlebury, too, sell Egyptians?'

'I don't know what he bought or sold. But he told Massey, and they both made money. Massey made quite a sum, but Skantlebury is cautious. Massey talks of reviving his projects; nothing short of millions will satisfy him. Well, we shall see; meantime, my dear, it is very hard on me, in my old age, to lose all my companions—first the boys, though we saw little of them. Yet it was pleasant to watch them going off to town every morning—their future all before them—what was it to be? The City is a wonderful place : there's a fortune for everybody who will work, and a splendid failure in store for the most lucky. Dear me ! and then Colliber went. Colliber is short in his temper, and he's got a sharp tongue, but we missed him very much.

He never seemed to understand his own greatness; he wasn't proud of his failure. I think he would rather not have failed at all. But Colliber was full of information. Well, he must needs go to the City—he knows why,' the garrulous old man went on talking. 'Then Massey and Skantlebury went. Massey is a conceited sort of a man, but he failed well; and he has ideas, though he is wanting in the respect due to rank and position. Skantlebury is a great loss to me; a most obliging creature, and deferential to his betters. I miss Skantlebury greatly.'

'Do they go every day to London?'

'Every day. They can't keep away. When men go off in that line they must always be in the City. I knew a man once, a clergyman he was, who used to speculate on the changes every hour, and stood at the window to see that his broker ran. Walking was too slow for him. Massey and Skantlebury go every day too; they sit and watch; they sneak one after the other to young Gallaway, and sometimes he swears at them, and sometimes he whispers a word. It is a gambling game, and it will end badly It is tossing for sovereigns. It is a game which a respectable man like Skantlebury, who knows what saving means, ought not to take up. A bad business, my dear, a bad business.'

I saw Olinthus very seldom. He came, however, one Saturday afternoon early in the spring of that year. He had only come to see me, he said; his mother and the girls could wait. I observed that he was looking ill at ease; his cheeks were flabby and pale; his eyes were red; his face was gloomy. I asked him what was the matter.

'Nothing that you can do any good for,' he replied roughly, but not rudely.

I asked no more, and he went on sucking the knob of his stick moodily.

'I did think, Claire,' he presently re-marked, 'that I should have some sympathy from you at least. You see I am down in the mouth, and yet you don't even ask me why.'

'I did ask you, but you refused to tell me.'

'I *can't* tell you, Claire,' he groaned. 'That is what makes me low. If I could tell you—if I could tell anybody—I should be better. But I can't. I can only wait till I am in my own rooms, and then swear at him.'

'If you want to tell me about it in order to swear at him—whoever he may be—I would rather you did not tell me anything.'

'I can't tell you anything,' he repeated. 'I'm like a man in a prison. Ah! you think it is all skittles, I suppose. Much you know! Look here, Claire,' he said with a sudden burst, 'I lead the life of a dog, I do, and daren't bite, because if I did——' Here he stopped suddenly, and turned ghastly pale. We were standing in the garden, and just then Mr. Colliber passed slowly by. He looked round, raised his hat to me, and nodded to Olinthus.

'What is the matter, Olinthus?' I asked, for he was quite white, and trembling. I thought he would faint.

'Nothing,' he replied, 'nothing at all. Do you think,' he whispered, 'do you think, Claire, that he heard me when I said—when I said—that I led the life of a dog?'

'Mr. Colliber? No, I should think not.'

'I don't want him to hear such words as these. He might—he might—put some wrong construction on them, you know. In the City credit is everything —yes, everything.'

'Your great fortune does not seem to bring you happiness,' I said.

'No, not yet ; but it will. I say to myself that when you consent——'

'Olinthus !'

'Well, then, if you consent—you know—I can then tell you everything, and it will be easier to bear. It's the dreadful loneliness of the thing that preys upon me. Other men can talk to each other ; I've got to shut up as tight as wax. Other men can drink and be jolly ; I've got to keep sober, except in my own chambers and by myself. Oh ! its dreadful. But the money comes in—yes, the money keeps coming in. Perhaps some day there will be the enjoyment of it.'

'And how is the Countess?' I asked.

'There again. Oh, Claire! I've been most cruelly deceived by the Countess. I thought she wanted my society; she only wanted my tips after all. I gave her one or two, and she plunged and made a little pile; and then she went on without me, and lost it all. Then she came to me again, and asked for more, but I couldn't give her any more. I dared not. It was as much as my berth—I mean—well—I couldn't—that's flat—and I told her so. And then she went on her knees—she did indeed. I never thought to have a Countess on her knees to me. But I couldn't do it; I'd been warned not to; and I refused. When she found that crying did no good, she sprang up in a rage—you never saw a real Countess in a rage; Claire, it's truly awful—she boxed my ears, she did indeed—who would have thought I should live to have my ears boxed by a Countess?—and called me a contemptible City cad—but of course her ladyship could say what she liked, and words don't break bones—and said her brother-in-law, the Honourable James, should come to the office with a horsewhip and cowhide me; and then she flung out of the office, and left word among the clerks that they had better not go away early, because a gentleman was coming with a cowhide for the contemptible cad within—meaning me. They grinned—the clerks. Hang 'em! I pay them their salaries, and don't order them about half so much as I am—never mind—and yet they grinned. I wish I had given them all the sack there and then.'

'And has the Honourable James called?'

'No; I sent him a letter. You see, Claire, when a Countess boxes your ears you can only grin and bear it. But as for her brother, whether he is an Honourable or not, if he comes with a horsewhip you can meet him with another. So I wrote to him and tossed the letter into the basket open for the clerks to read it. I told him first that he owed me seventy-five pounds, and I should be obliged by a cheque at once. Next, I was informed by his sister-in-law, the Countess, that he was going to cowhide me. I was going to lay in a guttapercha cane and a bludgeon, and was ready to accommodate him with either. He didn't call, and he hasn't sent that cheque.'

'It seems to me, then, that you have got rid of a very bad set of people.'

'And to think of the money they've won of me. Night after night it was baccarat, euchre, nap, écarté, poker, through the pack for sovereigns—every kind of game. I knew her ladyship was a gambler, well enough. But then'—he sighed heavily—'she could be very charming to a fellow, Claire. She was the only woman who ever made me feel that I could forget you. She had a way of pleasing a man and looking at him. Ah! those eyes of hers!' He sighed heavily. 'Then there are those two old idiots, Massey and Skantlebury. They keep coming to me. Sometimes I send them away. But if one goes the other comes. As for

Massey, he won't go. He sits down and crosses his legs and says he will wait as long as I like. But he won't go. They'll get me into an awful row one of these days. Why, if he should meet them this afternoon—any day—and they should tell him.'

Always this mysterious person in the background, of whom he was so much afraid. However, he said it had cheered him to let me know how miserable he was, and he presently went away. One thought of the copy-book moral maxims, and reflected that riches will not always make a man happy.

CHAPTER IV.

FOR ALLEN'S SAKE.

WHEN Gertrude—you must now let me speak of her by her Christian name—asked me, a few days later, to pay her a visit, I took it as another act of kindness to Allen, and accepted with the anticipation of going into a world quite new to me. If, however, it had been intended to confer a kindness on myself rather than on Allen, I could not have met with a more cordial welcome.

'Above all, my dear,' said Gertrude, 'call me by my Christian name. Let me still feel young—among the young; and recall my youth among the old. Nothing helps so much as to retain your Christian name. And now, my dear, how shall we amuse you?'

'We can get a box for any theatre you would like to see,' said Isabel, 'or tickets for any concert; and there are a few galleries open, and there are always the streets if the weather is fine.'

'I like the streets best,' I said. 'But, indeed, I do not want amusement. Let me watch your kind of life and learn why Allen loves it so much.'

It was easy to understand that, at any rate. After such a youth as the poor boy had passed, which made him loathe the name of money, he would love any kind of life which seemed free from the desire of making money or the fear of losing it, or the irksomeness of not having enough. The very last topic of conversation with Gertrude would be that of money. And then Gertrude's was a life spent among books and the talk was about books: and it was a life with many sides and sympathies, and keen for culture of many kinds. In this house Allen met with the appreciation and encouragement which I could not give him, because I never understood that worship of form and expression which to some makes a poem beautiful and delightful though it contains not a single new thought or a happy idea.

The first evening was Gertrude's evening at home. The rooms were very full, and most of the guests were men and women of some distinction, however small. It was exactly what Allen told me; all of them could do something; in the talk and instruction and discussions of the day they all took some part. What a difference—oh! what a great gulf between the world of Art and Letters, with its cleverness and brightness and apparent sinking of selfish interest, and the world of the City.

'Allen,' I whispered, 'can you picture to yourself Sir Charles set down in this drawing-room?'

'And his consternation when no one recognised the greatness of his colossal failure? Think of the universal stare! Tell me, Claire, do you like it?'

'It interests me very much. It seems so

bright and clever. Oh! Allen, this is indeed better for you than the City.'

He answered with his quick bright smile.

They all seemed to know each other and talked freely, and they all knew what was going on and what everybody was doing. Some of the ladies were dressed in æsthetic extravagances—I thank heaven, sometimes, that I am half a Parisienne—but many were dressed quite poorly, because, as I learned afterwards, the following of Art in its various branches is not always lucrative, and many of Gertrude's friends have to continue in poverty all their lives. As for the men, they were mostly middle-aged or old men who had done their work and made their mark. If you listened to them you would hear them talking of Lady Blessington and Disraeli and the Count D'Orsay and Lord Palmerston, when he was still a gay young fellow of sixty, and Taglioni and Madame Celeste and other people who flourished in the theatres and the forties. I think it is delightful to get old people who can talk and who have played a part in the things we read about, especially in the impossible time, the time just before one was born. When we were in France we went to see a certain Marquis of the ancient time, who had been a page in Napoleon's court. I expected to find a man who would remind me of Beranger. I found an old old gentleman sitting beside a stream fishing for gudgeon, and he could remember nothing at all. As for young men, the promise of the future was represented only by Allen and one or two others.

All the girls, for their part, seemed ready to contribute something to make the evening pleasant. I suppose there were some among them who only had the ordinary accomplishments, but those who performed for us exhibited a skill which was very far indeed beyond the amateur displays which one heard at my evenings, where some of us, including myself, could play prettily. For instance, there was one young lady of eighteen who played the violin in a duet with her sister. What would they think in the village of a girl playing the violin?   It would be considered ' unladylike.' Yet she played very beautifully, and looked as graceful as the Muse of Music.   And another played the zither (which I at once resolved to learn), while two more sang a Tyrolean song. And another played a brilliant piece on the piano, and another sang a most difficult song, with a sweet voice and highly trained.   Whatever they did was done well.   At my evenings everything was done only tolerably.   It was as if they had resolved on the mastery of the art, not the mere acquisition of an accomplishment. The violinist, for instance, presently told me, that it was her one occupation and the work of her life, so far, to play the violin well.   There was a portfolio of drawings—finished, beautiful drawings—lying on the table.   They were the fruits of a journey made by a young lady present.   This, too, was the chosen work of her life.   I am quite sure that there used to be, and still remains in some circles, a kind of prejudice that to do a thing well is below the dignity of a 'lady,' and savours of the 'professional.' But here, those who were not professional wished to be ; and I am quite sure that the lady who played the violin, the lady who painted the water-colour sketches, and the lady who sang, would have liked nothing better than a public exhibition. Why not? 'Art should belong to all,' said Gertrude ; 'it is treason to your genius to keep things hidden.'

It pleased me to observe how everybody knew and seemed to like Allen, and how my dear, shy, sensitive boy had developed into a young man who bore himself with confidence if not with assurance, and could hold his own with any, and was accepted as a man who was sure to rise.

'I am going to recite presently,' Isabel whispered to me. 'I always do, you know. It is my one poor talent. I cannot sing, nor can I write, nor paint; but I can recite. I have taken one of Allen's poems, which I hope will please you. But first I want you to sing.'

'Indeed,' I replied, 'I would rather not.'

'Allen tells me you have got the sweetest voice in the world and the most beautiful collection of French songs. Do sing one for us, only one.'

Perhaps the sweetness and novelty of the old French melody would make the people forget the want of training in the singer. I sang then, to my own accompaniment, because I could not stand up before everybody with the music in my hand, first one and then another of my French songs. One of them was set to an air taken by Clement Marot, when he translated the Psalms. I have heard it sung in the Protestant Temple at La Rochelle; it is a strange, unexpected air, with a sad yearning in it, which suggests thoughts and brings tears to your eyes. Will always loved it, and Allen used to walk about the room when I sang it, silent, dreaming, his eyes far off. I sang it to-night to please him. Happily, it pleased everybody.

'Claire,' said Allen, ' your voice was

never sweeter, and you never sang that song better.'

Amid the talk of the room I heard a voice, it was Gertrude's, saying—'and for once, believe me, nothing to do with literature or art at all. Yes; she is, indeed, very beautiful and sweet.'

Was she talking about me? Well: it is very pleasant to think that people call one beautiful and sweet. Yet it was all for Allen's sake.

Then Isabel stood up to recite. Surely the power of acting is a most wonderful gift. Isabel could act so well that we forgot a lovely and graceful girl was standing before us—at least, I did. I thought only of the words she uttered and the characters she assumed. As she stood before us, her slight figure swayed gently as if in rhythm with the verse; her hands were sometimes clasped and still, but sometimes lifted with quick, sharp gesture; her clear hazel eyes gazed through us and beyond us, as if she was, indeed, inspired, and saw nothing but the scenes of which she spoke, heard nothing but the words of the poem. She endowed the verse with an intensity of meaning, a fulness of purpose, a directness which I, who thought I knew all Allen's poetry so well, had never even suspected or felt.

When she finished there was again a murmur of applause, and the talk began again. And again I heard a voice—this time not Gertrude's, but the voice of a girl sitting beside me.

'Whose poem is it? Whose should it be? Of whom does Isabel think all day except of him?'

Yes. I had seen it already: in her eyes when they rested upon him; in her voice when she spoke to him; in the brightening of her colour when he approached her; in the jealous inquiring glance when she looked at him; in the very attentions which she lavished upon me, who had robbed her, she thought, of Allen's heart. Poor Isabel! Yet, who could

live with Allen so much and not love him?
Of course she loved him.

Sometimes I think, considering how many
men have to wait till they are far on in their
thirties before they marry, whether the women
who were young with them, and must have
loved them, ever forget them. Could I, for
instance, ever forget Will and Allen, even if
the time had gone by and they could not offer
to marry me, and I had accepted—if that were
possible—another man? I think there must
always, where there is a man who marries at
thirty or later, be some woman—perhaps more
than one—who loved him in his youth, when
as yet he had all the world before him, and
was unformed, and will never forget him as he
was then—young, ardent, full of life and
laughter and belief in the world, and love and
hope. I shall always remember Allen as he
was in those days: and *so will Isabel.*

'You know those verses, my dear?' asked
Gertrude.

'I thought I knew them well,' I said, ' but now I see very clearly that I did not know them at all.'

'There is no test,' she said, ' of good work so certain as the test of reading aloud or reciting. Always read your verses aloud, my dear. But I forget. You do not write. Oh! what a pity! I should like everybody whom I know to write. Let me tell Isabel what you have said.'

'It is quite true,' said Allen, who had joined us. 'Isabel has given the words stronger life and more reality than I could put into them. She knows that I can never thank her enough.'

Isabel smiled, and said that she was glad to interpret Allen's verses for me.

Then Gertrude, between the talk around her, began to speak of Allen.

'He is sure to succeed,' she said. 'He will become famous, if you care for fame, but of course you do.'

'Yes,' I replied; 'I suppose every woman must desire honour for her friends.'

'And he will do good work, lasting work. Is not that better still? My dear, tell me, do you think we have improved Allen for you?'

This assumption that it was all for me—the fame, and the good work, and the change in Allen—vexed me. Why should it be assumed that—— one does not like to finish the question even in thought.

'You must not say for me,' I whispered low. 'And besides, if it were for me, would it not be too much? What could I give him in return for so much?'

'You will give him what you have always given him—sympathy and encouragement, and—and love, my dear. He will want no more. Besides, you give him your beauty. Do not undervalue woman's most precious gift.'

'Gertrude, look at Allen, now.' Allen and Isabel were talking together earnestly. 'Can I—tell me—can I give him more than Isabel can give him? Can I give him half so much?

Her beauty is better than mine, and she knows
—what I do not—what he wants.'

'My dear, my dear,' she laid her hand in
mine; 'do not say such things. You must not
say them. Indeed you must not; do not
think them, even. We have always thought
of Allen as your own. Isabel can have no
such thought, believe me.'

'Yet, if I were to put such a thought into
her head——'

'And Allen has no such thought.'

'Perhaps not; yet.'

Gertrude's face was troubled. She looked
again at Isabel. No thought as yet. Her
sweet face calm and untroubled.

'Tell me, my dear,' she said; 'is—the
other—Will—is he, too, clever?'

'Not clever, as you count cleverness. But
others would call him full of cleverness. He is
not a man of books but of active work.'

Then we were interrupted, because Allen
brought his friend Lawrence to me, and our
talk for that evening was stopped. Nor did

Gertrude speak about it to me again for some time.

I found Mr. Lawrence Ouvry a very pleasant fellow, and quite as Allen had described him. He could not possibly be so wise as he looked, and beneath his thoughtful brow there dwelt a pair of eyes which seemed perpetually twinkling. He, too, began to talk about Allen, and seemed to regard him as already belonging to me. But one could not very well explain to a young man the exact situation. No one, among them all, I believe, conceived it possible that a mere country girl could refuse a man who had achieved literary distinction.

'We have done what we could for the illustrious poet and Maker,' said Lawrence. 'We have dragged him out of his solitude and made him go into the world. It was a recluse you sent to us, Miss Philipon, the hermit of Hainault. Have you preserved the original hermitage?'

'All Allen's friends ought to be very grateful to you, Mr. Ouvry.'

'Well; it is not every day that we get such a chance as a man with the real ring. Anybody can write; that is nothing—the current literature of the next generation will, I am quite certan, be written by the Board School boy—but only a few can write as Engledew writes.'

'You write, too, he tells me. Scientific papers—and—and——'

Here I laughed, because his eyes began to twinkle.

'You mean to say,' he whispered, 'that he has betrayed me?'

'Yes. He has told me all. I know your secret. But I will not reveal it.'

'The malady is hereditary,' he said. 'Sons take after their mothers. My mother wrote novels. That is the reason why I write— scientific papers.'

Then he began to tell me how he met Allen at a restaurant and how he began to talk with him, and how—well, I knew it all, but it was pleasant to be told it over again

It seemed as if a great many people wanted to be introduced to me that evening. Could they all know that I was such an old friend of Allen? That was impossible.

'My dear,' said Gertrude to me next day, 'do you think that the *beaux yeux* had something to do with it? As if the men—selfish creatures—were thinking about Allen!'

Somehow it had not occurred to me that men of letters and art should bestow a thought upon the face of a strange girl.

'It is strange, is it not?' said Gertrude. 'But men are wonderful, my dear. At every age, every man is ready to leave the most important things, put by the most wonderful work, in order to talk with a pretty girl. And the more nonsense they find to talk, the better they like it. The only chance for them is to lock themselves up in a study.' And then she began to say kind things about my face and figure, I suppose, to console me for not being an artist.

The next day we went to some studios and

saw unfinished pictures on the easels. As for the pictures one can say nothing. They are finished by this time and have been exhibited and bought, and are scattered over the whole world. The studios were charming, hung about with tapestry, bits of armour, trophies, weapons, brass things, old glass, mirrors, and all kinds of wonderful things. There were costumes lying about, and the artists seemed not at all disinclined to stop work and talk a little. As for the talk it was all about their work and their friends—artists seem to care for nothing else. One of them made a sketch of my head and face for me, and said it should be used for Helen of Troy—men talk nonsense, yet one likes these extravagancies. And always, everywhere, the same respect and deference shown to Gertrude, and the same *camaraderie* with Allen and Isabel.

One evening we went to the theatre and Lawrence Ouvry gave a little supper in his rooms after the performance. A young actor was one of the guests—we had seen him playing in the first piece. He had the most delightful manners, and kept us amused while he made me understand for the first time how his profession, like every other, wants hard work and constant study, and is a very serious profession indeed.

It has got nothing whatever to do with the story—except that Lawrence Ouvry had been so extraordinarily good to Allen that one likes to talk about him—but I cannot forbear to mention with what respect he was spoken of by his cousin as a man who had departed from the traditions of his family and gone off in quite another direction, as a cold, hard man of science who had no sympathy with Art.

'My dear,' said Gertrude, 'in all the practical concerns of life, and in every question connected with science, the calm judgment of that balanced mind is invaluable to us all—we greatly depend upon Lawrence. Yet it is a most surprising thing that a scientific man should come from among us. I suppose that he has by this time made a great name in science. Have you heard, Isabel, of anything that he has done?'

'Lawrence told me,' she replied, 'about a year ago, that he was thinking of a paper on the Validation of the Higher Kinetics— I remember the title because I made him write it down. But I have heard no more of it.'

I stayed with them for three or four days. Allen came every day, and of one thing I became daily more certain. What that was I will tell you presently. We talked on two subjects only. When Allen was with us we talked of literature, and of men and women of letters. When he was not with us, we talked of him.

I found, as I already suspected, that Allen's views on the subject of his profession were greatly modified. He thought more highly of his art and less highly of its followers. But to him, as to his friends, there were no interests worth consideration except those of literature. It was a new world to me, and it seemed as if, art being only one form of work, too much importance was given to one kind of work. But it was a congenial atmosphere for Allen; though it developed in him a spirit of separation which might do harm to his work. The world for such a man exists in order to supply him with materials. Men and women do all kinds of things; they live, love, work, quarrel, fight, hope, suffer, die—without any regard it is true to artistic grouping, yet in order to provide subjects and models for the painter. It was pleasant to hear this old lady, so kind of heart, speak of people as if they were all lay figures and puppets for the artist.

Allen must never give up his acquaintance with the people; he must always go about among them and learn their manner of life. ' Remember that, my dear'—always as if the future of Allen lay in my hands—' mankind affords an inexhaustible study; you can find a picturesque bit of life in every street. I have always lamented that women cannot get about like men; if we had greater freedom in this respect we should show greater breadth of treatment and more firmness of handling. If I were young I would go as nurse to the London Hospital for six months. Oh! what chances a nurse must have! Yet, my dear, I do not remember hearing of any nurse becoming a novelist. To be sure the profession of nursing is only thirty years old.'

'Do you not think the life a pleasant one, Claire?' Allen asked.

'It is very pleasant, Allen. And it suits you as no other life would. And you really think that your position is assured?'

'That I cannot say, but I hope so. What other hope have I? What other hope can I have? I am afraid to go on with the tales. Isabel wants me to undertake a three volume novel; but I doubt my strength,—yet—to write a good novel. And then, then—the Play.'

'Oh! The Play!'

'Gertrude does not know of it yet. We shall show it to her, when it is finished.'

'You have arranged it with Isabel, I suppose.'

. 'Yes. Isabel knows all my plans—Isabel and you, Claire. Tell me if you like her.'

'She is a little reserved with me. But yet I like her. She is clever, is she not?'

'Yes; she is very clever.'

'And I am sure she is sympathetic.'

'Yes; she has been a great help to me, Claire; I cannot tell you what I owe to these two ladies.'

'Shall I tell you, Allen, how to repay their kindness?'

'That is impossible.'

'No; it is very possible. And I will show you the way, Allen, but not this morning.'

I thought continually of Isabel and her secret; which she hardly knew herself. Allen filled so large a part of her thoughts and yet she did not know—I am sure she did not know—how much she thought about him. And if she considered me with curiosity and a little jealousy, it was only because she felt as if no one could be good enough for Allen.

'My dear,' said Gertrude, 'we grudge you our poet : not because you will not make him happy, but because a *grande passion* disturbs and hinders the current of his work. Allen has not yet caught that mysterious faculty which brings a man the best success—the love of the world. It is better, far better than success in a literary circle. We hope it for him. I am sure he will get it—some day. Strange quality ! Many of the greatest artists have never arrived at it. What can we call it ? I think it is *touch*.'

Then she began to talk about a poet's wife.

'She must,' said Gertrude, ' be content to become his shadow. She must remember that every help she gives her husband is sympathy and apprehension. She must receive his first thoughts.'

'His first thoughts,' Isabel repeated. 'They are the best and most beautiful.'

'Yes,' Gertrude went on very seriously, 'the most beautiful because they are the first fresh conceptions, the very inspiration. His wife has, therefore, her reward, if she wants any. It ought to be reward enough to see the work growing with the fame and honour, and to know that he will live long after her life is gone. My dear! It is a great thing: it is the greatest thing for a woman. It is better than to be a poet one's self, because in all woman's work in any art, there is none which touches the highest point And there never will be.'

On the last morning of my stay, Isabel spoke more freely to me. Of course she began on Allen.

'I am glad,' she said, ' that you think him improved. We see him so often that we are not conscious of the change which you find in him.'

I said what I thought best to say about her own share in the work of improvement, and she blushed very prettily as she hastened to explain .

that Allen was like a brother, or a son of the house. 'And oh!' she said, 'I have wanted to say it ever since you came; but I dared not, until now.'

'What is it, Isabel?'

'I understand now why Allen loves you.'

'Are you quite sure that he does?'

'Of course he does. And I am glad, too, that you are rich, because now he will not have to trouble his mind about money.'

'But, Isabel—do you not know? Has he not told you all the story?'

'A gambler in stocks and shares: and a merchant in China:—and Allen,' she replied, with a little laugh of contempt at the contrast.

'Does Allen ever talk to you about the merchant in China? Ask him, Isabel, to tell you about Will.'

CHAPTER V.

FROM WILL.

AND now the days lengthened apace; the first spring flowers were over, the primrose lingered yet in shady hedges, but the crocus and the daffodil were gone: the spring was ready to come upon us as soon as the east winds should cease to blow; already the lilac was in leaf and the blackthorn in flower, and the hawthorn ready to follow, and the great buds of the horse-chestnut were swelling. It was April, the month of which we expect so much and get so little. It wanted only two months more to the day when I should be asked to make my choice. Later in the month I received a letter from Will. He was coming home. 'I have asked and obtained a furlough. Another man has been sent out who will carry on my work while I am at home. There are many other reasons besides the chief one which fills my heart day and night, and has filled it for three years.' This was the only time that he had ever alluded to his 'chief reason.' Poor boy! His heart was filled with the thought of a simple girl. How can men so think of girls, when they have all the splendid work of the world before them? I thought when he went away to China that he would carry with him a kind memory of his old friend and playfellow, but not that he would always think of her. What a strong and constant heart! 'There are many other reasons,' said the letter. 'First, I hear privately from one of the junior partners that I may be more useful to the House at home, and that my work here has been appreciated. Next, I want to know what my father means. He writes that he is now on the eve of repairing his fortunes; that a great future awaits him; that he shall be able to die happy when his time comes, because he will leave me a colossal fortune.

I know that every one of his schemes was going to lead to boundless fortune, and I tremble. But my mother's money is held in trust. He cannot lose that. My poor father, with his imagination and ingenuity, might have made an excellent novelist, but in the City he was thrown away. Perhaps in a better ordered society men who are failures will be treated with the pity which should attach to those who have got into wrong grooves. A grocer who has compounded with his creditors, for instance, should be examined in order to find out whether he should not have been made a statesman or a divine, or a cobbler, perhaps; and so be instructed in the line for which nature intended him. Then everybody would be happy. Good-bye, Claire. Good-bye, Claire. Good-bye, Claire. It is nearly three years since I said that last, with Allen, in the dear old Forest. In four weeks more I shall be on board the mail. In ten weeks more I shall be in England again. WILL.'

I showed the letter to my father, who read

it with a serious face. 'Will is a brave and gallant lad,' he said. 'He is stronger than the artist. Yet Allen has a quick eye and a ready brain. And the third? He is very rich. He devotes himself to the robbery of the greedy, the credulous, and the ignorant. Admirable trade! Thus nature, who neglects nothing, finds pirates to pillage thieves and fools. Worthy Olinthus! Thus he gains the admiration and respect of the world. My daughter, will this illustrious maker of money join the other two in June?'

'I do not know, but I think he will.'

'He does us infinite honour. Claire, child.' My father took my head in his hands and kissed me, with soft eyes. 'Is it possible that in two or three months—only two or three months— my daughter will belong to some one else? Alas! why do we have daughters who go away when they are loveliest and best, and desert their old fathers for their young lovers? In a better world a woman's beauty will last her life, so that there shall be no excuse for falling in love while their fathers are living, unless they are not only old but also foolish and—and—*maussades*, and not worthy of a good daughter. Then they might go away and rejoice their husbands.'

He was always the kindest and most thoughtful of fathers, but in those days it seemed as if he anticipated every wish, even the slightest, and was continually devising some little surprise, some new gift for me. It rained gloves; there were showers of pretty trifles; he went to town and came back loaded with books and music; he would have ruined himself had I not begged him to give me nothing more. And I knew that he was counting the days left to him of his daughter's undivided heart. The jealous, fond father! As if there does not always remain as much love in a woman's heart as ever was taken out of it! 'With each child,' said once to me a poor woman of the village who had twelve, 'with each child I felt as if there was no more love left.' But the love came—yes—the love came! Love is a fountain which can never dry.

Will was coming home in order to ask that question again. Will and Allen would both ask that question. Did ever before a girl have to choose between two men, both of whom she loved alike? But then this girl was presently to discover that she did not love both these men alike but very differently. And how that came about she does not quite know, even now, and does not care to question herself too minutely.

In those days, with Will's letter in my hand, I used to wander alone in the recesses of the Forest, those places known only to the boys and myself, and try to take counsel of my heart, which would give no advice or counsel at all and remained obstinately silent.

Allen wrote to me as usual and told me of his work, how the play was advancing and would soon be finished, and how he was planning that three volume novel, and how he was asked to write for a new magazine. At all events, he had the desire of his heart: he was successful in the only way in which he desired success. Poor Allen! one remembered his early enthusiasm, his hero worship, his first poor, thin attempts, his eagerness to work in the way my father pointed out to him, his enthusiasm and his early disappointments. He was changed, indeed. The eagerness remained and the industry, but the old enthusiasms which were the golden haze of morning, the splendid dreams and illusions of youth, these were gone; to the imagination of a boy the round world and all that therein is seems so much more splendid than they are. He sees the type, the perfect model, and thinks that each individual example reaches perfection. As for me, I remembered also my father's illusions and designs. Allen was to have such a teaching as never any poet had before; he was to learn the unknown wants and wishes of the People; he was to lead the People—dream of an enthusiast who had never grown beyond the age of barricades. To lead the People! a noble dream, indeed, but not for Allen. Never at any time could it be possible for such as Allen.

It was in this month, I think, that in my daily walks and wanderings I became aware of a strange man. Even in the village, quiet as it is, the presence of a stranger does not excite universal interest; but this stranger came so often, and prowled about so mysteriously, that one got to suspect him of some design. He was about fifty-five years of age, rather a short man, with broad shoulders and a large grey beard; he wore coloured spectacles and a broad soft felt hat, rather like a clergyman's hat. He always smoked a cigar, and he sat about a great deal on stiles and gates looking always up and down the road as if he expected somebody. He seemed to come every fine day to the village, but I knew not where he came from.

One day as I passed him he took the cigar from his lips and addressed me.

'I beg your pardon, miss. May I ask a question?'

I permitted him to put his question.

'You know, I suppose, the names of most all the people who live in this village, now?'

I said that I knew them all, or nearly all. He had, I noticed, some touch of the American in his voice.

'Do you, now, happen to know a lady named Engledew? She would be a widow, and about five-and-forty by this time.'

'Yes, certainly, I know Mrs. Engledew. Do you want to see her? I can take you to her house. It is close by.'

'I should like to see her house, thank you. As for seeing her——' here he stopped short.

'The Mrs. Engledew I mean,' he went on, ' had a baby, I am told.'

'She has a son, now grown up.'

'Yes; it's four-and-twenty years ago. That seems a long time to you, no doubt, because you are young. It *is* a long time, whether to work out or look back upon, for people who have done things. But it isn't a long time for people who haven't done anything, and are consequently happy. For such it passes free and quick. Mrs. Engledew, now, is pretty happy, I dare say, being one of that sort?'

'No; she is not a happy woman. She has cause to be very unhappy. If you know her you know why.'

'I don't know her myself. But I am asked by one who does to come and make a few inquiries on the spot—cautiously, you know.'

'Cautiously? What is the need of caution? Mrs. Engledew lives here. You may see her any day. What do you mean by caution?' He avoided the question and made answer by another.

'Is her son, may I ask, in the Silk Line?'

'No; he is a man of Letters.'

The stranger whistled.

'Then I suppose they must want money,

both of them, pretty badly? A man of Letters!'

'Neither of them wants any money. Come down this lane and I will show you the house.'

He walked at my side in silence.

'There,' I said, when we came in sight of the cottage where Mrs. Engledew lived, 'that is her house, and there you will find her if you want to see her.'

'I don't think I want to see her to-day,' he said. 'Not to-day. No. I think I shall just look at the house and then go. That will be enough for once. Another time I can call. When you know where to call there's a great deal done already. No hurry about the rest. Not any hurry, you know.'

'There is Mrs. Engledew. You can go and speak to her.'

The widow stood at the door. She was going to tidy up her garden, and stood in the porch for a few minutes as one stands who is irresolute where to begin. The man with me began to tremble, and he dropped the stick he was carrying. He really was a most mysterious stranger.

'There is Mrs. Engledew.'

'She is thinner than she was, but then she is older. Many people get thin as they grow older.'

'She has grown thin from suffering and sorrow.'

'I did not think,' he said, 'that she would age so much.'

'If a woman's husband commits suicide on the eve of bankruptcy, caused by his partner's villainy, do you think that she is not likely to suffer?'

'No, no, of course'—he cleared his throat —'of course she must suffer in such a case. No one can blame a woman under these circumstances for getting thin. Through a partner's villainy. That's sad, now, isn't it?'

'You seem to know something about her.' I looked at him with increased wonder and suspicion.

'Yes, but she would not know me. It is

no use my speaking to her, not a bit of use.
I am only sent by another man to find out
about her.   Now that I have seen her I think
I will go.'

'This is very strange,' I said.

'You say that she is in no need of money.'

'I believe not.'

'Nor her son either.'

'I believe not.'

'Is she hard and unforgiving, now?   Does
she still feel bad—about that business we were
speaking of—the partner, you know?'

'Do you come from the man Stephens?'

'Maybe I do, maybe not.   Does she feel
bad about it still?'

'What can you think?'

'To be sure, to be sure; not a doubt of it.
You would yourself—naturally—and yet she
does not want money?   No.   And so, even if
she had all the money that the partner ran off
with, it wouldn't help her, would it?   No, certainly not.   Wherefore, I may as well go.'

He left me abruptly and walked away.

Two days afterwards I saw him again, sitting on a gate in sight of Mrs. Engledew s cottage. He was looking as if he waited on the chance of her coming out again. When he saw me he got off and walked away. Yet a week later I saw him again—and again after that. He was always sitting on the gate gazing steadily at the cottage, or he was walking backwards and forwards in an uncertain way, as if he was hesitating whether to go to the cottage door or not. He always came in the morning: in the afternoon he was gone.

What did it mean? I was so full of my own affairs at this time that I thought little about this strange visitor. Yet he gave me some anxiety. What did he watch the cottage for? Who was this man, who knew Mrs. Engledew and remembered her as she was twenty-five years ago? Why did he lurk about the place? And had I done right to tell a strange man where this poor widow lived?

CHAPTER VI.

WITH ALLEN.

In those last weeks I was grievously troubled in my own mind about Allen. Let us not ask too carefully whether there was jealousy. Why should not these ladies love Allen? To be sure one of them was young and beautiful. They had done far more for him than I could do; he was right in loving them in return. Who (not being in the City) could choose but love a young man so full of genius, so handsome, so modest, so free from affectation? And they began with what seemed perfect safety, because Allen was already in love with another girl. Brother and sister from the beginning; and so—and so—they went on without fear or caution, reading, talking, advising, planning, taking counsel together, till the heart of one was gone.

And the heart of the other? It was this that I wanted to find out. In order to do so I asked Allen if he would give me a whole day. It was already early May; the east wind had gone, and the showers of spring had begun. I contrived a little plot. I would make Allen feel exactly what coming back to me might mean. There was a broad gulf indeed between the Allen of the present and the Allen of three years before. I would make him step back and realise what life in the village would mean for him. Perhaps he still thought that he loved me; indeed, I am sure he did; he had been thinking so for a good many years; you do not easily break off such a habit of thought. Very well; then he should understand, without my telling him, how it would be to him were he to become my husband.

He came about noon. He brought with him his still unfinished play. He proposed to read it to me—always, he knew that I should like to hear what he was doing—and began at once upon the plot and the dialogue. But I put it aside, and talked of the village and its affairs. First, we must go and call upon his mother, a duty which he was perfectly willing to defer until the play had been discussed.

I think there is nothing more miserable than such a visit when confidence has been lost between mother and son. Mrs. Engledew asked no question about his prospects or his work, nor did she ask after his friends, she only said that he was looking well.

' And you, mother? '

'I am as well as I can now expect to be,' she replied ; and one really felt quite certain that if her son had remained in the Silk trade she would have been quite well.

The visit was constrained, and short. When we came away, Allen gave a sigh of relief.

'It is too late now,' said Allen afterwards, ' to hope that things will ever be different ; but I wish my mother could see things in a different light. If one were to become another Shakespeare, I suppose it would be the same thing. Oh! the City! the City!'

He shook himself impatiently.

We passed the green, where Sir Charles was basking in the sun.

'You must go and speak to him, Allen,' I said.

Sir Charles received him kindly. He said that he was glad to hear that Allen was getting on, so far as people in his line can be said to get on, considering that the profits, if any, go to the publishers. It was consoling to his friends to feel that, though he *had* left the plough after putting his hand to it, he was earning an honourable pittance. Allen smiled feebly. Sir Charles went on to say that he had not read the book called 'With the People,' and that he did not mean to read it, because he did not like the people, and found them low —contemptibly low. One of them at a Lord Mayor's Show once broke his carriage window with the neck of a bottle; they were a very low class; but if Allen would write a book on the Lord Mayors, or on knights, baronets, great merchants who have failed, and, generally, on the lives of gentlemen of exalted rank, he would promise to give it his very best attention.

When we left him, Allen seemed to me—but I may have been mistaken—to murmur strong words, as if he was choking.

And then we met Mr. Massey, ponderous and important. He was on his way to the City, but stopped to give Allen a condescending salute.

'You are looking thin, my boy,' he said. 'If you had remained in the City you would now be looking fat, like Gallaway. You should see young Gallaway. Well, it can't be helped, and I hope you won't fret over it. Perhaps—but I suppose it is now too late. Literature is but a poor trade, a poor trade.'

'Rich or poor,' said Allen, ' it is all I have.'

'All you have; very true. Tut—tut—tut. Dear! dear! All you have. Your poor mother feels it very much. I assure you, Allen. I tell her, whenever I find an opportunity, that literature is not generally regarded as disgraceful, though a sad falling off from the City. No literary man ever has a position, you know. If he goes to a City dinner, where is he to sit? Below the sheriffs, of course; below the aldermen; below the Common Council.'

'Of course,' said Allen, with a grin.

'I have now, myself, returned to the City. For some years I have been resting. I am, however, engaged in retrieving my fortunes. My son, I am happy to say, will, after all, be enriched by his father's exertions. I shall, on his return from China, buy him a partnership in one of the best Houses. Perhaps Brimage and Walton's. Good morning, Allen, good morning to you.'

'Venerable old jackass!' Allen murmured. 'Claire, let us get into the Forest quickly. Ugh! what a place it is!'

In the Forest I heard all about the play, and we decided that it would be a delightful thing to have it read in the old place where we used to run as children.

'Isabel shall read it,' cried Allen, kindling at the thought. 'Gertrude shall sit on the old trunk with your father.' Here a look of doubt fell upon his face. 'Do you think, Claire, that your father will like Gertrude?'

'You mean, Allen, will Gertrude like my father? I think she will.'

'Well, we will choose a fine day. What time of the day will be best, Claire? Shall we read it in the morning?'

'You will all dine with us, and after dinner we will walk into the Forest, and there Isabel shall read it. Will that do?'

He stayed all that day with us. I was curious to observe how my father and he would get on together. In the old days, when the boy was ignorant, he accepted his master's maxims as words of wisdom. Now, however, how would it be?

What actually happened was that Allen showed, involuntarily, how far he had drifted from the path in which he was designed to go.

My father began to talk of the things which were in his mind.

'For thirty years and more,' he said, 'I have been as one who sits upon the bank and watches the current of the river. It is not without its charm, the life of contemplation, though I own that the active life would be my choice had I the power to begin again and to choose again.'

'It would be a very good subject,' said Allen, 'the man who could begin again if he chose, and at any time he chose.'

'In these thirty years, what a change! How great the work achieved for the people! How stupendous the work that is to be done by the people!'

'And how monotonous the effect when the general level has been complete!' said Allen. 'Art is made up of contrasts.'

'I forgot,' said my father coldly, 'I forgot that you are now an artist.'

He proceeded to ask Allen about himself and his progress, but made no more remarks about the People; and after dinner he left, and went to smoke cigarettes in the garden.

'How does the village strike you, Allen, when you come back to it?'

'It is detestable.'

'But there is the Forest.'

'True, the Forest. Yet it seems so much smaller than of old.'

'That is because you have grown so much bigger, Allen.'

'Is it better, for instance, than Burnham Beeches, or Windsor, or even the Lake of Richmond Park?'

'I do not know. It is good enough for me, even now.'

'To me,' he said, 'the memory of the Forest will always be dear. It seems a pity, almost, to disturb the old recollections by coming back at all.'

'Your new life, Allen, has made the old impossible. You would never return here with any pleasure. The talk of the residents would be intolerable to you.'

He shuddered.

'You would not live happily so near your mother, unless, which seems unlikely, she would change her point of view.'

'No, I could not.'

'Even my father, Allen, whom you used to respect so much——'

'Oh, Claire! to him, at least, I have not changed. I respect him as much as I ever did. I am as grateful to him as I ever was. Believe me, there is no man whom I love and respect more.'

'Yet, Allen——'

'Yet we have so little in common. His views are not mine. That is all.'

'And Allen,' I went on, 'you could never give up, for the sake of anyone in the world, your new life, your club, your new friends, your new talk, to come back and live among your old friends in the old way.'

He turned pale: he shuddered.

'Ah, Claire,' he said, 'some things are worth life itself. This, my new life, is all the life I desire; yet I would give that up even at your bidding.'

'Poor boy! What would you have left if that were gone? What if I were to bid you say farewell to Gertrude, and to see Isabel no more?'

He blushed, and raised his eyes with a guilty look of suspicion.

'Isabel?' he asked. 'Isabel is a part of the life I would resign. She is my sister, Claire, my very dear sister. That is settled between us. You do not think—oh, Claire! you must not think—that there can be between Isabel and me anything——'

'Allen, I will always believe every word that you say; but the time for saying that has not quite come. It will soon be here—and, Allen, I asked you to come here to-day with a serious purpose. I want you, before Will comes home, to look round the old place again, to think of what you were three years ago, and of what you are. It will be good for you to think of this very seriously.'

He looked about him: he blushed and stammered.

'I cannot say what I should like to say, Claire. It is not quite time. You are always thoughtful for me. It was kind of you. Yes, I am changed, indeed, or else the place is changed. But you have not changed, except——'

'The place is so small. Is it not?'

'Yes, small, and its thoughts are mean. Yet there is the memory of the Forest and the place where we two dreamed away the summer evenings, while the bees droned and the late cuckoo called and the blackbird sang. Oh, happy time!'

'Go, make a poem of it, Allen. It will make a charming poem. Put in it your best and highest thoughts; then it will be a great poem. Isabel will recite it for you at one of the evenings.'

'I will, Claire,' he said quickly, 'I will.

Oh '—why, he seemed to begin the poem already—' do you feel the warm soft air, as it used to fan our cheeks? Do you hear the buzz of the insects, which was all our music? Do you catch the fragrance of the Forest, which kept our souls sweet and pure? Do you see the shadows lying across the glades, as they used to lie in the evenings, sinking into our hearts and filling us with thoughts? Do you see the boy and girl—such an eager boy, Claire, so eager to do far, far greater things than ever he will be able to do? I think of him sometimes with a kind of awe that he should have grown into so small a man. And the girl, too, so sweet a girl, so full of sym-pathy—the sweetest friend that ever boy had!'

'Allen,' I interrupted, 'write the poem, and I will come when Isabel recites it. Go now and think—think of what I have ven-tured to say.'

'I go, Claire; but in a few weeks——'

'Go, Allen. Good-night.'

'Art,' said my father, presently, 'should

be represented as a sorceress, who takes the strength from the hands of her lover, so that he can do nothing by himself but leaves him his eyes and ears. Then he watches and listens, and presently he imitates, groups, and copies. She is a beautiful sorceress, or else no one would fall in love with her. Yes, she takes away their strength; they can work no longer, and they have no heart for fighting.'

'They can sing and paint, and write romances and plays.'

'That is their reward, my child; but it is better to fight than to make songs of battle. Allen does not think so. Well, he has his reward.'

'And you yours,' I said. 'Why, who made the boy a poet?'

He lifted his shoulders and spread his hands.

The very next evening I had a visit from Olinthus. He came through the garden and walked through the open window. I did not see him at first; and, when I did, instead of offering me his hand, he began to groan in a most heartrending manner.

' What is the matter, Olinthus ? '

' Nothing—that is, everything. But it doesn't matter. You will only say it's a pity ; and the girls are provided for, and so is the old lady. It won't really matter to anyone.'

' But what is it? I suppose you are come here on purpose to tell me, are you not? '

' I have come to tell you, Claire, because you are the only person in all the world who will not jeer and sneer and grin. Even the girls will sniff. Oh ! I know I should have grinned myself and sniffed, very likely, if it had happened to anybody else except me. Everybody in the City always grins when a man goes wrong.'

' Have you gone wrong, then ? '

' Hush ! '—he stole like a conspirátor to the door and looked into the hall—' hush ! Where is your father, Claire ? '

' He is in the garden with Sir Charles. We are quite alone.'

'It's a dreadful thing. After two years and more of such success, it's a cruel thing —and I told him so—and a wicked thing. The man must be a devil. Yes, that's it. He can't be a man, he must be a devil; and he looks it.'

'If you will explain a little——'

He went on incoherently rambling.

'He led me into it; he gave me the taste for it, and made me feel the pride of it, and to seem clever and all; and then he wouldn't teach me how to do it, and I couldn't find out for all the trying in the world. Then he taught me to pretend. Ah! Claire, there's the sting when they find out that it was all pretence. The smash I could bear—anybody may smash —but it is the pretence that I can't stand up against. I shall go away to some place where they never heard my name, and live there for the rest of my life. I must. Why, they would laugh at me in the very streets if I were to go about. Oh, he's a devil! He must be.'

'What is pretence?'

'I will tell you all, Claire, just exactly as it happened, because you won't laugh. Besides, it was all done for your sake, every bit.'

'Every bit? Oh, Olinthus! And the Countess and the baccarat?'

'Very nearly all. The baccarat doesn't count. But I will tell you all, though I know very well what the consequence will be. I looked to coming here in two or three weeks with a diamond spray and an emerald ring. Yes! I've had my eye on the spray and the ring for a long time. And I've been looking for a house. None of your common four hundred a year Cromwell Road houses, but a palace in Kensington Palace Gardens. There is one to let now; a marble palace fit for a queen, or even for you, Claire. I was just going to close with the agent when I found that the place was let, and let to that—that man. Yes, I know what you were going to say, Claire, and it is like yourself to say it, but love in a palace is ten times as good as love in a measly villa.'

'I was not going to say that at all, Olinthus. I was going to say that it would have been a great pity for you to have built upon any hopes that—that——'

'Why, the other fellows are nothing at all: one of them only a literary scrub; and the other——'

'Will you please go on with your story?'

'And now it's all over. It's just as well that I did not take the house and order that spray, because now you won't even think of me. And yet I shall not be a pauper like Allen, or a clerk like Will. Perhaps you will consider that. Look here, Claire,' his voice sank to a whisper, 'I may be smashed, but it won't all go. There's a snug little sum in my mother's hands; I gave it to her to keep for me three months ago, when we had our last great shindy. And besides, you've got plenty of your own, and perhaps your father might live with us. I should not mind it much, if I had the buying of the claret.'

'Do pray get on with the story, or I will get up and go away.'

'No, no, I *will* go on. Listen then. I am a ruined man. That is the first thing.'

'But I thought you were so rich and so successful.'

'So I was. Now I am ruined.' His voice broke down, and he began to cry like a school-boy. It was undignified, but he could not help it, and indeed it was a very pitiful thing after so much greatness. I could think of nothing in the way of comfort. However, presently he recovered a little, and went on to tell me all.

It was a truly wonderful story that he had to tell. The boy whom we had first thought dull and stupid, and had afterwards been com-pelled to consider a miracle of cleverness, had never really done anything at all to make the world change its opinion. He was, indeed, so dull that he was persuaded to lend himself to a most extraordinary deception, entirely for the advantage of the contriver. He was believed by everybody to have a wonderful genius and insight into finance; he knew nothing whatever about it; while he was making thousands he knew no more of the science than any school-girl; *he would not even learn it.* He knew only the talk or jargon of it. I looked with a sort of amazement at a man who had so little dignity and self-respect as to play the part which he had played.

'I've made for Colliber,' he said, with con-viction, as if he really had made the money by his own sagacity and wisdom, 'I've made for Colliber over a hundred and fifty thousand pounds in two years. Why, my own share came to fifty thousand.'

'And where is it—all this money?'

'Some of it is spent; some of it is—where I told you,' he jerked his thumb in the direc-tion of his mother's house. 'Some of it the creditors will get.'

'But even now,' I said, 'you have not told me how it is that you are ruined.'

He then proceeded to explain with a great fulness how there was a rascally company established through the wicked cleverness of Mr. Colliber first, and next by himself, acting under Mr. Colliber's directions, and thirdly, by a selection of modern brigands, for the purpose of plundering English investors. The company was rotten, he said, from the beginning ; it had not the slightest chance of success as soon as the real facts were known. But in order to get the shares taken up it was necessary to hide these facts very carefully. So the prospectus was drawn up by Mr. Colliber himself, and was a masterpiece of suppression. Also in heightening and bringing out the few facts which could be of use to the new company the prospectus was unrivalled. The effect of this prospectus was that a great many of the shares were taken up and the company floated. And then began Mr. Colliber's usual game, which was to keep on forcing the shares by creating a demand and making a clatter about the company. More shares were taken up. But the facts came out. Then the shares went down to nothing at all, and the shareholders began to clamour.

'There is always some one,' said Olinthus, 'who won't lose his money without a fight for it. No one can deny that the prospectus was a bundle of lies. Colliber drew it up, so it must have been. All the prospectuses came out of my office, but at first nobody knew it. And now they've found it out, and they charge it upon me, and I've got to stand the racket.'

' What does that mean ? '

It appeared that it meant this. He would have to take up the whole of the worthless stock. Now all his available money would not suffice to take up a fourth part of the stock. Therefore he must go bankrupt, unless Mr. Colliber stood by him. And at this juncture Mr. Colliber deserted him ; told Olinthus that he had given him every opportunity for making his fortune ; that for his own part no one could come upon him, because he was not mixed up in the business at all, and, in fact, he was not known to be concerned in any part of the business ; but he had for some time been satisfied with the results of the partnership, and was, in fact, about to retire. He wished his partner success in the future; if he had to go bankrupt over this unlucky company it was only what he, Colliber, had done several years before; and that Olinthus, like himself, would be able to reflect with pride on his by-gone greatness. Doubtless, too, he added with a sneer, Gallaway would before long return to the work, bringing with him his old experience and the extraordinary sagacity which had astonished the whole world. He really was a most wonderful man, Mr. Colliber.

When I began to understand the story, I perceived that one was as much a robber as the other. I told Olinthus so. His sister's dowries, the gift of a house to his mother, the money he had placed in her hands—all these ought to be restored and given to the creditors

'As for my sisters,' said Olinthus, 'if I know the dear girls, they will see the creditors farther first; as for my mother, she won't give up her house unless she knows the reason why, nor the money, so long as she can stick to it.

And as for me, I mean to stick to every penny that I can.'

He could not understand the iniquity of his own share in the matter. That Mr. Colliber was a clever rogue he knew, and greatly admired his cleverness; but that he himself was anything but a deeply injured man he did not know or understand.

'If I had refused to put out that prospectus,' he moaned, 'he would have dissolved partnership at once; if ever I refused to do blindly what he ordered, he threatened that. And he was so greedy, and took three-fourths. And after all to make me liable!'

Mr. Colliber had then gone away. 'He has gone,' said his partner, 'with a hundred and fifty thousand in his pocket, and I have got to go bankrupt. As for consideration from the shareholders, not a bit, if you please. They'd tear me to pieces if they could. And if they did Colliber would look on with a grin.'

'Well, it is all over then.'

'All but the bankruptcy. That will happen

in a few days, I suppose—or weeks—or something. I don't know. I've been to a solicitor, and put my affairs in his hands. There's enough for him at any rate.'

'Then, now, Olinthus, you can return to honest work.'

'Oh! the old trade again. No, thank you, Claire. I've got enough to live on, and I shall do no more work, honest or not.'

He was resolute upon this point. As for dishonest work, he could do it no longer, because he did not know how to do it. And as for honest work and drudgery, his three years of riotous living and easy gains made it impossible to take up again the monotony of steady work and slow thrift.

It really was no use telling him that he might now turn his attention to honest work.

'There's one good thing I've done'—he began to laugh, and the effect was like a gleam of sunshine on a rainy day. 'This morning, while I was sitting in my office, pretty miserable, wishing Mr. Colliber would come back if only to call me an ass and a fool, who should call but the Countess? She pranced in, smiling sweetly, and she said she came to apologise for her bad temper six months ago. But I knew what she wanted. She had never forgiven herself, she said, after my kindness to her, and that she couldn't sleep at night for thinking of her ingratitude, and would I forgive her? Nobody can tell lies so sweetly as the Countess. Well : I said I would—I knew what she wanted very well; and would I forgive her brother, who, she heard with pain, had written an intemperate letter. I said I would—I knew, of course, what she was driving at—if he would pay his debt of honour, which was seventy-five pounds. Would I then shake hands? I did shake hands with her, Claire, knowing what would come next. So then her ladyship sighed and looked friendly—she's got the most beautiful eyes, I must say—eyes that go straight through a fellow and make him feel groggy in the knees—and said that as we were now good friends again, and she meant never, never, never to lose her temper any more, she wanted to consult me about a little transaction. She had been recommended to buy Argentines or Brazilians. Which could I recommend? Now it was only two days before that Mr. Colliber told me Brazilians would fall rapidly—he knew why, but did not tell me the reason. So I saw my chance. I was a cad, when she quarrelled with me: I was her dear friend, when she wanted me. And so I told her to go away at once and buy as much Brazilian stock as she could get. She sailed away with the liveliest smile, I do assure you. I wish I had asked her to give me a kiss. And both she and her brother have put on a pot for Brazilians and are telling all their friends; and won't there be a row in a fortnight?'

Then I asked him if anybody else had been told the whole story.

He said no one.

Would Mr. Colliber talk about it?

He said that he supposed Mr. Colliber's interests lay rather in keeping dark.

In that case I advised him to tell nobody else, unless, which perhaps might be best and yet would be a hard thing to do, he made a clean breast of the whole business.

It gave him great consolation to think that he might perhaps still, though bound to future obscurity, pass honourably for having been once a great financier. In the first dismay caused by the disaster, he felt as if all must be found out.

'I suppose,' he said, 'that it will take two or three months to get through the Court.— Oh! they are a vindictive crew. There's one man, a clergyman, who ought to be a Christian, and because he's lost a paltry five thousand pounds he heads the lot—says I made false representations. There's a pretty Christian for you! Well, Claire, I am glad I told you. Will that ten thousand make any difference in your views?'

'No, Olinthus. None.'

'And we might have been so happy together. We were made for each other. My mother says so, ever since you got your money. Before that, she said it was marrying beneath, and I ought to look higher.'

'Well—never mind. Thank you for thinking so much of me, Olinthus. I could never have married you, not if you had continued in your great success.'

'Never married me?'

'No; never.

'Not if I'd got the house in Palace Gardens?'

'Not even then. Oh! Olinthus, can't you understand that I would rather marry you in your poverty than when you were heaping up riches by defrauding and plundering widows and children and credulous persons?'

But that he could not understand.

CHAPTER VII.

A SECOND VICTOR HUGO.

THEN the time began to pass swiftly towards
the end. If you watch the flow of a river
over a weir you will see that the water seems
to linger and go slow a little before the point
where it leaps the little cataract; then with a
rush it sweeps forward, and is gone. For
three long years I had waited in patience, yet
never forgetting what was before me; at last the
time seemed to move more slowly; to others,
no doubt, it hastened forward, hurrying the
old towards their end, the dying towards their
death; but to me it seemed to linger so that
every hour could be felt and remembered.
Outside was the promise of the early summer
in the gardens, and in the Forest the first

fluttering foliage, on which the sunshine always, year after year, seems to lie like the bloom upon a peach.

I remembered a day long gone by, when we made a little picnic, one of many little picnics, in the Forest, and played about the glades, and the boys ran a race for what my father called the Prize of the Golden Apple, which was only an orange after all; and I held it for the victor. Now, after ten years, and more, the boys were to stand before me again. Why, just as before, one of them was out of the race altogether; and of the other two, just as before, no one could say which of the two came in first. I knew not who was the appointed judge; and yet the prize was no longer a golden apple, but a life's happiness. Not so much my own, but that of two men. Yet—the happiness of both? Of one there could be no doubt. He was so loyal, so steadfast, so true. Though he said no single word of love in his letters, it was clear of what his mind was full. And he was coming home—

all that long way!—on purpose to keep his appointment. Poor Will! could one send him empty away, and with a bleeding heart?

It was of Allen that I doubted. I am quite sure by this time that poets and men of imagination, who are always creating another world of their own filled with imaginary people, who are always studying those people, and watching them, and thinking about them, take less real hold upon things of actual life than men of action. They dwell continually in the unreal, so that things actual may grow to look like things imagined. They think much less about themselves than ordinary folk; they desire for themselves little beyond the success of their work; they are not troubled with the ambitions of ordinary men, except as on-lookers who are sometimes angered by the badness of a performance; the world is a stage to them, and men and women players. This is the reason, I suppose, why they do not grow old like their friends, but remain young in heart, and at fifty are still full of youthful thoughts.

All their waking hours they spend in dreams, among ghosts and shadows. When another man is in love he thinks all day long, and perpetually, of the girl he loves; but he who writes romances is always thinking of another woman as well, as well as of her whom he has married or is about to marry. She who marries such a man must be content to take a second place in her lover's heart without jealousy, because the first is occupied by the girl of his story, much lovelier, younger, cleverer than herself, and quite as real to him as the wife of his bosom. Again, a man who does not write can give all his best thoughts, if he is capable of fine thought, and his sweetest words, if he knows any sweetness of speech, to the girl he loves; but the man who does, keeps them for his own pages. He is a man of a thousand amourettes; he coquettes with every little insignificant girl who crosses the stage in his dramas; he secretly entertains, and continually feeds and fosters, for his heroines, *grandes passions*: he

is never out of love so long as he writes.
What spare love can such an one find for his
wife?   It is a strange life.   Does, one wonders,
the man who has written many stories ever
sit down to think of the long procession of
beautiful girls, tender, sweet, and true, with
their brave and gallant lovers whom he has
created for the world's delight?   Do they
delight him only to think of them?   Does he
raise his own heart by repeating to himself the
wise and noble things which his puppets have
said? or is he ashamed in meditating on the
foolish things he has allowed them to say? or
does he—it makes one sad to think that he
may do this—does he go away when his work
is finished and straightway forget it all—the
characters and their story, the lovers and the
maidens, the sadness and the joy; and put
them out of his mind lest they interfere with
the grouping and the dialogue of the next
story?   I thought of all this, and perhaps
thought too much of it.   I remembered how
Allen forgot and put out of his mind the girl

whom he had made to live for ever in the memories of those who .read his story. He must have loved her, while he wrote her life; yet he forgot her. Would he not forget me, too, if I were to go away out of his sight? And yet, on the other hand, why should one think of Allen in this way? There have been many poets, artists, and writers of fiction married happily for all that the world could see ; and, after all, a mistress of flesh and blood must always be a very different thing from a mistress of the imagination. There was no change in Allen. He came to me for advice and help as he always had done—a man who must always lean on some one, and be encouraged by praise and pleasant words. Never for a moment had I suspected the least change in Allen's feelings. To make those eager eyes sad would be indeed a dreadful thing.

Yet there was Isabel. Should not one think of her? For I had learned her secret, and she was born to be the wife of such a man. She would live for him, divine his

thoughts, lead him on, console and sympathise
with him in the way that only one who knows
the mystery and craft of literature can do.
What could I do for Allen compared with
what she could do?

Then it occurred to me that a way was
possible in which the true state of Allen's
mind might be discovered by him as well as
by myself.   It was simply that Gertrude
should pay her long-promised visit to us before
the day of Fate instead of after it.   I wanted
to watch Allen with Isabel again—even to
question him, because it is difficult for a woman
to read the mind of a man.

There wanted only a week of that day.   I
declare that I knew not, even so late, on
whom the choice would fall; nor did I suspect in the least that there would be no choice
to make.   Only a week !   Why Will must be
through the canal.   The ship must be driving
through the water day and night to land him
on the Italian shores.   Only three days and he

would be rolling across the Continent; only six and he would be among us again!

Gertrude was so good as to give up her evenings and her engagements, though it was the middle of the season, and the talk about the pictures and the concerts and all still in its freshness. It seems terrible to think that for the finest pictures, on which men have spent, it may be, years of work, there cannot be found more than a week or two of talk, even among people like Gertrude and her friends, who do not waste their time in society and scandal, and to whom the fashionable world is merely a spectacle when they choose to look at it for awhile. Only a week or two! And it is the same with the most beautiful book, the bravest deed, the finest work of music—only a week or two of talk, and then it is forgotten! But still it lives. In the world of London where new things follow each other so quickly needs must that to-day's event drives out the recollection of yesterday: but there is a world outside where new things last longer. Isabel brought with her Allen's manuscript play, now completed and intended to be read as a surprise for Gertrude. I was so foolish as to feel a little jealousy that she, and Allen with her, should be so eager about the play when a matter of so much importance was awaiting to be decided.

'You are wrong, my child,' my father said, reading my thoughts. 'To the artist his work is of more importance than his love. Let us read the play.'

Perhaps Allen had forgotten the nearness of the day. Gertrude, at all events, had not forgotten. She took both my hands in hers and pressed them as soon as we were alone.

'My dear,' she said in her sweet soft voice, 'I think it is wonderfully good of you to ask us at such a time. I thought you would wait until—until we had sent Allen to learn his fate.'

'Has Allen forgotten the day?' I asked, with a little jealousy.

'We talked of it yesterday,' she replied.

I suppose I looked surprised. Could Isabel

have discussed the subject? There is sometimes in women a courage greater than the
courage of man.

'My dear,' she added, 'you were quite
wrong. Indeed you were. Isabel looks on
Allen as her brother. We talked of you in
the twilight. I think the twilight in a London
house at this time of the year is delightful.
There is the scent of the lime blossoms—of
course I don't mean a house when there are
no trees and flowers—in the air, there are
flowers in the open windows, and as you sit in
the dusk, strange thoughts come upon one.
Yes, even to me, my dear, old as I am. And
then outside there are the mysterious voices
and steps of the people. What are they talking about? Whither are they going? Are
they spirits or are they real? Yes, we sat
beside the window and talked of you, my
dear. Allen told us over again the story of
his childhood and your early loves, and your
sweet sympathy with him. Oh, Claire, it is an
idyl of love.'

'Gertrude, you would not care for it unless you could dress it up and make it in your mind romantic.'

'It wants no dressing. There are some things which the imagination cannot improve. Why, you are a part of his life, Claire.'

'Yes, Allen loves me, I know that well enough. But yet——'

'But yet?'

'Will he not love me just as well and just the same if——'

'No, Claire—no, my dear; you must not think so.'

'Oh! Gertrude, can you not see? Are you blind? But listen, I have asked you here in order that Allen may find out for himself the difference. Gertrude, I could never make Allen so happy as Isabel will. And she loves him; I am jealous for Allen's happiness. I know that she loves him, even if she has never dared to let herself know the truth.'

Gertrude made no reply for a few moments; then she said, thoughtfully:

'Poor Isabel! and I never guessed. And you would let him go? My dear, it seems impossible. You would let this genius—this poet—go to another woman?'

'I would not, if I were Isabel; but I am not—and besides——'

'Besides, there is the other; but what is he like, then, the young hero? Is he an Apollo? Is he the Sun God? How does he outshine my poet?'

'You shall see him; he will arrive now in a day or two.'

'Before I knew you, my dear,' Gertrude went on, 'I was curious to find out who and what the girl was who drew all hearts. Now I know; yes, my dear,' she took my hands in hers, 'now I know very well indeed. But this Will, I cannot understand him yet.'

'You shall see him, Gertrude; but even then you may not understand him. Perhaps he will not be interesting to you, until you know him as Allen and I know him.'

Then my father came with Isabel and Allen, and our talk was stopped.

. . . . .

Naturally, we began with the Forest. There is one fault, and only one, which can be alleged against my Forest. It is sometimes undoubtedly wet under foot. The soil is clay, and the water lies in little pools. One cannot deny the charge. This day, fortunately, it was dry; there had been sunshine for nearly a week, a most wonderful thing for this rain-plagued climate of England. We could walk anywhere; through the narrow lanes arched over with the tender foliage of the spring, among the old trunks where there were no lanes at all, and over the broad stretches of turf which once had been our playground, our race-course, our theatre.

'This is the Forest,' said Gertrude, looking round her, 'which made Allen—what he is.'

'Nay,' said Allen, ' not the Forest only, my Master is here.'

Said my father—

'He who teaches a young man sows an unknown seed in an unknown soil. He knows not what may spring up. I thought to make a statesman, and behold! I make a poet.'

'You could not,' said Gertrude, 'oh! you could not make a greater than a poet. To be a statesman! to make large promises and not to be able to do the smallest things; to be continually reviled and held up to ridicule; to sacrifice truth and honour for the sake of Party—you would not, M. Philipon, desire such a life for Allen?'

'I did, mademoiselle, and still I would desire such a life. To a strong man blame would be nothing. But the strong man will not get blame, because he can perform what he promises. Do you know why your statesmen are continually reviled and ridiculed, and why they have to go out every three years? It is because they pretend to be, but are not, strong. The statesman of my hopes was one who would draw his strength from his own knowledge, not from the ignorant people who would send him to power. I dreamed of the strong man whom we all look for, but who never comes.'

'And then—and then,' said Gertrude, 'literature is the natural ladder by' which young men may climb.'

'That is, pardon a thousand times, perhaps the least suspicion of prejudice. It shows that the Republican idea has not yet touched the heart of mademoiselle. Why not a boy from a quiet and obscure village, taught by a Frenchman, as well as a young earl or the son of a cotton man?'

What my father said was true. Gertrude would have thought it a laudable ambition in a rich man to train his son for a political career. Yet it seemed to her absurd in the case of a poor lad born to be a city clerk. We know so little of the depth and reality of the Republican spirit which is abroad, outside our little island. It did not seem absurd to my father —this ambitious project.

'All statesmen,' said Isabel, 'seem to me

false and treacherous. Better the smallest ballad, if it is good, than the longest speech.'

' However,' said Gertrude, ' it was a noble dream, and this is a beautiful place. If you had not lived here, M. Philipon, Allen might have realised your hopes, and made speeches to the people. Let us sit a little and feel the silence. This is better than Richmond Park.'

It was so silent that afternoon, that we might have been fifty miles from any dwelling-place of man. No one was in the Forest except ourselves. We sat upon the fallen trunk which had been our friend so long, and were silent. There was a lark overhead, and there was a twitter of birds from the trees; a blackbird and a thrush were not far off, a cuckoo was close beside us; a long way off we heard the tinkle of a bell. I had never known the Forest more silent or sweeter. As we sat, the lark suddenly dropped straight down; the twitter of the birds ceased; there was a stillness which made itself felt, while overhead there hovered, motionless, a hawk.

Presently it darted away, and the birds began again.

'In this place,' said Gertrude, breaking the silence, 'one might dream away a lifetime. Of course Allen became a poet. Why did you not all dream in sweet verse? We must come, Isabel, and stay here a long summer through.'

'The Forest is not always so gracious,' I said; 'sometimes it is wet and muddy; sometimes, in cloudy weather, it loses its colour, and in cold east winds it loses its perfume.'

'A forest is like the sea,' said Gertrude. 'Its moods are many; they are never quite the same; and one never tires of it, and one is always tempted to say something about it; something which shall be new, a thing never said before. Like the sea, it satisfies; it is sympathetic; it responds to every thought.'

'And yet,' I said, 'you would long for London and your evenings after you had been here a month.'

She laughed. 'I believe I should. That

is my punishment, to love nature much, but society more. After all we are gregarious.'

Then it grew time to leave the Forest, and we came slowly back. I lagged behind with Gertrude, and Isabel between my father and Allen.

' Does your father never desire more society —a more active life ? '

' Not now. I think he did at one time. When we became rich—that is, what we call rich—his habits were formed ; he desired nothing more than to bask in the sunshine and to work in his garden. So we remained here.'

' But you will not remain here now——'

' I do not know.'

' You would not—oh ! Claire, you could not take Allen away ; yes, I know you have told me, but I cannot believe.'

' Could I take him from you, and from his present life, and from Isabel ? Do you think I could if I were to try ? '

' I think you can do with him what you please.'

'I can do a great deal, but not quite that. Without you, dear Gertrude—and Isabel—he would have no life.'

' Ah, Claire! do not make him unhappy.'

'Perhaps I will make him the happiest man in the world. Is he not a man who wants constant encouragement and sympathy?'

'Yes; more than any man I have ever known. And he seeks it of you.'

' Yes; he tells me of his anxieties, but he finds his encouragement—from Isabel.'

After dinner, we had arranged for Isabel to read Allen's play, of which Gertrude knew nothing. It was a three-act drama—a tale of the present day. We converted the drawing-room into a little theatre, of which the stage was one end. I was the orchestra at the piano, and we placed three chairs for the audience, consisting of Gertrude, my father, and Allen. My father was as yet not advanced much beyond the stage of compliment; he had made a great many of the dear old-fashioned kind about wit and beauty, and

Venus and the Muse, but I have suppressed them. Gertrude, however, liked them, and said that a woman never became too old to value a compliment, and that in the dear old days of the *salons* it was a man's chief study how best to turn a compliment. I think, indeed, that my father would have been better pleased if we had proposed to spend the evening in these harmless gallantries, especially with Isabel. But we gave him no choice, and he had to sit down and listen. I remembered a former occasion when Allen read his first verses, which were so execrable that I could have cried. My father assumed exactly the same critical attitude with a certain benevolent kindliness, as if he was prepared to sacrifice truth to compliment, because Englishmen, as is well known, cannot write plays, but must needs steal them from the French. Allen, doubtless, would be no exception ; still, he must be heard.

Then Isabel began. I suppose it was an easy thing for her to do, but to me it certainly seemed a very great thing. She had actually learned the whole drama; she rolled up the manuscript, holding it in her hand as an aid to gesture, and began to act the play. She acted it so well that my father quite forgot his critical attitude and his benevolent expression, and became, naturally, the Frenchman at a play; in other words, he sat with parted lips and wonder-stricken eyes, drinking in the scene. To see an actress on the stage among the painted scenes, dressed for her part, among the rest of the company, is one thing. To see her acting in ordinary evening dress, in a drawing-room, is another and a far greater thing. For to be carried away by the illusion of a stage is easy, but it is only a real actress who can carry her hearers out of themselves, with no scenic effects, no dress, no assistance of any kind.

This Isabel did; she played the parts each in turn herself; she became all the parts, one after the other; we did not want to be told who was speaking; by quick gesture, by sudden change of voice and manner, she sustained the whole. And I alone knew that she played it for one of her audience. Only my eye saw her quick glance at Allen, which said, although he saw it not, 'Is this the true interpretation of your thought? Poet, is this justice to your work?' No; Allen seemed not to see it. He looked nervously from Gertrude to me as if he read our verdict. Isabel had taken all this trouble for him; she was interpreting his thought; she was giving life to his puppets. He took her labour as if it was a gift of no consequence. Poor Isabel!

When she finished, at the very last words of the third act, her voice broke down, she stopped suddenly, and she fled. To the others it seemed an artistic finish: the drama ended, the actress disappeared. It was like the dropping of the curtain. I, who knew better, followed her. She had rushed to her own room, where I found her weeping and crying.

'Isabel,' I threw my arms round her and kissed her. 'Isabel, I have learned all.'

There was nothing to learn, she declared. It was the exertion; she was foolish; she would be better directly, she was better already.

She rose at once; she bathed her eyes and met my look with a calm and steady gaze. Yet she knew that I possessed her secret.

'Oh, Isabel' I whispered, 'can you think that I would take him from you?'

'But he loves you—you—you,' she replied passionately. 'We must make him happy. That is the first thing. We must make him happy. Come, Claire, what does it matter about ourselves? We have got to make him happy.'

We went back. Gertrude and my father were waiting for us. Then my father rose and solemnly bowed low to Allen.

'Poet and dramatist,' he said, 'I salute thee. Thou shalt be a Master, another Victor Hugo, a Chateaubriand.'

Allen blushed and trembled with pleasure.

Then he turned to Isabel. 'Mademoiselle,'

he said, 'it is the province of your art to interpret the art of the poet. Permit me to lay at your feet the assurance of my most profound admiration. Rachel could not have acted better.'

'You played it so well, Isabel,' I said, 'because no one knows Allen so well as yourself.'

'It is a great play,' said Gertrude. 'Give me the manuscript to-morrow. No, Allen, I will not dare to alter a single word. But I will suggest perhaps. Isabel, my dear, you played better to-night then you have ever played before.'

'What can I say to thank you enough, Isabel?' asked Allen.

'Oh!' she shook her head, 'I want no thanks. If Claire thinks that the play is good and worthy of you, that is enough.'

'Tell Allen, *mon père,*' I said, ' what we think of his play.'

'It is a play so good, my son,' he replied, ' that Claire shall translate it into French and we will offer it to the Français. Can I say more, my dear?'

Allen's face was soft and his eyes luminous with the joy of his work. I laughed in my heart to think that this man was to be judged as an ordinary lover. There was a mathematician once who forgot his wedding-day; there was a German scholar who so far observed that festival that he only read for twelve hours instead of fourteen; there was the case of Sir Isaac Newton, who used his mistress's finger as a tobacco-stopper; but I think I cannot remember any instance in history of a poet three or four days before the question which is supposed to mean a life's happiness has to be answered, who yet was carried away and absorbed in his own poem.

Isabel's eyes met mine, and made answer, 'What does it matter about ourselves? We have first to make them happy.'

CHAPTER VIII.

WILL'S RETURN.

THE next day and the day after, and the day after that, we showed our guests all our beautiful places; we drove about through leafy lanes and past picturesque cottages standing in the midst of flowers; we went to the quiet little town of Abridge, on the river Roding, standing in a circle as if it had once been within a round wall; we showed them the wild parts of Epping Forest and Copped Hall Park, and the burial place among the quiet trees of Harold and his brothers; we took them to Chigwell with its great trees and solemn churchyard, and to old Chingford Church, falling slowly and sadly to pieces, with shattered windows and bending roof and bare interior, and quiet old place of graves, which looks out upon the broad valley of the Lea. Everywhere there were trees with sunshine, flowers, and the singing of birds and a sweet calm.

'My dear,' said Gertrude, 'this is the true birthplace of a poet.'

'Yet at the West-end you know nothing of it.'

'I thought that Epping and all about it was given over to the mob who drink beer and break branches and shout,' she said.

'Only a little of the forest. Beyond High Beech you have solitude and quiet. At Hainault we are nearly always left in peace. And the quiet lanes beyond are never visited.'

'I am glad to have come here,' she said. 'Isabel, do you feel that we understand Allen better from seeing the place where he was brought up?'

Isabel was thinking about him, I suppose, because she started and blushed.

'To-night,' I said, 'you will meet some of

the people among whom Allen lived. They, at
least, did not help to make him a poet.'

It was my evening. They all came: Sir
Charles and Lady Withycomb, and Mr. and
Mrs. Massey, and Mrs. Gallaway with her three
daughters, and some of the girls from the
school and some from the village, and half-a
dozen young men. I was very careful that
Gertrude should talk to most of them. It was
delightful to witness her bewildered look when
the good old City knight told her of the
glorious failures of the leading residents and
related his story about the Prince of Wales. I
wanted her to understand perfectly, that in this
talk of money and of the City there was no
place for the lofty thoughts and splendid verse
on which Allen's soul had been nourished. I
wanted to make her feel that the only house in
the village where such things could be encouraged or comprehended was our own, and the
only man who could encourage them was my
father. He it was, and none other, who had
made a poet out of a City clerk. As for my

evening, it was not, to be sure, like Gertrude's. We had no people who had done anything, but we amused ourselves. The school-girls played a Proverb of De Musset's, and Sir Charles went sound asleep and snored ; one or two of us played and sang ; and presently we cleared away the chairs and began as usual to dance ; and while I played the first waltz, I heard Mr. Massey explaining to Gertrude the folly and wickedness of Allen in giving up his place and prospects in the City for the penniless and despised profession of letters. This annoyed me for the moment, because I thought she might be set against Will, since he had a father of mind so narrow. He also told Gertrude, but this I learned afterwards, that Allen had no chance with me at all, and his own son very little, because the third suitor, Olinthus Gallaway, had risen to so amazing a pitch of greatness that it was impossible for a dazzled maid to resist his attractions. Altogether Gertrude passed a very astonished evening.

It was eleven o'clock and our friends were

beginning to separate, some of the elder ones had already gone, we were dancing the last waltz, Isabel and Allen together, and I was sitting out.

Do you know that there are some sounds which you can hear above and among all others, however loud they may be? The sound I heard, above the music and the laughter and the talk, was the sound of a footstep on the gravel of the garden walk. I had not heard that step for three years. But yet I knew and heard it amid the buzz of talk, the sound of the piano and the laughter of the girls. It surprised me for the moment to think that Allen did not hear it. But he was dancing with Isabel. His arm was round her waist; her face was lying on his shoulder. How should he hear?

I sprang to my feet and stepped quickly through the window, which was open to the lawn. The night was dark, but I saw his figure standing within the garden rails as if in hesitation, and I ran across the lawn to meet him.

He seized me as I came by both hands and held them in his strong firm grasp, though his voice trembled.

'Claire!' was all he said. And I said nothing because I could not speak, and because at that moment I felt that there was no longer any doubt or hesitation possible, and that for me there was only one man in the world whom I could love, as Will wished me to love him.

Had he taken me in his arms that moment I should have told him all; but he did not. He only held my hands for a minute and let me go.

'Come, Will,' I said, ' and see my father.'

'I have not seen my own yet,' he replied. 'I came here straight from the station, where I have left everything till to-morrow. But you have a party, Claire.'

'It is only my evening. Come, Will, I have told you about my evenings.'

'One moment, Claire. You are well? Let me look at you.'

'We were on the lawn, and by the light

of the room he looked in my face, and I in his. My heart sank, and I felt humbled and ashamed because of the great love which I saw in those brave eyes of his. Never girl had braver lover.

Then I turned away, confused, and led him by the hand into the room; and my father sprang to his feet and cried 'Will!' and the dancers stopped, and Allen left Isabel, and the girls of the village all ran to shake him by the hand; and the school-girls caught hold of each other and looked at me, because they knew— dear me! everybody knew—my love-story, and gazed upon the suitor whom they had never seen, and whispered to each other that he was the tallest and properest of the three. Isabel stood by Gertrude's chair watching him curiously.

He was only a handsome lad when he went away; he returned to us a handsome man now, firm and well set up, his cheek a little bronzed with the sea-breezes; a strong man, his head erect, his bearing confident, his voice firm. He shook hands with all the girls, laughing, and then with my father, and, last of all, with Allen.

'I knew, Allen,' he said, 'what would happen. Tell me, Claire, does he know how proud we are of him?'

There was always a great contrast between the two; the one so eager, restless, and nervous, and the other so self-reliant, so calm and strong; but it seemed intensified. Allen's eyes had, more than ever, the far-off, expectant look of one who lives in imagination. Will's more than ever the steady, watchful look of one who works. His eyes were like the eyes of a pilot for trusty watch and ward. For him, the world was full of work to be done, and it was no place for dreams. To Allen, the only work was in dreams. Then I led him to Gertrude.

'Gertrude,' I said, 'this is Will; he landed this very day, and has come straight to see us. Will, this is Miss Gertrude Holt, and this is Miss Isabel Holt. They are Allen's very best and dearest friends, and have helped him to make the splendid beginning of which we are all so proud.'

Gertrude shook hands with him, saying something kind. After that, the evening was broken up. Everybody felt that we should like to be left alone, and they kindly went away. But the eldest Miss Gallaway whispered to me, with meaning, that Olinthus would be jealous if it was not for the fact that there were only three days left. She also said that Allen's disappointment would be easily consoled, and that something must be done in the village for the consolation of Will. Olinthus, she said, was talking of a house in Kensington Palace Gardens; of course, it mattered nothing to him what the rent would be; and he had let fall something about a carriage and pair; but that his wife would have every reason to expect, and it was, in fact, due to his position. Then she went away. Poor girls! They little knew that the greatness they thought so much of was destroyed already irrecoverably.

So they were all gone and we were left to talk.

At midnight Gertrude left us, and soon after my father. I made Isabel stay; I wanted to make her feel, somehow, as if Will belonged to her, as well, already, because he would in a way belong to her in the future. One could not look forward to any severance of the sweet ties of love and friendship between us all. We went into the garden and sat with shawls about our heads, talking through the short summer night.

First we made Will tell us all his adventures, or as many of them as he could think of, because it was absurd to suppose that a man had been away for three long years, and among Chinamen with pigtails and Chinawomen with flat faces and pinched-up feet, without having more adventures than he could tell in a summer night. Ridiculous to tell us that residence in Shanghai is as dull almost as residence in our village by the Forest.

'It is, indeed,' he said, as monotonous as

life in the City but for the people you meet, the people from all over the world, the people with stories of adventure to tell. You come across them on board the steamers; they are going no one knows whither and coming no one knows whence, and they live no one knows how. They are always ready to go on to Fiji, or to land on Borneo, or to take a place at Shanghai; only to talk with these men is worth going all the way to China.'

'And no adventures, Will, among the Chinese?'

'None at all, Claire. But a good many talks among them. Never believe that the Chinese are a worn-out race or the Chinese Empire rotten. They are as vigorous a people as any in the world. Wait till the tug comes of Cossack *versus* China.'

We all agreed that we would wait, and presently he began to tell us long stories of the places he had seen, the narrow seas, the beautiful islands of the Malay Archipelago, Singapore upon its hills, and green Penang.

'You have heard enough about myself,' he said.

Just then the church clock struck one, but nobody took any notice. As if we were going to be ruled by clocks on the night when Will came home!

'Come, Allen, you have done something for yourself worth doing. Tell me about yourself and how you have got on?'

Then Allen with much hesitation began to tell his story, all of which you know perfectly well already, and how he had made no money yet but plenty of hope, that is to say, no longer the vague hope of a boy but the hope grounded on work done and praise gained. Isabel helped him with a word or two. All the night she was considering Will curiously, as if wondering how such a splendid man could come from so mean a place. Why, it was all my father's doing. He made a man of action and ambition out of Will and a poet out of Allen, and both by the same method; but then there could never be another man like my father.

And then we had to tell about Olinthus and his surprising rise, so that he alone out of the three who went into the City resolved to emulate Whittington seemed to have succeeded. I, for my own part, felt horribly, dreadfully guilty, because I knew the shameful, foolish secret of it all, and could have foretold the conclusion. If a man has been away for three years, there is so much to be told that can never be told by letter. We had become rich, Will had been told that by letter, and he rejoiced; we had left our little cottage and taken a large house, Will was told that; we got together the people of the place and had a weekly evening, he was told that; he was told everything, and yet until he saw for himself, he did not understand the difference all these things made.

'When I went away,' he explained to Isabel, 'nobody ever met; there was no dancing or singing or any pleasant things at all, only talk about money and the horrible stories about the bankruptcies.' Allen shuddered. 'And Claire lived in a pretty little cottage with rooms about as big as cupboards, like a doll's house, didn't you, Claire?'

'I have shown Isabel the furniture we had,' I said. 'We have kept it all and put it into the smallest room of the house.'

'And then I come home and find a dance, actually a dance going on, in the village, and the girls looking as if they enjoyed it, and my dear old friend like a nobleman of the *ancien régime.* To be sure, he always had that air, but not so much.'

'And yet a Republican, Will.'

'I know, or rather a man filled with the enthusiasm of humanity.

'Oh! the dream—the dream,' Allen said impatiently. 'It was fortunate for me that I never knew, until too late, about that dream.'

'A noble dream,' Will said, 'the noblest of all dreams. Yet, Allen, you always longed for what you have. Are you happy at last, Allen?'

He laid his hand on Allen's shoulder in the old familiar way. When girls kiss each other, young men lay heavy hands on each other's shoulders.

'I am as happy as I can be,' Allen replied. ' Am I not, Isabel?'

'How can I tell?' she replied quickly. Then she added gently. ' If to have succeeded in what you most desired makes one happy, you ought to be happy, Allen. For you have already succeeded.'

Will looked at his old friend with a quick, involuntary glance of surprise, first at him and then at Isabel. I knew, very well, what he meant. Could Allen be happy, he thought, with that question still to be answered? And who was this girl who sat with us as if she were one of us, one of the little band of friends? Why did Allen turn to her? Next day, when an opportunity came, he asked me what these things meant. I told him—well, the convenient half truth which left him even more puzzled than before. In no society of which he had any experience did the young men and the maidens, who were neither brothers and sisters nor cousins

nor lovers, call each other by the Christian name
and talk with an absence of reserve so complete.
' Can a man be in love with two girls at once ? '
he asked.

' I think not, Will.   Perhaps these are the
manners and customs of the literary world, of
which, you see, you know nothing.   It is a
pretty custom, is it not ? '

' For a girl to be called by her Christian
name by all the men?   I am only a China-
man, Claire, and know nothing, but I shouldn't
like to see you, for example, called by your
name.'

' Perhaps it is only a custom of the house,
Will.'

He shook his head and laughed.   ' Perhaps it is only Allen's playful way,' he said.
' Poets must do what they please.   They are
privileged.   What does it matter if Allen is
happy ? '

Why, here was Will, like all the rest, falling into the universal plot and conspiracy to
make Allen happy !

So we talked, and the short night drew on to daylight. It was nearly three o'clock in the morning, and the sun rises, in June, before four.

'No one wants to go to bed,' I said. 'Let us all go into the Forest and see the sun rise.'

Isabel and I changed our dresses for short walking frocks and stout boots, and we sallied forth into the still and quiet morning. We crossed the dewy meadow and plunged into the Forest, where beneath the trees there were hanging about some shadows of twilight. I told Will to lead the way, if he remembered.

'As if I could forget!' he said, and led the way.

I went next, and Isabel followed. Allen came last, as Will led us from the open glade by a wet and narrow lane—but no one cared for the long wet grass—among low overhanging branches to where on a high ground we could stand and see the rising of the sun.

Did you ever see the sun rise? You may
see it, if you are awake, on an average, I suppose, about one day in six ; and in June, when
the mornings are mostly fine, about every other
day. In order to see it in the summer you
must sit up all night, as we did ; or you must
get up very early indeed when you are in the
middle of your sleep. I had seen it from my
bed-room window in the old days, and especially those sad days when the boys first went
away, and I used to lie awake at night wondering how one could live three years without
them. Then I used to sit at the window and
watch the east for the first streak of day,
though when it came it very often found me
sleeping in the chair. But it is best to see it in
the Forest with the trees behind you, the grand
old trees which seem like yourself to be waiting
for the sunrise, and trees beside you and trees
sloping away before you, and far away in the
distance the country dark, silent and mysterious. But in the trees there is the twitter of
the birds, they are only half-awake and they

are dreaming. And in the branches there is the rustling of the leaves, as if the morning breeze was waking them from their slumbers. Then in the east the grey light which lies all round the horizon on a summer night begins to put on colour; and faint beautiful shades of opal, sapphire, and colours which have no name, and have never yet been caught by painter, lie in broad belts one above the other, each for a few moments only, and then long fingers of light shoot upwards into the sky, and the belts of colour melt and blend together, and all the birds wake up together and break into the morning hymn of praise, and the sun rolls upwards and warms the cold bosom of the earth. And who am I that I should try in feeble words to speak of this grand pageant of the dawn?

Suddenly a lark began to sing high over our heads, and we started and looked at each other.

' Claire,' whispered Isabel, catching my hand, her eyes filling with tears, ' I shall never forget this night, never—never. Oh! my dear. I know not what to think or say.'

'It is a fitting end to our talk,' I said. ' Will has come back, and Allen has succeeded, and we are at another dawn of a better day. Come, Isabel, let us go home.'

We left the boys and went back together, hand in hand, but silent.

'I have suffered, dear Isabel,' I said, ' because I did not know; but now I know and I am happy. It is the dawn of a happy day for you, dear Isabel, who love one of the two so much, and for me, because I love— the other. Kiss me, dear. Let us always be sisters. You have taken Allen's heart from me, and you have only made me happier for the loss. Remember what you said, " Above all things we must make him happy." '

'Oh, Claire!' the tears came again into her eyes. ' Can you, can any girl, give up Allen? And besides, you do not know——'

'Hush, Isabel! I know very well; but let us keep our secret.'

It was half-past four by this time. I suppose we ought to have gone to bed and lain awake thinking of our lovers. Alas! we were both outrageously hungry, and we went to the supper-room and ate cold chicken and drank claret-cup, and went to bed laughing as if there were no such thing as love in the world.

As for our lovers, I believe they had cigars and did not go to bed at all. And I know for certain that temper was exhibited in certain quarters when it became known that Will, after three years' absence, actually went first of all to see Claire, with whom and Allen Engledew he sat up all the night, only calling upon his own mother in the morning. I went to bed and to sleep, and perhaps I dreamed the thing and perhaps I heard it, but when I awoke a voice was in my ears—the voice of my father—and words saying, ' She will choose between the two, the man who acts and the man who writes, and I think that she will surprise us both. But let us wait, and find consolation for the others.'

Could Gertrude and my father have talked together in the garden while I was still asleep? and could I, in half-waking dreams, have heard them?

The man who acts. Surely it is best for a man to act. Men have to do the work of the world. That man who does it carries out the purpose for which he was born better than the man who talks about the worker. My choice? Why I never had any choice. Although I thought I was going to sit down and exercise a deliberate judgment, I could not do otherwise, when the time should come, but hold out both my hands and say, 'Take me, Will, I am your own.' I believe, if you rightly consider it, that this is the case with every woman. She does not choose, but she gives her love—because she cannot choose but give it.

CHAPTER IX.

THE OPINIONS OF A CHINAMAN.

THE return of one native is, I suppose, a great event in a quiet village, and here were two natives returned, one at least, carrying his sheaves with him, although to the general eye he seemed as if he was laden with straw and chaff and stubble and tares, instead of golden grain. So that the return of Will, who had certainly 'got on' in a material way, created more general interest. Besides, Allen had never been really away, and rumours were always afloat of his starving agonies and mad ambitions. Most of the residents pictured him as sitting with a tight belt round his waist, to keep down the pangs of hunger while he wrote poems which nobody would buy, or paragraphs for daily papers at a penny a line—they were very eloquent on that penny a line—Mr. Skantlebury especially, knew all about it; or else he was imagined as forming one of a madcap crowd of roysterers, singing and drinking with the accompaniment of tobacco. Mr. Massey it was who knew how literary men always sit up o' nights together, and get drunk and sing and smoke pipes. It was, I think, rather a disappointment to most of us when Allen came back, certainly well fed, well dressed, and not, so far as could be seen, greatly given to drink.

'I have been talking to Sir Charles, Claire,' said Will to me, ' and I have been having it out with my father. I have received the congratulations of Mr. Skantlebury on my arrival. I have been wept over by Allen's mother, who said that I was the supplanter of her son ; but she did not blame me. I have been warned by Mrs. Gallaway '—here I believe I blushed— 'and I have been to town and called upon

Tommy—Tommy the Great—Trismegistus—thrice greatest Tommy!'

'Did you call at his office?'

'Yes, I did, at eleven in the morning. Claire, there is something wrong with His Greatness. He looks pale. He pulled out a pint of champagne while I was with him, and because I would have none he drank it all himself. He grinned in a ghastly way when I congratulated him on his success. There is something wrong with Olinthus.'

I knew very well indeed what was wrong with him, but I would not tell him.

'Tommy did not pretend the ordinary polite rejoicing at my return; did not say he was glad to see me; did not ask me to dine with him at his club or anywhere else; did not show, or pretend, the least interest in my movements, and he seemed mightily relieved when I came away. But perhaps he had his work upon his mind—another fortune to make before noon, I dare say.'

This was just what one would have expected

of the poor man. With ruin staring him in the face, the visit of his old schoolfellow would only distract him.

'His cheeks are flabby and his hand shakes, and his eyes are blood-shot. On the whole, Claire, I would rather not be in poor old Tommy's shoes. But what a fellow he is! Fancy his hiding away those wonderful powers of his! And fancy ourselves being such donkeys as to call him stupid! We used to laugh at him, Allen and I, because he couldn't understand things at school. He was stupid, was he? Why, this finance business, which I take to be pure plundering and robbery, is a thing which wants a quicker brain and wider knowledge than any other trade in the world. Where did he pick up his knowledge?'

I knew that as well, but I could not tell him.

'When I asked him he sighed and said that he did't know whether the thing was worth the trouble it had cost him. Trouble! it must have been downright, resolute work of the hardest kind, coupled with the most extraordinary sagacity. You see it means nothing more or less than to find out for certainty the things which are kept in the background. You must know all the secrets and all the motives. Perhaps he kept a detective branch in his own service. I asked him what he had made in the three years; but he refused to tell me, and altogether looked so glum that I came away. I expected to find him swaggering over his money after the old fashion. What does it mean?'

It meant that the great financier was going to be horribly punished, and perhaps held up to ridicule. But that I could not reveal. Will went on.

'Coming home in the train I heard some talk which adds to my presentiments about him. There were two men talking about some company or other. I heard the name of Gallaway mentioned, and one of them began to tell a long story about the way in which Mr. Olinthus Gallaway has been making money. I partly suspected it before. It seems that he has been following the same game as that carried on ten years ago or so by Colliber. This man seemed to know something about it. There is a row impending, it appears. They are going to make an attempt at fixing a certain prospectus on Olinthus. If he can be proved to have framed this prospectus, an action will be brought against him. It is quite certain that he took up and sold the shares. I wonder if that is the reason why Tommy looked so glum. The man in the train said that if such an action could be brought, and was successful, the result would make one of the richest men in the City a bankrupt. Another man, who seemed vindictive, remarked that for his own part he should like nothing better than to see him and all such fellows on the tread-mill. I suppose he was a shareholder in one of the illustrious Tommy's companies.'

I changed the subject.

'You have not told me, Will, how you find the place and all the people in it. Allen says it has grown so small. The Forest is only a wood of very limited extent; he can no longer feel lost in it, and he has ceased to feel any awe for the glorious bankrupts.'

'I do not find the place any other than it used to be, but the people are changed. Mr. Colliber is gone, which seems a good thing for everybody. The man used to remind me of a hawk, with his hooked nose and sharp eyes and quick savage manner. I never think of a financier without supposing him greatly to resemble Mr. Colliber; when I called upon Tommy I fully expected to find that his features were changed, and I am disappointed. He might be thought to look a little like an owl, with his fat cheeks, but not at all a hawk.'

'Yes, Mr. Colliber went away without telling any one he was going.'

'As for the Gallaways, I suppose it is quite natural that they should be proud of their brother; but perhaps they are a little more inflated than one would like to see. And they did dwell upon the contrast between my position and Tommy's. I wonder if they understand at all what it means. Do you think they *can* understand? Why, if they could, the reading of the eighth commandment every Sunday would strike them dumb with terror and shame.'

He could not forget the story of the company which he had heard in the train.

'And I've been to see Allen's mother. The poor lady told her tale of woe; her son is no richer, she says, and has no prospect whatever before him of making any money. It is a dreadful thing to her. She looks upon these ladies as his most mischievous friends. As for his book it is only a proof and visible sign of degradation. How can a book make money, or even a bare living? Only one thing would reconcile her.'

'What thing?'

'If they were to elect Allen, Lord Mayor of London, and she were to see him in his coach of state with chaplain and swordbearer.'

'Poor Mrs. Engledew! And the rest, Will?'

' I found Sir Charles as well as ever. He flourished about Olinthus, of course, and regrets that he is not likely to live long enough to see his failure. This, he says, is sure to be colossal. He also expressed his hope that I had brought back from China the true spirit of British enterprise, for which my father is so distinguished.'

' Oh, Will! but you know——'

' Yes, Claire, I know.' His face fell. ' I know, and I am ashamed. My father, at the age of sixty-five, has gone back to the City with that old donkey Skantlebury, and is gambling, with nothing to lose, and no chance of getting any scraps of information, except what Tommy throws him. I am ashamed, I say, when I think of those two old men going one after the other and humbly begging for advice and instructions.'

' Will,' I cried, ' please tell your father to take no more advice from him. No, it is not on account of the shame, but the danger. Tell him at once.'

' I have no influence with him. I have

tried to represent the danger to him, but he has made a little money by his transactions, and is full of his former ardour for making a fortune. The old projects are brought out; the money he is to make by his new speculations is to be applied to the revival of the old. I am an unnatural son because I will advance no money to push off the scheme at once.'

'Then the end is certain,' I said, thinking of what I knew.

'I suppose it is very certain,' he replied, from his own knowledge. 'And there will be the glory of a second bankruptcy in which there will be nothing to lose.'

'And now tell me if you think my father much altered.'

'Nothing will ever alter him,' said Will. 'You know that I was not his favourite pupil. Therefore, I have not disappointed him, as Allen has. He expected nothing from me.'

'Yes; and yet, it was but a dream—an impossible dream.'

'Impossible—perhaps, But a noble dream. Do you know, Claire, that the things he put into our heads, the things he made us see and hear, have always been with me? So they have with Allen. I see in every one of his stories the presence of these ideas. I am not clever in his way. I cannot create a figure and make her represent a multitude. Where Allen sees one girl, I see half a million. Where he sees one couple, I see a million. And I have been thinking about them ever since.'

'I know you have, Will. I found you out from your letters. Does my father know too?'

'I do not suppose he does. How should he know?'

'He read all your letters, Will.' But it occurred to me that he had not perhaps read them so carefully as I had done, and I was confused.'

'He seems happier in being rich,' Will said. 'This house and his large garden are more pleasant to him than the little cottage. He is proud of his library, and it pleases him to have no work, especially no distasteful work, to do. I think Frenchmen become idle more gracefully than we restless Englishmen. Look at my father and Skantlebury.'

In the evening we had a great talk. It began with Gertrude, who could see the artistic merit of a picture or a romance whatever the subject, but had, I think, little sympathy with the inartistic and ignorant multitude who get through their lives somehow with so little joy. Perhaps she was too old for the sentiment of the sympathy, which seems to me quite a modern thing in England and an importation from France, who is the mother of all ideas. She was speaking of the separation from the ordinary world which belongs to the literary and artistic life. ' What,' she said, ' is to other people the earnest business of a life is to the literary and artistic life only a curious subject of study. This is the reason why such men are bad at business. They look on from the outside and draw their pictures. If they have to go into the fight they get struck down and come off badly. Their work is outside.'

'Yet,' said Will, with diffidence, 'they cannot cease to be human. Art without sympathy is like a picture without atmosphere.'

'It is well said,' observed my father.

'The sympathy,' said Isabel, 'comes from the real humanity of the artist. He would not, if he could, cease to be human.'

'How can a man,' said Will, 'look on without longing to engage in the struggle? We are fighting animals.'

'You are not an artist, Mr. Massey,' said Gertrude. 'The artist is not a fighting man. He wants an atmosphere of calm——'

'Yet Benvenuto Cellini—' Will interrupted.

'You cannot,' Gertrude went on, 'act' as well as observe and meditate. The artist must keep a steady hand and a clear eye. He must be superior to the ignoble struggles and ambitions of the common life.'

These were the ideas in which the dear lady had been brought up. A poet or an artist was a sacred creature who watched the movements of mankind, but had no part in them. Allen murmured approval. Will knocked the proposition all to pieces.

'A great many poets and writers,' he said, 'have been men of action, and even excellent men of business. Shakespeare, for instance; Lamartine tried statesmanship; Cervantes was a soldier; Byron, Pope, and Dryden were all able to look after their own affairs. And, then, why should not a man join in the ambitions of other men?'

'Because it is so much more noble to look on than to struggle in the ignoble fight,' said Allen grandly.

'I don't know that. But even if it were, I do not see that the fight is ignoble. The people work to keep wife and children. Work therefore means love, which is not ignoble. The first desire is to improve the material condition. That is not ignoble. There is not much art among the mob, it is true, and no desire for art. Art is imitation and representation, and means some kind of ease. As for the people, I think that the spectacle of the whole world from the very beginning, looking for some one who will tell them how equal justice may be had, is not ignoble.'

'There spoke my pupil,' said my father. But Gertrude shook her head.

'We live in a land where there *is* equal justice,' she said. Indeed, she had always been told so, and was now too old to learn anything different.

'You should ask the better-class workman what he thinks about equal justice,' said Will. 'You remember the old walks and talks, Allen?'

'Oh! yes,' Allen replied, going without a blush straight over to the opposite side. 'I remember, of course I remember now. The people are always asking how things are to be set right. There are a thousand wrongs of which we feel hardly any, and they feel all. I had forgotten. Do you remember, Will, the shoemaker we met one Sunday afternoon at Walthamstow, and how he spoke of rich men's law and poor men's law? I should have gone with him and learned how he lived. We miss our best chances. He was a splendid subject and I let him go.'

'But—ignoble, Allen?'

'No, not ignoble; I was wrong. The life of the man who works is not ignoble. The ignoble life begins a little higher up—or lower down—with the small trader.'

'Allen does well,' said Gertrude, 'to study the common people. They are splendid material for him; they are his workshop. As for me, I find them coarse in manner and rough in speech. I prefer my own kind.'

'Allen might have done better for himself,' said Will, 'if he had studied the people a little longer. He observed and made pictures. I suppose, Allen '—he laid his hand on Allen's shoulder, the familiar trick—'I suppose that nature made you an artist, so that you see picturesque situations where I saw only things ugly and mean. Perhaps the more you study the people the more picturesque things you will see. Let us begin the old walks again.'

'We will,' said Allen; 'we will have a thousand walks together. I shall get new ideas just as I used to get them when we were boys together, and every walk brought a flood of thoughts.'

'There are two ways,' Will went on, ' of watching things. One is, yours, to study the effect; the other is, perhaps, mine, to look for the cause.'

' After all,' said my father, ' it was Will who learned my lesson aright. Then my life has not been thrown away.'

' Yes,' Will went on, 'I have not Allen's genius : but still I have ambitions. I do not know yet how I shall begin or what may be attempted. When one lives abroad, far away from the things which at home distract the thoughts, one can sit down and think. Then the memory of our old walks and talks came back, and I began to wonder if it was possible to find out a way.'

'Always for the people?' my father asked.

'Always for the people. It may be that I have found out some of their wants. I do not say; only I hope that I have found something.'

'He hopes,' repeated my father. 'It is modestly said. For he who leads the people must not expect to be taught by the people, because the people have no voice or power of speech, but wait for him who can speak for them. Yet, my son, he who works for the people, must trust the people.'

'There is nothing else to trust,' Will replied. 'Everything else has been tried and has broken down. If this, too, fails, there will be no more hope. Trust them? Why, is there not the safety of that divine instinct in their hearts which cries continually for justice?'

'Will,'—my father sprang to his feet and

caught his pupil by both hands,—'you, too, have heard it. Listen!'—he held up his finger. 'You too can hear it. It is the breaking of the wave which will overwhelm the world.

'Oh!' said Gertrude half laughing, half in complaint. 'Then there will be no stalls, but all pit; no half-crown days, but all shilling days; no beautiful books, but all cheap literature; no place at all, my poor Allen, for you and me!'

CHAPTER X.

JOHN STEPHENS.

I was walking across the green in the morning
on some household business, when I saw in the
lane, where stood Mrs. Engledew's cottage, the
strange man of whom I have already spoken.
He was a long way off, but my eyes were good.
Besides, it was impossible to mistake his broad
felt hat and his great beard.   He was sitting on
a rail as usual, and had a cigar in his mouth.

I went on to the shop without thinking
much about the man.   On my way back,
seeing him still sitting there and in an attitude so observant, I reflected that it was a
favourable opportunity, now that Allen was
at home, to ask him why he came there and
what he wanted.

He did not hear my step until I was quite close to him. When he saw me, he made as if he would get down and walk away. But when I spoke to him he put his hands in his pockets and remained sitting on the rail.

'This is the fourth time,' I said, 'that I have seen you watching Mrs. Engledew's house. What do you want with her? Why do you perpetually sit and look at her door?'

'The party,' he replied, without looking me in the face, 'who takes an interest in the lady has sent me to inquire.'

'To inquire what? To sit on a gate all day and look at the house?'

'I told you about that party,' he replied, 'at the beginning.'

'What can you learn by looking at the house? Why do you not go and see her for yourself? What do you mean?'

He said that by standing where he was he could see very well, and sometimes the lady sat working at the window, and sometimes she came out into the garden. Very well indeed he could see her. That was what he did for the party who took an interest in the lady. The manner of the man was rough but not offensive. He did not seem to resent my questions.

'But why do you not go and tell her of this person who takes an interest in her?'

'Because,' he replied, 'there are reasons. If this person knows that the lady is comfortably off and wants for nothing and that she is happy—that is, as happy as most people can expect to be at her time of life, and widows of bankrupts and all—that person is satisfied. If she was hard up now——'

'Who is the person, then? Who can be the man who sends a stranger to hang about the house and ask questions of the people? Mrs. Engledew's cousins and relations do not hide themselves. Your employer must have some good reason for hiding himself.'

'Perhaps he has,' the man laughed, a low chuckle without any mirth in it. 'Perhaps he has excellent reasons. Oh! yes, he doesn't want to show at all.'

'The only man who can have such reasons is her husband's late partner, the wicked wretch who stole his money and ruined his credit—and murdered him.'

'Which he certainly did, Amen. Of course you mean Stephens, John Stephens, Stephens is the man,' his voice became husky, 'who stole and spent and ruined all. If it had not been for Stephens, her husband would have been a rich man this day. If it had not been for him, all this grief would never have been. As for me I always say that John Stephens is nothing better than a murderer. Very good reasons why Stephens should keep out of the way; murderers must lie snug. He was a forger, too, and it might be proved after all these years—forgers must sit in the dark; he falsified the accounts; he stole the money; he ran away with all that was left. Thieves, embezzlers, falsifiers, and such must at all times lay low, mustn't they? You bet, John Stephens has got very good reasons.'

'Then you are employed by this man?'

'Put it, if you like, that I am. Put it this way, young lady. You say to yourself this. If Stephens has got money, it's Stephens's bounden duty, being a forger and a thief, to give that money up. But if the lady doesn't want the money and Stephens does, why give up that money? Why give it up? What's the good of giving it up? It won't bring back the past; it won't prevent Engledew being bankrupt. It won't prevent him—look here, young lady, John Stephens couldn't know he would kill himself. Now, could he?'

I suppose it was just then that I began to suspect who the man might be. I remembered, too, the strange knowledge he had shown of Mrs. Engledew's early appearance. He went on talking in an incoherent way, repeating himself as if his mind was oppressed.

'Stephens, you see, young lady, considering all things, does well to lay low. But perhaps you are quite right. Very likely it may be John Stephens himself—no other—who put me on this job.'

I was quite certain now that it was Stephens. What could he want with the poor lady? You may tell him, then,' I said, 'that he has ruined two lives and done his best to ruin a third. Good heavens! that such a wretch should live!'

'It is no use telling him what he knows. As for his living with the knowledge of *that* behind him, he thinks he'd better go on living as long as he can.'

He got down from his gate, when he had made this grim reply, and leaned against it, with his hands in his pockets, as if he was disposed to carry on the conversation as long as I pleased.

'Does he repent then, this man?' I asked. 'You know him well; that is clear. Does he repent?'

'As for repentance, now, that is according as you read the word. Stephens is sorry—he is always sorry that he did it. Sometimes he gets mad just in thinking about it. But as

for repentance, young lady, when I was young
I used to go to church. When I think of
that I laugh. I just laugh. Now repentance
in church meant being sorry and hoping for
forgiveness. I don't think Stephens ever
thought, even when he was as mad as a hatter,
that anybody would forgive him.'

'I see. But he is sorry?'

'That is so. It is close upon five-and-
twenty years since he did it. What he claims
is this, though perhaps you won't believe it:
most every night for all these years he has
seen the face of the man he murdered—yes—
murdered. And it looks upon him with anger.
Sometimes, too, there comes the face of his
wife ; but not so often.'

He stopped, looking before him as if he
saw that face still.

'It does one good to talk to some one.
I've talked to no one since—well—a long time.
Nobody to talk to—that is the very devil.
Then you get to see faces and to hear voices ;
when the voices go on too long people take

and lock a man up, and say he's gone off his chump for a spell.'

He stopped again.

'Five-and-twenty years at three hundred and sixty-five days in the year. That makes about nine thousands ghosts; doesn't it?' The man ticked off the amount on his fingers as if he was adding up an account. 'Nine thousand one hundred and twenty-five ghosts it is exactly. I counted up this morning. Wherever Stephens goes the face goes too. Every night when he blows his candle out the face comes back. If he leaves the candle alight, the face gets between him and the candle. You can't dodge a ghost, anyhow, if you try all the time. Stephens has tried going to bed drunk—but that's no good, bless you! and sitting up all night, but that's no good either. Always that face; sometimes, that other face. There's a curious thing about the other face. Before Carry lost her husband she was as pretty a woman as you wished to see. You would have thought that Stephens would have seen that pretty face. Not at all. What he sees is a sharp and worn face—see there.'

I looked. The widow at the moment threw open the window and looked out into the sunshine. I thought that, set as the face seemed in sunlight, flowers, and bright leaves, it ought to have been a happy face, contented with fortune and glad to live. A foolish thought.

'That is the face he has always seen, growing older and thinner too. Strange, isn't it?'

'Very strange—go on.'

'There are lots more things as strange as you ever heard. When Stephens bolted there was very little money left for him to take, because he had lost it all. But what there was he took—say, two hundred pounds, not more; and he went to America by a French steamer from Havre. You would think that such a man would spend a couple of hundred in no time. Well, he did: some of it he gambled; some of it he drank; some of it he fooled; he kept on throwing it away. Yet, as fast as he threw away, the money came back to him. Never any more. Then, what with the faces at night and the voices, and the way in which that money behaved just as if it meant to remain with him, Stephens's head got a little queer and they locked him up. I think he was locked up for twenty years or thereabouts. When he came out they gave him back his two hundred pounds. And that money has stuck to him and grown more. Yes, it's now just exactly enough to pay back all, at compound interest. Seems strange, doesn't it?'

'Very strange.'

'He has been working and saving; and it occurred to him that if he were to go and get rid of this money by giving it back to Carry, he might get rid of the faces, too.'

'Very likely he would.'

The man pulled a bit of paper with figures on it from his pocket, and he looked at it.

'If you write out that sum at three and a half per cent. interest, which is a fair rate, you will find that two hundred pounds in twenty-five years, becomes five hundred and thirty pounds, two shillings and a penny. I've worked it out, though it's a longish sum. The dollars came in then, and Stephens put them away till they had got up to what he wanted.'

' Why did he not send the money over? '

' No ; that wouldn't do. He must bring it himself.'

' And so, Mr. Stephens,' I said, ' you have got the money in your pocket now? '

He made no reply, and seemed not at all surprised that I knew him.

' Why do you not go and give it to her? '

' It is always in my pocket. If she was poor——'

' Come with me and give it to her.'

' To-morrow I will go. I can stand one night more. To-morrow.'

' No ; come to-day.'

' It is all I have got in the world,' he replied, with a strange eagerness. ' All I have in the world. She does not want it. The money would make her no happier. She lives in a beautiful little cottage covered with flowers. Why should I make myself a beggar? The past is gone ; it can't be brought back.'

'You owe her the money—come with me.'

I took him by the hand, but he pushed me back and turned to walk away. In another moment he would have gone, but just then I heard steps on the road. Thank heaven, it was Allen.

'Stop,' I said. 'Do you know that young man ? It is Allen Engledew—her son.'

He made no more hesitation. He stood still until Allen reached us.

'Allen,' I said, 'this man wishes to see your mother. Will you come with us? He has an important thing to say.'

'Who is he ? ' Allen asked. 'Who are you, and what do you want with my mother ? '

'You have got her face,' Stephens replied.

No more was said. We walked down the lane, the man between us like a criminal, and entered the cottage, the door of which was open.   The widow looked up surprised.

'Mother,' said Allen, 'this stranger wishes to make some communication to you.'

'First,' I said, 'let him pull off his spectacles and his hat.'

He took them off, without a word, looking with strange and curious eyes at Mrs. Engledew. Suddenly she recognised him and sprang to her feet and seized him by the collar, crying :

'It is the robber and the forger!   It is John Stephens.'

'It is,' he replied, quietly.   'You have not forgotten me.'

'Allen, hold him tight.   Do not let him escape, while I run for the police.   Claire, you are younger, do you run, my child.   Allen and I will hold him.'

'Stay, mother,' said Allen, gently taking her hand from the man's coat collar, 'let us hear first what he has to say.'

'He is the forger and the thief, Allen, do I not tell you?   Quick, villain, say what you

please, and then the police. Oh! At last, at
last!'

'I carried off,' said Stephens, apparently
unmoved, 'a couple of hundred pounds. Here
it is.' He lugged out of his pocket a little
bag with bank notes and gold in it. 'The
debt has been mounting at compound interest.
Now it has come to 530*l.* 2*s.* 1*d.* Count it,
you will find it correct.'

'The money, Allen,' said the widow, coldly,
'can be placed in the hands of the Court. It
is, I suppose, evidence of confession.'

'Have you anything more to say?' asked
Allen.

'Well, yes, I should like to say in your
presence, young gentleman, that it is all true.
I am everything that your mother says. If it
had not been for me, your father would have
become rich and lived long; your mother
would have been a contented and happy
woman; you, well, I don't know much about
you. If you like I will go to prison. Prison
or mad-house makes very little odds. That

won't give you back your father. If it is any
satisfaction to you I will confess and give
no trouble to anybody and work out my
sentence.'

He addressed Allen, but he spoke to the
woman whom he had wronged. He could not
take his eyes from her.

'Carry,' he added, 'I say that nothing can
ever restore what has been destroyed. Do
you think that the man who has done the
mischief has ever been happy, either, for a
single day?'

'Allen,' said his mother, 'we waste time.
Let us rid ourselves of this monster. Let him
be locked up.'

'You have suffered through my doing,' he
went on, not as if pleading for pardon but as
stating a plain fact. 'I have suffered through
my own. Which do you think has been the
more miserable?'

'Allen,' she repeated. 'Quick, let him go
with you to the police office. If he attempts
to escape, knock him down—kill him. I will

get you, if you like, your father's gold-headed stick.'

'I will go with your son if he wishes. I will not try to escape. Why should I? I have seen you. I have given you the money. I have told you what I came to say. What matter for the rest?'

Allen gave him his hat and pointed to the door.

'Go,' he said, 'you are free. Mother, tell him that you forgive him. We are Christians, mother. Forgive him. We must all forgive.'

'I cannot,' she cried, bursting into tears. 'Oh, Allen! I cannot, I cannot. The sight of him makes me remember all—how happy I should have been. It is easy for you to say forgive; but you never knew your father, Allen. There was no one like him in all the city, no one. Forgive this man? Why I have cursed him every day since he ran away.'

'I have been cursed,' the man said. 'I have had nothing but bad luck. I've been in prison for what another man did. I have had

agues and fevers and pains. I have been in a
mad-house most all the time——'

'Forgive him, mother,' said Allen. 'Forgive him. Let him go.'

'Say it for me, then, Allen. I cannot say
that I forgive him.'

'My mother freely and fully forgives you,'
said Allen. 'I forgive you as well; you can
go. As for the money, you had better take it
with you. We do not want it.'

The man shook his head. He would not
have the money, he said. Then he turned to
the widow, 'Do you mean it, Carry?' he said.
'Do you mean it, from your heart?'

She made no reply.

'Carry!' the man held out his hands in a
helpless way. 'Carry, I don't know what I
shall do or where I shall go. I think my life
is ended. But I have given back the money.
That is done. The faces will go now, perhaps,
and the voices. If ever you think of me again,
Carry, try to think of me as in the old, old
days, before I became—what I am. Yes, I

will go.' He turned to go, hesitated, turned again, and threw himself at the feet of the woman he had wronged with a cry,

'Carry—Carry—oh! Carry. We were boys and girls together. I used to love you. . . . . I have ruined you . . . . forgive me.'

She put out her hand; he touched it with his lips, rose and left the house. Then I went too, leaving Allen alone with his mother.

CHAPTER XI.

A GLORIOUS FAILURE.

THE storm broke upon poor Olinthus sooner than he expected. But as there was no escaping from it, the sooner it fell the better.

The first sign of the coming disturbance which came to us was in an excited and noisy meeting of the village Parliament upon the Green. There were gathered together, Sir Charles, Mr. Massey, and Mr. Skantlebury. My father was with them too, though he took no part in the talk.

' As for me,' cried Mr. Skantlebury, waving his arms, ' I will have justice, if there is justice to be had I will have it—Gallaway or no Gallaway. What? Do you think I am going to sit down and be robbed?'

'Patience, Skantlebury,' said Sir Charles. 'You don't know yet that you have lost your money. The shares may go up again.'

'Never; they never can. I knew from the first that it was a hollow thing,' said the victim.

'Then what did you buy the shares for?' Sir Charles asked.

'I bought them to sell, of course. He told me to; he said he held twenty thousand; but we will have justice.'

'In this country everybody can get justice,' said the ex-Lord Mayor. 'I have myself sat on the bench, and I ought to know. Fine with costs, or imprisonment in case you can't pay. I have meted out with impartiality to all alike—rich and poor. The rich pay up, and the poor go to prison. This is the country for justice, Skantlebury, so long as a Lord Mayor sits to administrate it.'

'It was Gallaway who started the company—that shall be proved. It was Gallaway who wrote the prospectus—that shall be proved; he dictated it, and we have got . the boy who took it down in shorthand. We will make him give back the money in full.'

'How much will it be, do you think, Massey?' asked Sir Charles.

'Fifty thousand shares at five pounds each. One pound on deposit, one pound ten on allotment, the rest at call. But the directors confidently anticipated——'

'I asked for two thousand shares; I sent up two thousand pounds; they allotted all; I sent up three thousand more. If I could get the money back. I've lost five thousand. Oh! it's hard; it's a dreadful hard thing, after working and slaving, to think that it may be gone. Five thousand pounds!'

His voice rose to a shriek, and he threw up his hands in a kind of bewilderment. He could not understand how the money he had so slowly accumulated should melt away so suddenly. 'He told me to buy the shares; he said he had twenty thousand; he told me to hold on, and I held; and they went up, and I might have

sold; and where are they now? At nothing
—anything — you can't sell them; nobody
will buy; they won't even speculate with 'em.
And he's sold all he had, and I've lost my
money.'

'But you've got some money left, Skantlebury?' said Sir Charles anxiously. 'You
wouldn't, surely, fail for so pitiful a sum as
five thousand? Why, think of the discredit
you would bring upon the village.'

Mr. Skantlebury turned away with an angry
gesture.

'It really would be nothing short of disgrace
to all of us,' Sir Charles went on. 'And you,
Massey, are you hard hit too?'

'I took up all I could afford,' replied the
sanguine speculator. 'But, Lord! it's nothing.
Gallaway's a man of a million. A man of his
resource is equal to anything. If we lose our
money, he will make it up to us, only Skantlebury has no faith. And suppose they bring it
home to him—what is it? Fifty thousand, we
will say, allotted at two pounds ten. It is not

much more than a hundred thousand after all. Gallaway can meet the bill and laugh.'

'Some of them sold at a premium, though,' said Sir Charles. 'I dare say it would run up to a hundred and thirty thousand. That would be a very creditable failure.'

'Don't,' groaned Mr. Skantlebury, 'don't, Sir Charles. Please don't speak of failure. You heard what they said at the meeting, Massey.'

There had been an excited meeting of the unhappy shareholders, nearly all of whom, I believe, were in the same position as Mr. Skantlebury; that is to say, they held shares in the hope of selling at a premium, and not with any belief in the company or the soundness of the scheme. One of the victims made a very strong speech, charging Mr. Gallaway with dreadful things, and especially with fraud, robbery, and dishonest representations. Of course the unhappy Olinthus was legally responsible and guilty of everything, and only I knew how he had done nothing except at the dictation of his partner, who was now furnishing a great

house with the proceeds of his three years'
plunder. The speaker, who was a clergyman,
the very clergyman of whom I had heard,
certainly showed a most astonishing energy
and vigour in action as well as in speech. It
was he who had traced this prospectus to the
office; who had got hold of the hand which
wrote it out at Olinthus's dictation, and it was
by his exertions that the great promoter, wire-
puller, financier, and operator could be made
responsible for statements by which people had
been robbed of thousands. He had got the
opinion of counsel; Mr. Gallaway was, that
opinion stated, legally responsible; a test action
could be brought; if that was successful he
might be made to disgorge all.

'And I make no doubt, Skantlebury,' said
Mr. Massey cheerfully, ' that he will have to pay
up. But what is it? Say a hundred thousand.
Very good; do you suppose that Gallaway is
not worth a good deal more than that? Why,
they say he lives in simple chambers; he's got
neither wife nor child; he can't spend more than

a thousand a year; and he has been making money hand over hand—hundreds of thousands. Keep up your courage, Skantlebury; you shall get your money paid back.'

My father told me all this, and how they fortified each other's opinion, though Mr. Massey, strong in his belief, pointed out that action or no action, young Gallaway would certainly see them through. Alas! what would be their despair when they knew what I already knew?

'Nobody knows,' said Mr. Massey, ' the money that young man has made. A temporary check : that is what it is. Consider, Skantlebury, three years of such success as the world has never seen.'

'Ah ! ' said Mr. Skantlebury.

'Did he ever tell you what he lost ? ' asked Sir Charles.

'I don't believe he ever lost anything. All he touched turned to gold. There never was and there never will be a man in the City to compare with him.'

'Not Colliber? his failure was a quarter of a million.'

'Not even Colliber,' said Mr. Massey. 'When I think of the companies he has floated. Why, between ourselves, don't we know that he wrote all the prospectuses himself, got the directors, and floated the shares, all by himself? And has any one of those companies ever paid any dividend; or, will one of them pay a dividend? Come, Sir Charles, as an old City man you know that.'

'If all the shareholders,' said Sir Charles, thoughtfully, 'were to bring home all those prospectuses against him, they might make him a bankrupt for millions! And only five-and twenty!! For millions!!! What an honour, what a guide and example for the young people of the village! what a joy to his widowed mother! Glorious! Glorious, indeed!'

He rubbed his hands and chuckled, but Mr. Skantlebury shuddered.

And now I must anticipate, because the

circumstances of Olinthus's fall belong to a somewhat later time.

The case created a very great interest. There were reports and rumours in the City—which, so far as a woman can learn, seems as much given to gossip as a country town; some said that Gallaway would be tried by the Public Prosecutor, others that he would get clear off, and float dozens more companies; some said that he would have to go bankrupt, and others that he could face half-a-dozen storms such as these. Some said that he would be put into the box, when extraordinary revelations would be forced from his reluctant lips; and others, that he would square the action, and that nothing more would be heard of it. But the clergyman was conscientious; he had a public duty to perform, and he did it.

On the day—the appointed day—when Olinthus should have come with the other two, he did not appear, but he sent me a letter. He said in it, first, that I was to consider his communication as strictly private, confidential, and privileged. The game, in fact, was now up, and it only remained to get out of the mess as comfortably as possible. Since his partner had deserted him he had been speculating heavily, but somehow, not wisely. In short, he had lost great sums of money. Then the action would most certainly proceed, and he was hopelessly ruined. There was one gleam of comfort—the Countess, with all her brothers, sisters, cousins, and friends, had followed his advice and 'gone in,' with most disastrous results. The worst of it was the want of credit, because people would expect the estate to cut up well. In fact, they all thought him worth hundreds of thousands, and there would be, in fact, no more than enough to pay the lawyers and accountants, while as for creditors and shareholders they would have to go whistle. Yet, he added, all might yet be retrieved if Mr. Colliber would only come back; but he made no sign and answered no letters—from which we perceived that poor Tommy had been humbling himself. As for the City it would be closed to him for a good while, and, of course, under the circumstances, he should cease his financial operations. He went on to add very kindly, that he knew the tenderness of my heart, and he was quite sure that his misfortunes would make no difference at all in my feelings towards him. The ten thousand pounds which he had had the forethought to deposit with his mother would produce four hundred a year, and with what my father would give me, there would be plenty to live upon in a quiet way. Therefore, he still laid himself, as he had always promised to do, with the wreck of his fortunes at my feet, and so on, with many protestations of earnest affection. It was a very humble letter and pitiful to read, if only for the contrast of his former talk and his strange inability to discern the infamy of his conduct, both as regards his fraudulent

companies and his robbery of the ten thousand
pounds.

Of course the thing was not settled in a
day. The action was brought, the great
Olinthus Gallaway was put in the witness box
and examined, but he had very little to say.
He acknowledged that the prospectus was
drawn up by himself; he admitted, in fact,
that he was responsible for the formation of
the company; he hoped to make a very good
stroke of business out of the company; he had
done his best to give the company a good shove
off; he had done his best also to run up the
shares; and he had done it all, he declared on
oath, in full confidence that the company was
founded on the soundest possible principles, in
ignorance of the damaging circumstances which
afterwards came to light, and in certainty that
it would succeed if managed well. They cross-
examined him at great length; he had to confess all sorts of damaging things—as that he
knew nothing at all concerning points about
which the prospectus went into elaborate

details, and had consulted nobody who did; that he accepted important statements made by interested persons without question; and that he accidentally forgot to consider one or two very important facts which he was proved to have learned. This he regretted, but confessed the fact manfully, and after all he adhered to his statement, which was, no doubt, perfectly true, that he had no reason to doubt the substantial truth of the prospectus put forth. The judge summed up dead against him: the jury had no hesitation; he lost his case; and the result was what Mr. Skantlebury predicted—that he had to take up the worthless shares on account of which the action was brought. This meant that he had to take up all the fifty thousand at the price for which they were issued, namely, two pounds ten a share. So that here was a debt of a hundred and twenty-five thousand pounds to begin with. Mr. Skantlebury came home jubilant that evening.

'We've nailed him,' he said, rubbing his

hands. 'We've got him at last. A hundred and twenty-five thousand pounds he'll have to pay. They say he's worth twice that money and more.'

But when in the course of a few days it was announced that Mr. Olinthus Gallaway had suspended payment, a nervous qualm seized Mr. Skantlebury and he only partly recovered confidence when Mr. Massey assured him that the estate would fully meet the liabilities.

'And if it doesn't,' he added, 'do you think young Gallaway will not make it good for us?'

This confidence bore Mr. Massey through another trouble. In fact, following advice given after the withdrawal of Mr. Colliber, he had gone in for a certain stock, I forget whether it was a bull or a bear, but he came out, Sir Charles said, a lame duck—afterwards I learned the nature of the joke. As Mr. Massey's gains were all invested in the unlucky company, he had no means of meeting the day of settlement.

The broker found that he had nothing at all, and that it was of no use making the man a bankrupt, so that after all Mr. Massey was no worse off after the catastrophe than before it. He returned, therefore, to the contemplation of his former projects and his lamentations over the undutiful character of his son who will advance him nothing.

Alas! when the estate came to be examined, it was found to consist of a few hundreds, which the lawyers and the accountants got together, with a great quantity of worthless scrip. Several theories were advanced to account for the wretched sum which represented the estate. One was that the bankrupt had spent his money in the most shameless extravagance and profligacy. This theory prevailed for some time till the question was asked what ground there was for supposing Mr. Gallaway to have made such immense sums. Then everybody went straight round in the opposite direction, and said, 'Oh! of course. It was all exaggeration. His transactions, after all, were not so out of the common,' and poor Tommy's reputation was quite snuffed out. I do not know how much in the pound was paid, but I am sure that it was only a few pence, and the name of Gallaway now takes the place of Colliber as a proverb and byword of execration. Most of the victims were men like Mr. Skantlebury, who had retired from business with their few thousands, the savings of a life's work, and thought four per cent. a miserable return for their money, remembering the large profits they had made in trade. It seems to me a most dreadful thing when a man like this loses his money. All his life he has been thinking of nothing else than how to save it : his only idea of success is to save a great deal : his chief hope is to retire in his old age and lead a tranquil life on the money he has saved. And then to lose it ! I believe that the unfortunate Mr. Skantlebury had saved no more than seven or eight thousand pounds; enough, however, to afford him all that he wanted. Now five thousand was gone, and he was left with an income of about a hundred and fifty pounds a year. He went away: where he went to I do not know; or why he went; but we saw him no more. And then the great Bankrupt returned to his native village. His sisters refused to give back the little fortunes with which he had endowed them, and said strong things about the folly which had thrown away such splendid chances. And until they married and went away, they reproached him continually with eating the bread of idleness, and asked him why he did not go back to the City and make another fortune; and what was the use of being clever if he did not use his cleverness; and was it not a flying in the face of Providence to do nothing when he had shown such extraordinary power of doing anything he pleased? I think that it was not, in those days, a happy household: the daily papers were full of articles which said most unkind things about the operations conducted by Mr. Gallaway: the system which he had so successfully pursued was laid bare, and all could see for themselves with what ease and yet with what dexterity they had been fooled: it was shown to be no new system, but one which he must have been taught by an older hand. Who was this older hand? It was dreadful to read these things: the poor girls put the newspapers out of sight and refused to look at them. Somehow their brother did not mind so much. He cut out all the articles and preserved them in a portfolio, just as an author might cut out and preserve laudatory reviews of his last book. He read them through over and over again. He rubbed his hands over them: and when he came to any passage which acknowledged the extraordinary audacity and cleverness of the whole history, he scored this passage with a red pencil. 'You see, Claire,' he said to me, once, 'they know nothing, and they do not suspect. Colliber can't let out now, because no one would believe him. And they will go on believing in my cleverness. That's a comfort to a man, isn't it? And nobody knows except yourself.' It is, in fact, a secret which I have kept. I am quite sure that as Olinthus grows old he will forget Mr. Colliber's part in this business altogether, and believe firmly that he alone did it all with his own wonderful brain and his own strong right hand.

He has not yet gone back to the City. I think he never will. He is perfectly idle and would be happy but for his mother's rule, which is despotic. First of all she refused to give up any part of the ten thousand pounds, saying that a man who had let a hundred thousand slip through his fingers was not to be trusted with money at all. If, she added, she had insisted on living with him all the time, she would have known how to keep the money —action or no action, there should have been nothing lost. And for a long time she incessantly demanded of him an account of the various ways in which he had contrived to waste so great a fortune. She allows him a pound a week for pocket money and dress, and makes him go to church three times every Sunday—I suppose for penance.

At first, Olinthus was visited by a good many persons who hoped to suck advantage from his wonderful knowledge. No one, I have reason to believe, has ever gone away the wiser for the interview. And to Mr. Massey's entreaties and prayers he has remained obdurate. One man, he told me, actually proposed the same kind of partnership as that which existed between himself and Mr. Colliber. This greatly pleased him, and nothing, I am sure, would delight him more than to enact Mr. Colliber's part again, especially the last magnificent passage, the timely retirement with all the spoil in the hour of danger.

' A brilliant failure, indeed, Gallaway,' said Sir Charles, ' at your age, with the promise of your life before you, truly brilliant. Not so colossal as Colliber's, but very solid and substantial. And who knows what you may do the second time?'

'As for that, Sir Charles ——,' Olinthus began.

'As for that, my dear boy; think of the leading articles in all the papers. How many young men of five-and-twenty have achieved such a reputation as your own?'

Olinthus folded his arms and frowned.

'Or ruined so many people?' added my father.

Olinthus put his hands in his pockets and smiled.

'We shall have him with us,' said the ex-Lord Mayor, regarding him with thoughtful admiration, 'for a short time only. Then we shall lose him.'

'What?' cried Olinthus, turning pale. 'Why do you think I am going to die?'

'Not die, Gallaway. Not yet for a great many years, I trust. No; but you will leave us. You will rise to greater glories. You have settled here for a little rest, like a tired eagle after a long flight.   You now plume your feathers'—Olinthus agitated an elbow.   'Soon, you will soar aloft once more, and we shall gaze upon you in the clouds.'

Olinthus shook both elbows.

'If you come down again,' continued the garrulous old man, 'let it be for millions.   But I shall not live to see it.   I remember—' Sir Charles wiped away a tear—'I remember as if it was but yesterday, when you were but a little boy, how you said your only ambition was to make money, to become Lord Mayor, and to fail for millions.   A promising lad!   A bright and hopeful boy!   See what you have done—and Allen after all nothing but a common writing person.'

'If the respectable Skantlebury were here,' said my father, 'he would say—deplorable!'

CHAPTER XII.

THE PRIZE OF THE GOLDEN APPLE.

So my last words, like the first, tell how a prize was won, if, in truth, I may call myself a prize. If Will thought I was, cannot I think so too? And if it was the heart's desire of my lover, was it not the fulness and completion of my life to me? Great as is the love of man for a woman, there is one thing which is greater, the happiness and contentment of the woman who possesses that love. For whoso findeth love findeth life, and hath obtained favour of the Lord.

On the eve of the appointed day neither of the boys came to the house. I believe that they walked away together somewhere, and spent a day walking side by side in silence absolute. We passed a quiet evening; my father wrapt in a profound dejection. Isabel played to us; Gertrude and I sat side by side and whispered.

'Your mind is quite made up, my dear?' she asked.

'Quite. I see now that it could never be otherwise. Isabel will make him far, far happier than I could ever hope to do. And besides, oh! Gertrude, you will understand me. You know I love Allen as much as you do; yet—I do not know why—there would always be in my heart, if I were to marry him, the sense of something wanting.'

'And with Will?'

I could not answer. But with Will there would be nothing wanting. I know now what it is—the one thing lacking. But Gertrude knew it not. It was the helplessness of Allen's nature. He wants continually the encouragement, praise, and sympathy which a woman looks for from her husband. Without this support he would droop, and fall into melancholy and distrust,

'He is a strong man, my dear,' Gertrude whispered after a silence. 'He has great ambition, and he is clever, though not in our way. Can it be that Art is, after all, not so great a thing as administration? Yet Art will always much more fire the imagination and touch the heart. My dear, I would rather—if I were young again and beautiful—I would rather marry Allen than Will.'

I exchanged no more confidences with Isabel. We had said enough. She trusted me now, though, with a woman's doubts and fears, she could not understand that Allen could love her more than he loved me, and, for her sake, be ready to give up the hope in which he had seemed to live for three years. Now, I know not whether the words I had said to Allen awakened him to a sense of his own feeling, or whether he began to understand that he might have to live apart from the two ladies who had become necessary to his life. Certainly one could observe in him signs of doubt and trouble. These were shown in a nervous and restless manner, and in the way in which his eyes fell now on Isabel and now on myself. As if I could not read the thoughts of Allen whom I had studied so long! They were thoughts which he did not put into words. They were contrasts which he dared not face between a life with me and my father—with whom he no longer had any kind of common interest—and a life with Isabel, and Gertrude, and Art, and the followers of Art: they were reproaches—that I know full well: they were temptations to resign his pretensions: they were jealousies. But the time was come and the thing, with all its consequences, was before him. Like the girl with the thistle-down he might have tried his fortune, saying, ' I love her—love her not.'

When the others were gone to bed, I went into the garden, where my father was walking backwards and forwards alone. He threw away his cigarette and drew me into his arms and kissed me twice.

' My daughter,' he said, ' my dear daughter —my best of daughters—it is the last time.

To-morrow, your cheek, and your lips, and your forehead, and your hand will belong to one of the boys. One of the boys! I hoped it, always. Yet, now—you will go away—this house will be empty—there will be no more sunshine in it, no more music, no more laughter. What am I to do, my child, when you are gone?'

'But, *mon père*, I am not going to leave you.'

'You must, Claire. Between Allen and myself there is no more confidence. We are not *sympathiques*. I know it not, his world of art.'

'But oh! *mon père*, suppose I do not— suppose it is not—Allen after all!'

He held me at arm's length and looked into my face as if he could read my secret there; yet we were standing in the shadow of a cherry-tree, and it was past ten o'clock and a cloudy night.

'Claire,' he whispered, 'you will give up the boy of books?'

' Yes.'

' Remember, he is a poet—he is a *romancier* —he writes things which make people cry. To be his wife is to be the wife of a great man, as people think——'

' It is not Allen,' I replied.

' Then it is Will.'

He kissed me again, and then began to talk in his old, quick, impatient way.

' *Quoi donc?* I am stupid. I grow old. I have no more eyes than a pig. You love not Allen, yet he is a poet. One thinks that a poet makes all girls to fall in love with him. He captures hearts. Yes, he is clever. He has a quick eye, and he knows words. He is of the first force in words. He is a maker of phrases, like Malherbe. For me, the maker of phrases is not the great man. I love better the man who acts than the man who talks. And I thought he had your heart. *Que je suis bête.* For you are my daughter. Then comes —the other. Yes, the other. Ah! I did not know him. I thought he was stupid—an

English boy with a brain of beer—a boy for the shop. But he is not stupid—not stupid at all. He remembers what I have taught him. He knows things; he is wise; he is not afraid. And—yes—it is where the English are better than the French—he is good. My daughter, if Will, this young Prince from China, gives you his word, it will be true *parole d'honneur*. You will not have cause for jealousy. What do I say? It is not in England that wives are jealous of their husbands. This young man is like the Chevalier Bayard for honour. It is strange. His father is a fool, who would be a rogue, like the Honourable Gallaway, if he were not so great a fool. Perhaps it is his mother who is wise. Perhaps the example of his father has driven the boy into wisdom. He is *gentilhomme*. Everybody is gentleman now, but everybody is not *gentilhomme*. But I have one fear, my daughter. Yes, one anxiety tears my heart. I fear, Claire, that he will become rich. It is an instinct with the English; they are the only people who can grow rich without cheating and stealing and lying. It is a great virtue with them. Will, no doubt, must become rich. Well, no man is without faults. We must forgive him, and pretend that we are poor.'

'We have enough,' I said, 'if he does not. Why, we are quite rich ourselves.'

'We have enough,' he repeated gravely. 'Thanks to the good brother, who also became rich, with his vast Beddery. I find that I made a mistake. You were always right—can Woman ever be wrong? I thought that because a boy was fond of books and open to ideas I could make of Allen a great man. It is of such stuff that artists are made. Boys who become great men must have the clear head and the brave heart. Kiss me again, my daughter. In your marriage, as well as in all your life before, you will make your father happy.'

And so the morning came at last. But I no longer felt any trouble or anxiety, except that kind of fear with which one meets new happiness. It is as if no joy was to be granted to men and women without some pains which shall go before. This is part of the mystery of life; it begins, so joyful and happy a thing as it is for some, with helplessness and pain: it ends, so joyful a resurrection awaiting us, with helplessness and pain. There is no happiness in it which is not preceded by suffering. So, to me, the contemplation and thought of this great gift of a man's whole heart and soul, the endowment of his brain and his labour, the honour of his honour, the joy of his joy, the pain of his pain, the faith in his faith, filled my heart with a tumult of fear and shame as of my own unworthiness. Is that not a strange thing that we should ardently desire the best things that heaven can give, yet should feel, when they are granted, so unworthy to possess them?

The boys would come, I was sure, to the Forest in the evening, to the place where we parted, and at the time. But there were many things to be said, first, to Allen. In the afternoon I sent him a note, begging him to come and see me in my own room. He came at once. He was very pale, and trembled, and his eyes were downcast. These were signs of a guilty conscience, and made me rejoice. My task would be the easier; yet it was not very easy. It is always hard to explain when one is on the brink of a great mistake. First, I begged him to consider again the very great difference there was between the Allen of to-day and the Allen of three years ago : how he had made new friends and got into new lines of thought; how the old ways, mine still, were no longer his; how I was hardly able to understand and appreciate his life, so that my counsel would no longer be of use to him, nor my sympathy intelligent, and how, as his wife, I should only be a hindrance and an encumbrance to him.

'No, no,' he said hoarsely, 'never an encumbrance, Claire.'

'In the old days, when we were both ignorant together, Allen, you could come to me and could tell me of what you were doing, and I could encourage you. That is no longer possible unless you are satisfied with my saying, "Well done, Allen," when you succeed, and "Poor Allen," when you fail.'

'But I have loved you always, Claire,' he said.

So he had, I knew that, and he loved me still in exactly the same way and as much as he had ever loved me. I told him so.

'And what has Will done, then?' he asked, stung with a momentary pang of jealousy. There was no need to answer that question.

'You must marry, Allen,' I said, 'when you find a woman who has become a part of your daily life—the daily life that you desire most: who will enter into your thoughts, and understand your work, the manner and meaning and *technique* of it. The woman who will make you happy, Allen, must be like yourself, an artist. I desire only the practical and real world.'

He changed colour, but made no reply.

'In your world,' I went on, 'you and your friends are happiest when they live apart from the rest of us. They regard everything from another point of view. Your wife must be one of them. Allen, let me save you from disappointment and unhappiness.'

He had been sitting at the table, his head upon his hand. He sprang to his feet, crying—

'Claire, your way would become my way, or else mine should become yours. Unhappiness? With you? Claire, let what you have said be as if it never had been said. Let me remember the hopes of three years ago.'

'Oh, Allen! ask your heart again. It is not a question of consistency. How could you know three years ago? I told you long ago to think well what you would do.'

He made no reply, but he sat down again.

'You must not bring your wife a divided love, Allen. You most not leave a door open for regret and repentance. You must never be able to say, " Had I not married her—but the other—all would have been well with me." Have you considered?'

Still he made no reply. He was of so truthful a nature that his silence replied for him.

'My poor Allen!' I gave him my hand. 'I have never loved you otherwise, or more, than I love you now. I think I could never have married you, even if there had been no Will in the case at all. I have loved you so long that I have watched every one of your moods. I know you so well that I think I can read your thoughts.'

'Read them now,' he said, with down-dropped eyes. 'Read them, Claire, so that I need not speak.'

'You think that the offer of three years ago binds you to me in honour—it does not, Allen, it never did. You think that it is shame-ful to come to me and say, " Claire, I love you as much as I always did; but I love another woman more." It is not shameful, Allen. You think that in honour you are bound to endeavour to make one woman miserable though you cannot make the other woman happy. You must think so no longer. Have I read your thoughts, Allen?'

'Forgive me, Claire, you have.' He bowed his head as he replied almost in a whisper.

'There is nothing to forgive, dear Allen. Kiss me and tell me what you please about it. You know you always used to tell me all.'

He kissed my hand—the foolish, soft-hearted boy. He let a tear fall upon it.

'Who could help loving you always? Oh! Claire, I am, indeed, not worthy of you.'

'Tell me about it, Allen. I want to have your confidence in this as in all other things.'

'They were so kind to me, both of them. We used to talk together about you, Claire.'

'But you talk about me no longer, do you?'

'No, we talk very little to each other. A

constraint has grown up between us, now; it is because I have found out—yes, Claire, you have always had my secret thoughts—I have found out that I love her. She is always in my mind night and day.'

'I have seen it, Allen. And I? Am I never in your mind?'

'It is strange; you are with me as much as you ever were. You are a part of myself. If I think of Isabel it is as if I ought to go straight to you and tell my thought.'

'That is not strange at all. It proves only that you love me just as you always have done. You shall make her happy, Allen. Go, I refuse your offer, sir, I cannot marry you.'

I made him as grand a curtesy as I knew, one of those magnificent sweeping reverences which ladies make on the stage, after they have first thoughtfully swept their trains out of the way.

'Are you content, my dear old play-fellow?'

'Could I ever have thought,' said Allen,

his face like a boy's face still for smiles and tears, ' could I ever have believed that the day would arrive when you would make me happy by refusing to marry me?'

'You foolish boy! oh, Allen, I love you so much that I am jealous for your happiness. But Isabel loves you more because she will make you happy. Go and find her; she is somewhere in the house or garden. Go, Allen, take her, too, into your confidence.'

He stooped again and kissed my fingers.

'There is no one—there never will be any one—like you, Claire. And now that I have made you cry. Forgive me.'

So he left me. Presently I joined Gertrude, who was in the drawing-room.

'Gertrude,' I said, 'congratulate me. I have made a man happy.'

'Which one! Oh! Claire, my dear Claire, which is it?'

'It is Allen,' I replied.

Her face showed her disappointment.

'I must go to congratulate him,' she said

slowly. 'After all, what chance had poor Will against our poet? I knew how it must end.'

'None,' I said; 'I sincerely hope and pray she will accept him.'

'Claire!' she caught me by both hands. 'Tell me at once, you wicked woman; I am so anxious, and you are laughing at me.'

'I have made Allen happy—by refusing him. He has gone to find Isabel. Poor Will! I think he will indeed have a poor chance against our poet.'

'Kiss me, my dear, you are a dear, delightful, beautiful, kind-hearted girl. Are you quite, quite sure, my dear, that you do not love Allen?'

I whispered, because although no one was in the room, there are some things which must not be said aloud.

'Gertrude, I found out, three days ago, that there is only one man in all the world for me; and I am going now to tell him so.'

She threw her kindly arms round my neck

and prayed that I might be happy. This dear lady had spent her life in writing love stories—think of that!—her whole life without any love story of her own, and yet her heart was as fresh as when she first began, and her interest as strong in every pair of lovers. This is what comes of the dreaming life. Perhaps it is the best.

I went, with beating heart, to the old trysting-place beside the fallen tree in the Forest. No girl ever had a sweeter evening or a more delightful retreat to hear the tale of love. And yet no tale of love was poured into my ears at all. To be sure I did not want it at the time, but afterwards it seemed as if something should have been said. It is too bad to take a poor girl's heart by storm. Will was before me. Of course, I knew he would be; and he came to meet me. Oh, the impatient boy! He could not even wait for me to reach the appointed spot. He threw down his hat and walked across the turf.

' Claire ! ' he said.

'Will!'

And that was all, except that he took me
in his arms in the open Forest, though no one
was there to see except the larks above our
heads, and showered kisses upon me with never
a word; and every kiss a holy sacrament of
love. When we walked back, hand-in-hand,
the sun was set and the twilight was upon us.
Then a strange old feeling came upon me. It
was as if I was a child again, and once more
walked through the Forest in the summer
twilight holding Will by the hand, and half
afraid. I was half afraid again, yet full of faith
and hope and joy. Just as they had done
when we were children together, the trees of
the Forest threw up tall arches above our
heads, and made a great cathedral in which we
could lift up our hearts and sing praises;
again the black shadows lay on either hand full
of possible dragons for my brave boy to slay;
again the sweet fragrance of the early summer
filled the air and the soft breath of the west
wind played upon our cheeks. Again I was a

little child going out into the unknown world with Will's strong hand to support me.

'My dear—my dear,' it was the first time Will called me by that sweet and simple name. 'The life of which Allen writes so well, the better life, the nobler life; we will teach each other how to lead it.'

'Nay, Will, I shall learn from you.'

When we got home we found that my father had spread a most beautiful supper for us. It was in memory, he said, of the evening, three years before, when he bade the three young men wait for three years more. It was a supper just like that memorable feast; all flowers, fruit, vegetables, and little things. I would tell you all about that supper, but, in fact, it was a failure. My father tried to make a speech but broke down and shed tears, and so did some others. Isabel sat with blushing cheeks, and Allen looked guiltily happy, as if he had climbed into the Garden of Eden over the wall, as indeed he had.

Will is still young and his work lies

before him. If you should sometime hear something of him, as of a man who is doing good work and true, I pray you all remember that he learned how to do it of my father.

THE END.

LONDON : PRINTED BY
SPOTTISWOODE AND CO., NEW-STREET SQUARE
AND PARLIAMENT STREET

CHATTO & WINDUS'S
LIST OF BOOKS.

About.—The Fellah: An Egyptian Novel. By EDMOND ABOUT. Translated by Sir RANDAL ROBERTS. Post 8vo, illustrated boards, 2s.; cloth limp, 2s. 6d.

Adams (W. Davenport), Works by:

A Dictionary of the Drama. Being a comprehensive Guide to the Plays, Playwrights, Players, and Playhouses of the United Kingdom and America, from the Earliest to the Present Times. Crown 8vo, half-bound, 12s. 6d.   [*In preparation.*

Latter-Day Lyrics. Edited by W. DAVENPORT ADAMS. Post 8vo, cloth limp, 2s. 6d.

Quips and Quiddities. Selected by W. DAVENPORT ADAMS. Post 8vo, cloth limp, 2s. 6d.

Advertising, A History of, from the Earliest Times. Illustrated by Anecdotes, Curious Specimens, and Notices of Successful Advertisers. By HENRY SAMPSON. Crown 8vo, with Coloured Frontispiece and Illustrations, cloth gilt, 7s. 6d.

Agony Column (The) of "The Times," from 1800 to 1870. Edited, with an Introduction, by ALICE CLAY. Post 8vo, cloth limp, 2s. 6d.

Aide (Hamilton), Works by:

Carr of Carrlyon. Post 8vo, illustrated boards, 2s.

Confidences. Post 8vo, illustrated boards, 2s.

Alexander (Mrs.).—Maid, Wife, or Widow? A Romance. By Mrs. ALEXANDER. Post 8vo, illustrated boards, 2s.; cr. 8vo, cloth extra, 3s. 6d.

Allen (Grant), Works by:

Colin Clout's Calendar. Crown 8vo, cloth extra, 6s.

The Evolutionist at Large. Crown 8vo, cloth extra, 6s.

Vignettes from Nature. Crown 8vo, cloth extra, 6s.

Architectural Styles, A Handbook of. Translated from the German of A. ROSENGARTEN, by W. COLLETT-SANDARS. Crown 8vo, cloth extra, with 639 Illustrations, 7s. 6d.

Art (The) of Amusing: A Collection of Graceful Arts, Games, Tricks, Puzzles, and Charades. By FRANK BELLEW. With 300 Illustrations. Cr. 8vo, cloth extra, 4s. 6d.

Artemus Ward:

Artemus Ward's Works: The Works of CHARLES FARRER BROWNE, better known as ARTEMUS WARD. With Portrait and Facsimile. Crown 8vo, cloth extra, 7s. 6d.

Artemus Ward's Lecture on the Mormons. With 32 Illustrations. Edited, with Preface, by EDWARD P. HINGSTON. Crown 8vo, 6d

The Genial Showman: Life and Adventures of Artemus Ward. By EDWARD P. HINGSTON. With a Frontispiece. Crown 8vo, cloth extra, 3s. 6d.

Ashton (John), Works by :

A History of the Chap-Books of the Eighteenth Century. With nearly 400 Illustrations, engraved in fac-simile of the originals. Crown 8vo, cloth extra, 7s. 6d.

Social Life in the Reign of Queen Anne. Taken from Original Sources. With nearly One Hundred Illustrations. New and cheaper Edition, crown 8vo, cloth extra, 7s. 6d.

Humour, Wit, and Satire of the Seventeenth Century. With nearly 100 Illustrations. Crown 8vo, cloth extra, 7s. 6d.

Balzac's " Comedie Humaine " and its Author. With Translations by H. H. WALKER. Post 8vo, cloth limp, 2s. 6d.

Bankers, A Handbook of London; together with Lists of Bankers from 1677. By F. G. HILTON PRICE. Crown 8vo, cloth extra, 7s. 6d.

Bardsley (Rev. C.W.), Works by :

English Surnames: Their Sources and Significations. Crown 8vo, cloth extra, 7s. 6d.

Curiosities of Puritan Nomenclature. Crown 8vo, cloth extra, 7s. 6d.

Bartholomew Fair, Memoirs of. By HENRY MORLEY. A New Edition, with One Hundred Illustrations. Crown 8vo, cloth extra, 7s. 6d.

Beauchamp. — Grantley Grange: A Novel. By SHELSLEY BEAUCHAMP. Post 8vo, illustrated boards, 2s.

Beautiful Pictures by British Artists: A Gathering of Favourites from our Picture Galleries. In Two Series. All engraved on Steel in the highest style of Art. Edited, with Notices of the Artists, by SYDNEY ARMYTAGE, M.A. Imperial 4to, cloth extra, gilt and gilt edges, 21s. per Vol.

Bechstein. — As Pretty as Seven, and other German Stories. Collected by LUDWIG BECHSTEIN. With Additional Tales by the Brothers GRIMM, and 100 Illusts. by RICHTER. Small 4to, green and gold, 6s. 6d.; gilt edges, 7s. 6d.

Beerbohm. — Wanderings in Patagonia; or, Life among the Ostrich Hunters. By JULIUS BEERBOHM. With Illusts. Crown 8vo, cloth extra, 3s. 6d.

Belgravia for 1883. One Shilling Monthly, Illustrated.—" Maid of Athens," JUSTIN McCARTHY's New Serial Story, Illustrated by FRED. BARNARD, was begun in the JANUARY Number of BELGRAVIA, which Number contained also the First Portion of a Story in Three Parts, by OUIDA, entitled "Frescoes;" the continuation of WILKIE COLLINS's Novel, "Heart and Science;" a further instalment of Mrs. ALEXANDER's Novel, "The Admiral's Ward;" and other Matters of Interest.

*** Now ready, the Volume for JULY to OCTOBER, 1883, cloth extra, gilt edges, 7s. 6d.; Cases for binding Vols., 2s. each.*

Belgravia Annual : Christmas, 1883. With Stories by JAMES PAYN, F. W. ROBINSON, DUTTON COOK, J. ARBUTHNOT WILSON, and others. Demy 8vo, with Illustrations, 1s.

[In preparation.

Bennett (W.C.,LL.D.),Works by :

A Ballad History of England. Post 8vo, cloth limp, 2s.

Songs for Sailors. Post 8vo, cloth limp, 2s.

Besant (Walter) and James Rice, Novels by. Each in post 8vo, illust. boards, 2s.; cloth limp, 2s. 6d.; or crown 8vo, cloth extra, 3s. 6d.

Ready-Money Mortiboy.

With Harp and Crown.

This Son of Vulcan.

My Little Girl.

The Case of Mr. Lucraft.

The Golden Butterfly.

By Celia's Arbour.

The Monks of Thelema.

'Twas in Trafalgar's Bay.

The Seamy Side.

The Ten Years' Tenant.

The Chaplain of the Fleet.

Besant (Walter), Novels by :

All Sorts and Conditions of Men: An Impossible Story. With Illustrations by FRED. BARNARD. Crown 8vo, cloth extra, 3s. 6d.

The Captains' Room, &c. With Frontispiece by E. J. WHEELER. Crown 8vo, cloth extra, 3s. 6d.

All In a Garden Fair. Three Vols., crown 8vo, 31s. 6d.   *[Shortly,*

Birthday Books:—

The Starry Heavens: A Poetical Birthday Book. Square 8vo, handsomely bound in cloth, **2s. 6d.**

Birthday Flowers: Their Language and Legends. By W. J. GORDON. Beautifully Illustrated in Colours by VIOLA BOUGHTON. In illuminated cover, crown 4to, **6s.**

The Lowell Birthday Book. With Illusts., small 8vo, cloth extra, **4s. 6d.**

Blackburn's (Henry) Art Handbooks. Demy 8vo, Illustrated, uniform in size for binding.

Academy Notes, separate years, from 1875 to 1882, each **1s.**

Academy Notes, 1883. With Illustrations. **1s.**

Academy Notes, 1875–79. Complete in One Volume, with nearly 600 Illustrations in Facsimile. Demy 8vo, cloth limp, **6s.**

Grosvenor Notes, 1877. **6d.**

Grosvenor Notes, separate years, from 1878 to 1882, each **1s.**

Grosvenor Notes, 1883. With Illustrations. **1s.**

Grosvenor Notes, 1877–82. With upwards of 300 Illustrations. Demy 8vo, cloth limp, **6s.**

Pictures at South Kensington. With 70 Illustrations. **1s.**

The English Pictures at the National Gallery. 114 Illustrations. **1s.**

The Old Masters at the Nationa. Gallery. 128 Illustrations. **1s. 6d.**

A Complete Illustrated Catalogue to the National Gallery. With Notes by H. BLACKBURN, and 242 Illusts. Demy 8vo, cloth limp, **3s.**

The Paris Salon, 1883. With over 300 Illustrations. Edited by F. G. DUMAS. (English Edition.) Demy 8vo, **3s.**

At the Paris Salon. Sixteen large Plates, printed in facsimile of the Artists' Drawings, in two tints. Edited by F. G. DUMAS. Large folio, **1s.**

The Art Annual, 1882–3. Edited by F. G. DUMAS. Demy 8vo, **3s. 6d.**

The Art Annual, 1883–4. Edited by F. G. DUMAS. With 300 full-page Illustrations. Demy 8vo, **5s.**

Blake (William): Etchings from his Works. By W. B. SCOTT. With descriptive Text. Folio, half-bound boards, India Proofs, **21s.**

Boccaccio's Decameron; or, Ten Days' Entertainment. Translated into English, with an Introduction by THOMAS WRIGHT, F.S.A. With Portrait, and STOTHARD'S beautiful Copperplates. Cr. 8vo, cloth extra, gilt, **7s. 6d.**

Bowers'(G.) Hunting Sketches:

Canters in Crampshire. Oblong 4to, half-bound boards, **21s.**

Leaves from a Hunting Journal. Coloured in facsimile of the originals. Oblong 4to, half-bound, **21s.**

Boyle (Frederick), Works by:

Camp Notes: Stories of Sport and Adventure in Asia, Africa, and America. Crown 8vo, cloth extra, **3s. 6d.**; post 8vo, illustrated bds., **2s.**

Savage Life. Crown 8vo, cloth extra, **3s. 6d.**; post 8vo, illustrated bds., **2s.**

Brand's Observations on Popular Antiquities, chiefly Illustrating the Origin of our Vulgar Customs, Ceremonies, and Superstitions. With the Additions of Sir HENRY ELLIS. Crown 8vo, cloth extra, gilt, with numerous Illustrations, **7s. 6d.**

Bret Harte, Works by:

Bret Harte's Collected Works. Arranged and Revised by the Author. Complete in Five Vols., crown 8vo, cloth extra, **6s.** each.

Vol. I. COMPLETE POETICAL AND DRAMATIC WORKS. With Steel Plate Portrait, and an Introduction by the Author.

Vol. II. EARLIER PAPERS—LUCK OF ROARING CAMP, and other Sketches—BOHEMIAN PAPERS — SPANISH AND AMERICAN LEGENDS.

Vol. III. TALES OF THE ARGONAUTS—EASTERN SKETCHES.

Vol. IV. GABRIEL CONROY.

Vol. V. STORIES — CONDENSED NOVELS, &c.

The Select Works of Bret Harte, in Prose and Poetry. With Introductory Essay by J. M. BELLEW, Portrait of the Author, and 50 Illustrations. Crown 8vo, cloth extra, **7s. 6d.**

Gabriel Conroy: A Novel. Post 8vo, illustrated boards, **2s.**

An Heiress of Red Dog, and other Stories. Post 8vo, illustrated boards, **2s.**; cloth limp, **2s. 6d.**

The Twins of Table Mountain. Fcap. 8vo, picture cover, **1s.**; crown 8vo, cloth extra, **3s. 6d.**

The Luck of Roaring Camp, and other Sketches. Post 8vo, illustrated boards, **2s.**

Jeff Briggs's Love Story. Fcap 8vo, picture cover, **1s.**; cloth extra, **2s. 6d.**

Flip. Post 8vo, illustrated boards, **2s.**; cloth limp, **2s. 6d.**

Brewer (Rev. Dr.), Works by:

The Reader's Handbook of Allusions, References, Plots, and Stories. Third Edition, revised throughout, with a New Appendix, containing a COMPLETE ENGLISH BIBLIOGRAPHY. Crown 8vo, 1,400 pages, cloth extra, **7s. 6d.**

A Dictionary of Miracles: Imitative, Realistic, and Dogmatic. Crown 8vo, cloth extra, **7s. 6d.**   [*In preparation.*

Buchanan's (Robert) Works:

Ballads of Life, Love, and Humour. With a Frontispiece by ARTHUR HUGHES. Crown 8vo, cloth extra, **6s.**

Selected Poems of Robert Buchanan. With Frontispiece by T. DALZIEL. Crown 8vo, cloth extra, **6s.**

Undertones. Crown 8vo, cloth extra, **6s.**

London Poems. Crown 8vo, cloth extra, **6s.**

The Book of Orm. Crown 8vo, cloth extra, **6s.**

White Rose and Red: A Love Story. Crown 8vo, cloth extra, **6s.**

Idylls and Legends of Inverburn. Crown 8vo, cloth extra, **6s.**

St. Abe and his Seven Wives: A Tale of Salt Lake City. With a Frontispiece by A. B. HOUGHTON. Crown 8vo, cloth extra, **5s.**

The Hebrid Isles: Wanderings in the Land of Lorne and the Outer Hebrides. With Frontispiece by W. SMALL. Crown 8vo, cloth extra, **6s.**

A Poet's Sketch-Book: Selections from the Prose Writings of ROBERT BUCHANAN. Crown 8vo, cl. extra, **6s.**

Robert Buchanan's Complete Poetical Works. Crown 8vo, cloth extra, **7s. 6d.**   [*In preparation.*

The Shadow of the Sword: A Romance. Crown 8vo, cloth extra, **3s. 6d.**; post 8vo, illust. boards, **2s.**

A Child of Nature: A Romance. With a Frontispiece. Crown 8vo, cloth extra, **3s. 6d.**; post 8vo, illustrated boards, **2s.**

God and the Man: A Romance. With Illustrations by FRED. BARNARD. Crown 8vo, cloth extra, **3s. 6d.**

The Martyrdom of Madeline: A Romance. With a Frontispiece by A. W. COOPER. Crown 8vo, cloth extra, **3s. 6d.**

Love Me for Ever. With a Frontispiece by P. MACNAB. Crown 8vo, cloth extra, **3s. 6d.**

Annan Water: A Romance. Three Vols., cr. 8vo, **31s. 6d.**   [*Immediately.*

Brewster (Sir David), Works by:

More Worlds than One: The Creed of the Philosopher and the Hope of the Christian. With Plates. Post 8vo, cloth extra, **4s. 6d.**

The Martyrs of Science: Lives of GALILEO, TYCHO BRAHE, and KEPLER. With Portraits. Post 8vo, cloth extra, **4s. 6d.**

Letters on Natural Magic. A New Edition, with numerous Illustrations, and Chapters on the Being and Faculties of Man, and Additional Phenomena of Natural Magic, by J.A. SMITH. Post 8vo, cloth extra, **4s. 6d.**

Brillat-Savarin.—Gastronomy

as a Fine Art. By BRILLAT-SAVARIN. Translated by R. E. ANDERSON, M.A. Post 8vo, cloth limp, **2s. 6d.**

Browning.—The Pied Piper of

Hamelin. By ROBERT BROWNING. Illust. by GEORGE CARLINE. Large 4to, illum. cover, **1s.**   [*In preparation.*

Burnett (Mrs.), Novels by:

Surly Tim, and other Stories. Post 8vo, illustrated boards, **2s.**

Kathleen Mavourneen. Fcap. 8vo, picture cover, **1s.**

Lindsay's Luck. Fcap. 8vo, picture cover, **1s.**

Pretty Polly Pemberton. Fcap. 8vo, picture cover, **1s.**

Burton (Robert):

The Anatomy of Melancholy. A New Edition, complete, corrected and enriched by Translations of the Classical Extracts. Demy 8vo, cloth extra, **7s. 6d.**

Melancholy Anatomised: Being an Abridgment, for popular use, of BURTON'S ANATOMY OF MELANCHOLY. Post 8vo, cloth limp, **2s. 6d.**

Burton (Captain), Works by:

To the Gold Coast for Gold: A Personal Narrative. By RICHARD F. BURTON and VERNEY LOVETT CAMERON. With Maps and Frontispiece. Two Vols., crown 8vo, cloth extra, **21s.**

The Book of the Sword: Being a History of the Sword and its Use in all Countries, from the Earliest Times. By RICHARD F. BURTON. With over 400 Illustrations. Square 8vo, cloth extra, **32s.** [*In preparation.*

Bunyan's Pilgrim's Progress.

Edited by Rev. T. SCOTT. With 17 Steel Plates by STOTHARD, engraved by GOODALL, and numerous Woodcuts. Crown 8vo, cloth extra, gilt, **7s. 6d.**

Byron (Lord):

Byron's Letters and Journals. With Notices of his Life. By THOMAS MOORE. A Reprint of the Original Edition, newly revised, with Twelve full-page Plates. Crown 8vo, cloth extra, gilt, 7s. 6d.

Byron's Don Juan. Complete in One Vol., post 8vo, cloth limp, 2s.

Cameron (Commander) and Captain Burton.—To the Gold Coast for Gold: A Personal Narrative. By RICHARD F. BURTON and VERNEY LOVETT CAMERON. With Frontispiece and Maps. Two Vols., crown 8vo, cloth extra, 21s.

Cameron (Mrs. H. Lovett), Novels by:

Juliet's Guardian. Post 8vo, illustrated boards, 2s.; crown 8vo, cloth extra, 3s. 6d.

Deceivers Ever. Post 8vo, illustrated boards, 2s.; crown 8vo, cloth extra, 3s. 6d.

Campbell.—White and Black: Travels in the United States. By Sir GEORGE CAMPBELL, M.P. Demy 8vo, cloth extra, 14s.

Carlyle (Thomas):

Thomas Carlyle: Letters and Recollections. By MONCURE D. CONWAY, M.A. Crown 8vo, cloth extra, with Illustrations, 6s.

On the Choice of Books. By THOMAS CARLYLE. With a Life of the Author by R. H. SHEPHERD. New and Revised Edition, post 8vo, cloth extra, Illustrated, 1s. 6d.

The Correspondence of Thomas Carlyle and Ralph Waldo Emerson, 1834 to 1872. Edited by CHARLES ELIOT NORTON. With Portraits. Two Vols., crown 8vo, cloth extra, 24s.

Century (A) of Dishonour: A Sketch of the United States Government's Dealings with some of the Indian Tribes. Crown 8vo, cloth extra, 7s. 6d.

Chapman's (George) Works: Vol. I. contains the Plays complete, including the doubtful ones. Vol. II., the Poems and Minor Translations, with an Introductory Essay by ALGERNON CHARLES SWINBURNE. Vol. III., the Translations of the Iliad and Odyssey. Three Vols., crown 8vo, cloth extra, 18s.; or separately, 6s. each.

Chatto & Jackson.—A Treatise on Wood Engraving, Historical and Practical. By WM. ANDREW CHATTO and JOHN JACKSON. With an Additional Chapter by HENRY G. BOHN; and 450 fine Illustrations. A Reprint of the last Revised Edition, Large 4to, half-bound, 28s.

Chaucer:

Chaucer for Children: A Golden Key. By Mrs. H. R. HAWEIS. With Eight Coloured Pictures and numerous Woodcuts by the Author. New Ed., small 4to, cloth extra, 6s.

Chaucer for Schools. By Mrs. H. R. HAWEIS. Demy 8vo, cloth limp, 2s. 6d.

Cobban.—The Cure of Souls: A Story. By J. MACLAREN COBBAN. Post 8vo, illustrated boards, 2s.

Collins (C. Allston).—The Bar Sinister: A Story. By C. ALLSTON COLLINS. Post 8vo, illustrated boards, 2s.

Collins (Mortimer & Frances), Novels by:

Sweet and Twenty. Post 8vo, illustrated boards, 2s.

Frances. Post 8vo, illust. bds., 2s.

Blacksmith and Scholar. Post 8vo, illustrated boards, 2s.; crown 8vo, cloth extra, 3s. 6d.

The Village Comedy. Post 8vo, illust. boards, 2s.; cr. 8vo, cloth extra, 3s. 6d.

You Play Me False. Post 8vo, illust. boards, 2s.; cr. 8vo, cloth extra, 3s. 6d.

Collins (Mortimer), Novels by:

Sweet Anne Page. Post 8vo, illustrated boards, 2s.; crown 8vo, cloth extra, 3s. 6d.

Transmigration. Post 8vo, illustrated boards, 2s.; crown 8vo, cloth extra, 3s. 6d.

From Midnight to Midnight. Post 8vo, illustrated boards, 2s.; crown 8vo, cloth extra, 3s. 6d.

A Fight with Fortune. Post 8vo, illustrated boards, 2s.

Colman's Humorous Works: "Broad Grins," "My Nightgown and Slippers," and other Humorous Works, Prose and Poetical, of GEORGE COLMAN. With Life by G. B. BUCKSTONE, and Frontispiece by HOGARTH. Crown 8vo, cloth extra, gilt, 7s. 6d.

Collins (Wilkie), Novels by.
Each post 8vo, illustrated boards, 2s;
cloth limp, 2s. 6d.; or crown 8vo,
cloth extra, Illustrated, 3s. 6d.

Antonina. Illust. by A. CONCANEN.

Basil. Illustrated by Sir JOHN GIL-
BERT and J. MAHONEY.

Hide and Seek. Illustrated by Sir
JOHN GILBERT and J. MAHONEY.

The Dead Secret. Illustrated by Sir
JOHN GILBERT and A. CONCANEN.

Queen of Hearts. Illustrated by Sir
JOHN GILBERT and A. CONCANEN.

My Miscellanies. With Illustrations
by A. CONCANEN, and a Steel-plate
Portrait of WILKIE COLLINS.

The Woman in White. With Illustrations by Sir JOHN GILBERT and
F. A. FRASER.

The Moonstone. With Illustrations
by G. DU MAURIER and F. A. FRASER.

Man and Wife. Illust. by W. SMALL.

Poor Miss Finch. Illustrated by
G. DU MAURIER and EDWARD
HUGHES.

Miss or Mrs.? With Illustrations by
S. L. FILDES and HENRY WOODS.

The New Magdalen. Illustrated by
G. DU MAURIER and C. S. RANDS.

The Frozen Deep. Illustrated by
G. DU MAURIER and J. MAHONEY.

The Law and the Lady. Illustrated
by S. L. FILDES and SYDNEY HALL.

The Two Destinies.

The Haunted Hotel. Illustrated by
ARTHUR HOPKINS.

The Fallen Leaves.

Jezebel's Daughter.

The Black Robe.

Heart and Science: A Story of the
Present Time. New and Cheaper
Edition. Crown 8vo, cloth extra,
3s. 6d.   *[In preparation.*

Convalescent Cookery: A
Family Handbook. By CATHERINE
RYAN. Post 8vo, cloth limp, 2s. 6d.

**Conway (Moncure D.), Works
by:**

Demonology and Devil-Lore. Two
Vols., royal 8vo, with 6- Illusts., 28s.

A Necklace of Stories Illustrated
by W. J. HENNESSY. Square 8vo,
cloth extra, 6s.

The Wandering Jew. Crown 8vo,
cloth extra, 6s.

Thomas Carlyle: Letters and Recollections. With Illustrations.
Crown 8vo, cloth extra, 6s.

Cook (Dutton), Works by:

Hours with the Players. With a
Steel Plate Frontispiece. New and
Cheaper Edit., cr. 8vo, cloth extra, 6s.

Nights at the Play: A View of the
English Stage. New and Cheaper
Edition. Crown 8vo, cloth extra, 6s.

Leo: A Novel. Post 8vo, illustrated
boards, 2s.

Paul Foster's Daughter. Post 8vo,
illustrated boards, 2s.; crown 8vo,
cloth extra, 3s. 6d.

Copyright. — A Handbook of
English and Foreign Copyright in
Literary and Dramatic Works. By
SIDNEY JERROLD, of the Middle
Temple, Esq., Barrister-at-Law. Post
8vo, cloth limp, 2s. 6d.

Cornwall.—Popular Romances
of the West of England; or, The
Drolls, Traditions, and Superstitions
of Old Cornwall. Collected and Edited
by ROBERT HUNT, F.R.S. New and
Revised Edition, with Additions, and
Two Steel-plate Illustrations by
GEORGE CRUIKSHANK. Crown 8vo,
cloth extra, 7s. 6d.

Creasy.—Memoirs of Eminent
Etonians: with Notices of the Early
History of Eton College. By Sir
EDWARD CREASY, Author of " The
Fifteen Decisive Battles of the World."
Crown 8vo, cloth extra, gilt, with 13
Portraits, 7s. 6d.

Cruikshank (George):

The Comic Almanack. Complete in
Two SERIES: The FIRST from 1835
to 1843; the SECOND from 1844 to
1853. A Gathering of the BEST
HUMOUR of THACKERAY, HOOD, MAY-
HEW, ALBERT SMITH, A'BECKETT,
ROBERT BROUGH, &c. With 2,000
Woodcuts and Steel Engravings by
CRUIKSHANK, HINE, LANDELLS, &c.
Crown 8vo, cloth gilt, two very thick
volumes, 7s. 6d. each.

The Life of George Cruikshank. By
BLANCHARD JERROLD, Author of
"The Life of Napoleon III.," &c.
With 84 Illustrations. New and
Cheaper Edition, enlarged, with Ad-
ditional Plates, and a very carefully
compiled Bibliography. Crown 8vo,
cloth extra, 7s. 6d.

Robinson Crusoe. A choicely-printed
Edition, with 37 Woodcuts and Two
Steel Plates, by GEORGE CRUIK-
SHANK. Crown 8vo, cloth extra, 7s. 6d.
100 Large Paper copies, carefully
printed on hand-made paper, with
India proofs o the Illustrations,
price 36s.   *[In preparation.*

Cumming—In the Hebrides. By C. F. GORDON CUMMING, Author of "At Home in Fiji." With Autotype Facsimile and Illustrations. Demy 8vo, cloth extra, 8s. 6d.

Cussans.—Handbook of Heraldry; with Instructions for Tracing Pedigrees and Deciphering Ancient MSS., &c. By JOHN E. CUSSANS. Entirely New and Revised Edition, illustrated with over 400 Woodcuts and Coloured Plates. Crown 8vo, cloth extra, 7s. 6d.

Cyples.—Hearts of Gold: A Novel. By WILLIAM CYPLES. Crown 8vo, cloth extra, 3s. 6d.

Daniel. — Merrie England in the Olden Time. By GEORGE DANIEL. With Illustrations by ROBT. CRUIKSHANK. Crown 8vo, cloth extra, 3s 6d.

Daudet.—Port Salvation; or, The Evangelist. By ALPHONSE DAUDET. Translated by C. HARRY MELTZER. New and Cheaper Edition. Crown 8vo, cloth extra, 3s. 6d. [*Shortly*

Davenant. — What shall my Son be? Hints for Parents on the Choice of a Profession or Trade for their Sons. By FRANCIS DAVENANT, M.A. Post 8vo, cloth limp, 2s. 6d.

Davies' (Sir John) Complete Poetical Works, including Psalms I. to L. in Verse, and other hitherto Unpublished MSS., for the first time Collected and Edited, with Memorial-Introduction and Notes, by the Rev. A. B. GROSART, D.D. Two Vols., crown 8vo, cloth boards, 12s.

De Maistre.—A Journey Round My Room. By XAVIER DE MAISTRE. Translated by HENRY ATTWELL. Post 8vo, cloth limp, 2s. 6d.

Derwent (Leith), Novels by:
Our Lady of Tears. Crown 8vo, cloth extra, 3s. 6d.; post 8vo, illustrated boards, 2s.
Circe's Lovers. Crown 8vo, cloth extra, 3s. 6d. [*In preparation.*

Dickens (Charles), Novels by:
Post 8vo, illustrated boards, 2s. each.
Sketches by Boz.
The Pickwick Papers.
Oliver Twist.
Nicholas Nickleby.

DICKENS (CHARLES), *continued*—
The Speeches of Charles Dickens. Post 8vo, cloth limp, 2s. 6d.

The Speeches of Charles Dickens, 1841–1870. With a New Bibliography, revised and enlarged. Edited and Prefaced by RICHARD HERNE SHEPHERD. Crown 8vo, cloth extra, 6s.

About England with Dickens. By ALFRED RIMMER. With 57 Illustrations by C. A. VANDERHOOF, ALFRED RIMMER, and others. Sq. 8vo, cloth extra, 10s. 6d.

Dictionaries:

A Dictionary of Miracles: Imitative, Realistic, and Dogmatic. By the Rev. E. C. BREWER, LL.D. Crown 8vo, cloth extra, 7s. 6d. [*Preparing.*

A Dictionary of the Drama: Being a comprehensive Guide to the Plays, Playwrights, Players, and Playhouses of the United Kingdom and America, from the Earliest to the Present Times. By W. DAVENPORT ADAMS. A thick volume, crown 8vo, half-bound, 12s. 6d. [*In preparation.*

Familiar Allusions: A Handbook of Miscellaneous Information; including the Names of Celebrated Statues, Paintings, Palaces, Country Seats, Ruins, Churches, Ships, Streets, Clubs, Natural Curiosities, and the like. By WM. A. WHEELER and CHARLES G. WHEELER. Demy 8vo, cloth extra, 7s. 6d.

The Reader's Handbook of Allusions, References, Plots, and Stories. By the Rev. E. C. BREWER, LL.D. Third Edition, revised throughout, with a New Appendix, containing a Complete English Bibliography. Crown 8vo, 1,400 pages, cloth extra, 7s. 6d.

Short Sayings of Great Men. With Historical and Explanatory Notes. By SAMUEL A. BENT, M.A. Demy 8vo, cloth extra, 7s. 6d.

The Slang Dictionary: Etymological, Historical, and Anecdotal. Crown 8vo, cloth extra, 6s. 6d.

Words, Facts, and Phrases: A Dictionary of Curious, Quaint, and Out-of-the-Way Matters. By ELIEZER EDWARDS. Crown 8vo, half-bound, 12s. 6d.

Dobson (W. T.), Works by :

Literary Frivolities, Fancies, Follies, and Frolics. Post 8vo, cloth limp, 2s. 6d.

Poetical Ingenuities and Eccentricities. Post 8vo, cloth limp, 2s. 6d.

Doran. — Memories of our Great Towns; with Anecdotic Gleanings concerning their Worthies and their Oddities. By Dr. JOHN DORAN, F.S A. With 38 Illustrations. New and Cheaper Edition, crown 8vo, cloth extra, 7s. 6d.

Drama, A Dictionary of the. Being a comprehensive Guide to the Plays, Playwrights, Players, and Playhouses of the United Kingdom and America, from the Earliest to the Present Times. By W. DAVENPORT ADAMS. (Uniform with BREWER'S "Reader's Handbook.") Crown 8vo, half-bound, 12s. 6d. [*In preparation.*

Dramatists, The Old. Crown 8vo, cloth extra, with Vignette Portraits, 6s. per Vol.

Ben Jonson's Works. With Notes Critical and Explanatory, and a Biographical Memoir by WM. GIFFORD. Edited by Colonel CUNNINGHAM. Three Vols.

Chapman's Works. Complete in Three Vols. Vol. I. contains the Plays complete, including the doubtful ones; Vol. II., the Poems and Minor Translations, with an Introductory Essay by ALGERNON CHAS. SWINBURNE; Vol. III., the Translations of the Iliad and Odyssey.

Marlowe's Works. Including his Translations. Edited, with Notes and Introduction, by Col. CUNNINGHAM. One Vol.

Massinger's Plays. From the Text of WILLIAM GIFFORD. Edited by Col. CUNNINGHAM. One Vol.

Dyer. — The Folk-Lore of Plants. By T. F. THISELTON DYER, M.A. Crown 8vo, cloth extra, 6s. [*In preparation.*

Edwards, Betham-. — Felicia: A Novel. By M. BETHAM-EDWARDS. Post 8vo, illustrated boards, 2s. ; crown 8vo, cloth extra, 3s. 6d.

Edwardes (Mrs. A.), Novels by :

A Point of Honour. Post 8vo, illustrated boards, 2s.

Archie Lovell. Post 8vo, illust. bds., 2s. ; crown 8vo, cloth extra, 3s. 6d.

Early English Poets. Edited, with Introductions and Annotations, by Rev. A. B. GROSART, D.D. Crown 8vo, cloth boards, 6s. per Volume.

Fletcher's (Giles, B.D.) Complete Poems. One Vol.

Davies' (Sir John) Complete Poetical Works. Two Vols.

Herrick's (Robert) Complete Collected Poems. Three Vols.

Sidney's (Sir Philip) Complete Poetical Works. Three Vols.

Herbert (Lord) of Cherbury's Poems. Edited, with Introduction, by J. CHURTON COLLINS. Crown 8vo, parchment, 8s.

Eggleston.—Roxy: A Novel. By EDWARD EGGLESTON. Post 8vo, illust. boards, 2s. ; cr. 8vo, cloth extra, 3s. 6d.

Emanuel.—On Diamonds and Precious Stones: their History, Value, and Properties; with Simple Tests for ascertaining their Reality. By HARRY EMANUEL, F.R.G.S. With numerous Illustrations, tinted and plain. Crown 8vo, cloth extra, gilt, 6s.

Englishman's House, The: A Practical Guide to all interested in Selecting or Building a House, with full Estimates of Cost, Quantities, &c. By C. J. RICHARDSON. Third Edition. With nearly 600 Illustrations. Crown 8vo, cloth extra, 7s. 6d.

Ewald (Alex. Charles, F.S.A.), Works by :

Stories from the State Papers. With an Autotype Facsimile. Crown 8vo, cloth extra, 6s.

The Life and Times of Prince Charles Stuart, Count of Albany, commonly called the Young Pretender. From the State Papers and other Sources. New and Cheaper Edition, with a Portrait, crown 8vo, cloth extra, 7s. 6d.

Eyes, The.—How to Use our Eyes, and How to Preserve Them. By JOHN BROWNING, F.R.A.S., &c. With 37 Illustrations. Crown 8vo, 1s.; cloth, 1s. 6d.

Fairholt.—Tobacco: Its History and Associations; with an Account of the Plant and its Manufacture, and its Modes of Use in all Ages and Countries. By F. W. FAIRHOLT, F.S.A. With Coloured Frontispiece and upwards of 100 Illustrations by the Author. Crown 8vo, cloth extra, 6s.

Familiar Allusions: A Handbook of Miscellaneous Information; including the Names of Celebrated Statues, Paintings, Palaces, Country Seats, Ruins, Churches, Ships, Streets, Clubs, Natural Curiosities, and the like. By WILLIAM A. WHEELER, Author of "Noted Names of Fiction;" and CHARLES G. WHEELER. Demy 8vo, cloth extra, 7s. 6d.

Faraday (Michael), Works by:

The Chemical History of a Candle: Lectures delivered before a Juvenile Audience at the Royal Institution. Edited by WILLIAM CROOKES, F.C.S. Post 8vo, cloth extra, with numerous Illustrations, 4s. 6d.

On the Various Forces of Nature, and their Relations to each other: Lectures delivered before a Juvenile Audience at the Royal Institution. Edited by WILLIAM CROOKES, F.C.S. Post 8vo, cloth extra, with numerous Illustrations, 4s. 6d.

Fin-Bec. — The Cupboard Papers: Observations on the Art of Living and Dining. By FIN-BEC. Post 8vo, cloth limp, 2s. 6d.

Fitzgerald (Percy), Works by:

The Recreations of a Literary Man; or, Does Writing Pay? With Recollections of some Literary Men, and a View of a Literary Man's Working Life. Crown 8vo, cloth extra, 6s.

The World Behind the Scenes. Crown 8vo, cloth extra, 3s. 6d.

Post 8vo, illustrated boards, 2s. each.
Bella Donna.
Never Forgotten.
The Second Mrs. Tillotson.
Polly.
Seventy-five Brooke Street.

Fletcher's (Giles, B.D.) Complete Poems: Christ's Victorie in Heaven, Christ's Victorie on Earth, Christ's Triumph over Death, and Minor Poems. With Memorial-Introduction and Notes, by the Rev. A. B. GROSART, D.D. Crown 8vo, cloth boards, 6s.

Fonblanque. — Filthy Lucre: A Novel. By ALBANY DE FONBLANQUE. Post 8vo, illustrated boards, 2s.

Francillon (R. E.), Novels by:
Crown 8vo, cloth extra, 3s. 6d. each; post 8vo, illust. boards, 2s. each.
Olympia.
Queen Cophetua.
One by One.

Esther's Glove. Fcap. 8vo, picture cover, 1s.

French Literature, History of. By HENRY VAN LAUN. Complete in 3 Vols., demy 8vo, cl. bds., 7s. 6d. each.

Frost (Thomas), Works by:
Crown 8vo, cloth extra, 3s. 6d. each.
Circus Life and Circus Celebrities.
The Lives of the Conjurers.
The Old Showmen and the Old London Fairs.

Fry. — Royal Guide to the London Charities, 1883-4. By HERBERT FRY. Showing, in alphabetical order, their Name, Date of Foundation, Address, Objects, Annual Income, Chief Officials, &c. Published Annually. Crown 8vo, cloth, 1s 6d.

Gardening Books:

A Year's Work in Garden and Greenhouse: Practical Advice to Amateur Gardeners as to the Management of the Flower, Fruit, and Frame Garden. By GEORGE GLENNY. Post 8vo, cloth limp, 2s. 6d.

Our Kitchen Garden The Plants we Grow, and How we Cook Them. By TOM JERROLD, Author of "The Garden that Paid the Rent," &c. Post 8vo, cloth limp, 2s. 6d.

Household Horticulture: A Gossip about Flowers. By TOM and JANE JERROLD. Illustrated. Post 8vo, cloth limp, 2s. 6d.

The Garden that Paid the Rent. By TOM JERROLD. Fcap. 8vo, illustrated cover, 1s.; cloth limp, 1s. 6d.

My Garden Wild, and What I Grew there. By FRANCIS GEORGE HEATH. Cr. 8vo, cl. extra, 5s.; gilt edges, 6s.

Gentleman's Magazine (The) for 1883. One Shilling Monthly. "The New Abelard," ROBERT BUCHANAN's New Serial Story, was begun in the JANUARY Number. "Science Notes," by W. MATTIEU WILLIAMS, F.R.A.S., is also continued monthly.

*** Now ready, the Volume for JANUARY to JUNE, 1883, cloth extra, price 8s. 6d.; Cases for binding, 2s. each.*

Gentleman's Annual (The). Christmas, 1883. Containing Two Complete Novels by PERCY FITZGERALD and Mrs. ALEXANDER. Demy 8vo, illuminated cover, 1s. [*Preparing.*

Garrett.—The Capel Girls: A Novel. By EDWARD GARRETT. Post 8vo, illustrated boards, **2s.**; crown 8vo, cloth extra, **3s. 6d.**

German Popular Stories. Collected by the Brothers GRIMM, and Translated by EDGAR TAYLOR. Edited, with an Introduction, by JOHN RUSKIN. With 22 Illustrations on Steel by GEORGE CRUIKSHANK. Square 8vo, cloth extra, **6s. 6d.** gilt edges, **7s. 6d.**

Gibbon (Charles), Novels by:

Each in crown 8vo, cloth extra, **3s. 6d.**; or post 8vo, illustrated boards, **2s.**

  Robin Gray.
  For Lack of Gold.
  What will the World Say?
  In Honour Bound.
  In Love and War.
  For the King.
  Queen of the Meadow
  In Pastures Green.

Post 8vo, illustrated boards, **2s.**
The Dead Heart.

Crown 8vo, cloth extra, **3s. 6d.** each.
  The Braes of Yarrow.
  The Flower of the Forest.
  A Heart's Problem.
  The Golden Shaft.
  Of High Degree.

Fancy-Free. Three Vols., crown 8vo, **31s. 6d.** [*In the press.*

Gilbert (William), Novels by:
Post 8vo, illustrated boards, **2s.** each.
  Dr. Austin's Guests.
  The Wizard of the Mountain.
  James Duke, Costermonger.

Gilbert (W. S.), Original Plays by: In Two Series, each complete in itself, price **2s. 6d.** each. FIRST SERIES contains The Wicked World—Pygmalion and Galatea—Charity—The Princess—The Palace of Truth—Trial by Jury. The SECOND SERIES contains Broken Hearts — Engaged — Sweethearts—Gretchen—Dan'l Druce —Tom Cobb—H.M.S. Pinafore—The Sorcerer—The Pirates of Penzance.

Glenny.—A Year's Work in Garden and Greenhouse: Practical Advice to Amateur Gardeners as to the Management of the Flower, Fruit, and Frame Garden. By GEORGE GLENNY. Post 8vo, cloth limp, **2s. 6d.**

Godwin.—Lives of the Necro- mancers. By WILLIAM GODWIN. Post 8vo, cloth limp, **2s.**

Golden Library, The:
Square 16mo (Tauchnitz size), cloth limp, **2s.** per volume.

Bayard Taylor's Diversions of the Echo Club.

Bennett's (Dr. W. C.) Ballad History of England.

Bennett's (Dr. W. C.) Songs for Sailors.

Byron's Don Juan.

Godwin's (William) Lives of the Necromancers.

Holmes's Autocrat of the Breakfast Table. With an Introduction by G. A. SALA.

Holmes's Professor at the Breakfast Table.

Hood's Whims and Oddities. Complete. All the original Illustrations.

Irving's (Washington) Tales of a Traveller.

Irving's (Washington) Tales of the Alhambra.

Jesse's (Edward) Scenes and Occupations of a Country Life.

Lamb's Essays of Elia. Both Series Complete in One Vol.

Leigh Hunt's Essays: A Tale for a Chimney Corner, and other Pieces. With Portrait, and Introduction by EDMUND OLLIER.

Mallory's (Sir Thomas) Mort d'Arthur: The Stories of King Arthur and of the Knights of the Round Table. Edited by B. MONTGOMERIE RANKING.

Pascal's Provincial Letters. A New Translation, with Historical Introduction and Notes, by T. M'CRIE, D.D.

Pope's Poetical Works. Complete.

Rochefoucauld's Maxims and Moral Reflections. With Notes, and Introductory Essay by SAINTE-BEUVE.

St. Pierre's Paul and Virginia, and The Indian Cottage. Edited, with Life, by the Rev. E. CLARKE.

Shelley's Early Poems, and Queen Mab. With Essay by LEIGH HUNT.

Shelley's Later Poems: Laon and Cythna, &c.

Shelley's Posthumous Poems, the Shelley Papers, &c.

Shelley's Prose Works, including A Refutation of Deism, Zastrozzi, St. Irvyne, &c.

White's Natural History of Selborne. Edited, with Additions, by THOMAS BROWN, F.L.S.

Golden Treasury of Thought,
The: An ENCYCLOPÆDIA OF QUOTATIONS from Writers of all Times and Countries. Selected and Edited by THEODORE TAYLOR. Crown 8vo, cloth gilt and gilt edges, 7s. 6d.

Gordon Cumming. — In the
Hebrides. By C. F. GORDON CUMMING, Author of "At Home in Fiji." With Autotype Facsimile and numerous full-page Illustrations. Demy 8vo, cloth extra, 8s. 6d.

Graham. — The Professor's
Wife: A Story. By LEONARD GRAHAM. Fcap. 8vo, picture cover, 1s.; cloth extra, 2s. 6d.

Greeks and Romans, The Life
of the, Described from Antique Monuments. By ERNST GUHL and W. KONER. Translated from the Third German Edition, and Edited by Dr. F. HUEFFER. With 545 Illustrations. New and Cheaper Edition, demy 8vo, cloth extra, 7s. 6d.

Greenwood (James), Works by:

The Wilds of London. Crown 8vo, cloth extra, 3s. 6d.

Low-Life Deeps: An Account of the Strange Fish to be Found There. Crown 8vo, cloth extra, 3s. 6d.

Dick Temple: A Novel. Post 8vo, illustrated boards, 2s.

Guyot. — The Earth and Man;
or, Physical Geography in its relation to the History of Mankind. By ARNOLD GUYOT. With Additions by Professors AGASSIZ, PIERCE, and GRAY; 12 Maps and Engravings on Steel, some Coloured, and copious Index. Crown 8vo, cloth extra, gilt, 4s. 6d.

Hair (The): Its Treatment in
Health, Weakness, and Disease. Translated from the German of Dr. J. PINCUS. Crown 8vo, 1s.; cloth, 1s. 6d.

Hake (Dr. Thomas Gordon),
Poems by:

Maiden Ecstasy. Small 4to, cloth extra, 8s.

New Symbols. Crown 8vo, cloth extra, 6s.

Legends of the Morrow. Crown 8vo, cloth extra, 6s.

The Serpent Play. Crown 8vo, cloth extra, 6s.

Half-Hours with Foreign Novelists. With Notices of their Lives and Writings. By HELEN and ALICE ZIMMERN. A New Edition. Two Vols., crown 8vo, cloth extra, 12s.

Hall. — Sketches of Irish Character. By Mrs. S. C. HALL. With numerous Illustrations on Steel and Wood by MACLISE, GILBERT, HARVEY, and G. CRUIKSHANK. Medium 8vo, cloth extra, gilt, 7s. 6d.

Halliday. — Every-day Papers.
By ANDREW HALLIDAY. Post 8vo, illustrated boards, 2s.

Handwriting, The Philosophy
of. With over 100 Facsimiles and Explanatory Text. By DON FELIX DE SALAMANCA. Post 8vo, cloth limp, 2s. 6d.

Hanky-Panky: A Collection of
Very Easy Tricks, Very Difficult Tricks, White Magic, Sleight of Hand, &c. Edited by W. H. CREMER. With 200 Illustrations. Crown 8vo, cloth extra, 4s. 6d.

Hardy (Lady Duffus). — Paul
Wynter's Sacrifice: A Story. By Lady DUFFUS HARDY. Post 8vo, illust. boards, 2s.

Hardy (Thomas). — Under the
Greenwood Tree. By THOMAS HARDY, Author of "Far from the Madding Crowd." Crown 8vo, cloth extra, 3s. 6d.; post 8vo, illustrated boards, 2s.

Haweis (Mrs. H. R.), Works by:

The Art of Dress. With numerous Illustrations. Small 8vo, illustrated cover, 1s.; cloth limp, 1s. 6d.

The Art of Beauty. New and Cheaper Edition. Crown 8vo, cloth extra, with Coloured Frontispiece and Illustrations, 6s.

The Art of Decoration. Square 8vo, handsomely bound and profusely Illustrated, 10s. 6d.

Chaucer for Children: A Golden Key. With Eight Coloured Pictures and numerous Woodcuts. New Edition, small 4to, cloth extra, 6s.

Chaucer for Schools. Demy 8vo, cloth limp, 2s. 6d.

Haweis (Rev. H. R.). — American
Humorists. Including WASHINGTON IRVING, OLIVER WENDELL HOLMES, JAMES RUSSELL LOWELL, ARTEMUS WARD, MARK TWAIN, and BRET HARTE. By the Rev. H. R. HAWEIS, M.A. Crown 8vo, cloth extra, 6s.

Hawthorne (Julian), Novels by.
Crown 8vo, cloth extra, 3s. 6d. each;
post 8vo, illustrated boards, 2s. each.
> Garth.
> Ellice Quentin.
> Sebastian Strome.

Mrs. Gainsborough's Diamonds. Fcap. 8vo, illustrated cover, 1s.; cloth extra, 2s. 6d.

Prince Saroni's Wife. Crown 8vo, cloth extra, 3s. 6d.

Dust: A Novel. Crown 8vo, cloth extra, 3s. 6d.

Fortune's Fool. Three Vols., crown 8vo, 31s. 6d.   [*Shortly.*

Heath (F. G.). — My Garden
Wild, and What I Grew There. By FRANCIS GEORGE HEATH, Author of "The Fern World," &c. Crown 8vo, cloth extra, 5s.; cloth gilt, and gilt edges, 6s.

Helps (Sir Arthur), Works by:
Animals and their Masters. Post 8vo, cloth limp, 2s. 6d.

Social Pressure. Post 8vo, cloth limp, 2s. 6d.

Ivan de Biron: A Novel. Crown 8vo, cloth extra, 3s. 6d.; post 8vo, illustrated boards, 2s.

Heptalogia (The); or, The
Seven against Sense. A Cap with Seven Bells. Cr. 8vo, cloth extra, 6s.

Herbert.—The Poems of Lord
Herbert of Cherbury. Edited, with an Introduction, by J. CHURTON COLLINS. Crown 8vo, bound in parchment, 8s.

Herrick's (Robert) Hesperides,
Noble Numbers, and Complete Collected Poems. With Memorial-Introduction and Notes by the Rev. A. B. GROSART, D.D., Steel Portrait, Index of First Lines, and Glossarial Index, &c. Three Vols., crown 8vo, cloth boards, 18s.

Hesse - Wartegg (Chevalier
Ernst von), Works by:
Tunis: The Land and the People. With 22 Illustrations. Crown 8vo, cloth extra, 3s. 6d.

The New South-West: Travelling Sketches from Kansas, New Mexico, Arizona, and Northern Mexico. With 100 fine Illustrations and 3 Maps. Demy 8vo, cloth extra, 14s.   [*In preparation.*

Hindley (Charles), Works by:
Crown 8vo, cloth extra, 3s. 6d. each.

Tavern Anecdotes and Sayings: Including the Origin of Signs, and Reminiscences connected with Taverns, Coffee Houses, Clubs, &c. With Illustrations.

The Life and Adventures of a Cheap Jack. By One of the Fraternity. Edited by CHARLES HINDLEY.

Holmes (Oliver Wendell), Works by:
The Autocrat of the Breakfast-Table. Illustrated by J. GORDON THOMSON. Post 8vo, cloth limp, 2s. 6d.; another Edition in smaller type, with an Introduction by G. A. SALA. Post 8vo, cloth limp, 2s.

The Professor at the Breakfast-Table; with the Story of Iris. Post 8vo, cloth limp, 2s.

Holmes. — The Science of
Voice Production and Voice Preservation: A Popular Manual for the Use of Speakers and Singers. By GORDON HOLMES, M.D. Crown 8vo, cloth limp, with Illustrations, 2s. 6d.

Hood (Thomas):
Hood's Choice Works, in Prose and Verse. Including the Cream of the Comic Annuals. With Life of the Author, Portrait, and 200 Illustrations. Crown 8vo, cloth extra, 7s. 6d.

Hood's Whims and Oddities. Complete. With all the original Illustrations. Post 8vo, cloth limp, 2s.

Hood (Tom), Works by:
From Nowhere to the North Pole: A Noah's Arkæological Narrative. With 25 Illustrations by W. BRUNTON and E. C. BARNES. Square crown 8vo, cloth extra, gilt edges, 6s.

A Golden Heart: A Novel. Post 8vo, illustrated boards, 2s.

Hook's (Theodore) Choice Humorous Works, including his Ludicrous Adventures, Bons Mots, Puns and Hoaxes. With a New Life of the Author, Portraits, Facsimiles, and Illustrations. Crown 8vo, cloth extra, gilt, 7s. 6d.

Horne.—Orion : An Epic Poem,
in Three Books. By RICHARD HENGIST HORNE. With Photographic Portrait from a Medallion by SUMMERS. Tenth Edition, crown 8vo, cloth extra, 7s.

Howell.—Conflicts of Capital and Labour, Historically and Economically considered: Being a History and Review of the Trade Unions of Great Britain, showing their Origin, Progress, Constitution, and Objects, in their Political, Social, Economical, and Industrial Aspects. By GEORGE HOWELL. Crown 8vo, cloth extra, 7s. 6d.

Hugo. — The Hunchback of Notre Dame. By VICTOR HUGO. Post 8vo, illustrated boards, 2s.

Hunt.—Essays by Leigh Hunt. A Tale for a Chimney Corner, and other Pieces. With Portrait and Introduction by EDMUND OLLIER. Post 8vo, cloth limp, 2s.

Hunt (Mrs. Alfred), Novels by:

Thornicroft's Model. Crown 8vo, cloth extra, 3s. 6d.; post 8vo, illustrated boards, 2s.

The Leaden Casket. Crown 8vo, cloth extra, 3s. 6d.; post 8vo, illustrated boards, 2s.

Self-Condemned. Crown 8vo, cloth extra, 3s. 6d. [*Shortly*.

Ingelow.—Fated to be Free: A Novel. By JEAN INGELOW. Crown 8vo, cloth extra, 3s. 6d.; post 8vo, illustrated boards, 2s.

Irving (Henry).—The Paradox of Acting. Translated, with Annotations, from Diderot's "Le Paradoxe sur le Comédien," by WALTER HERRIES POLLOCK. With a Preface by HENRY IRVING. Crown 8vo, in parchment, 4s. 6d.

Irving (Washington),Works by: Post 8vo, cloth limp, 2s. each.
Tales of a Traveller.
Tales of the Alhambra.

James.—Confidence: A Novel. By HENRY JAMES, Jun. Crown 8vo, cloth extra, 3s. 6d.; post 8vo, illustrated boards, 2s.

Janvier.—Practical Keramics for Students. By CATHERINE A. JANVIER. Crown 8vo, cloth extra, 6s.

Jay (Harriett), Novels by. Each crown 8vo, cloth extra, 3s. 6d.; or post 8vo, illustrated boards, 2s.
The Dark Colleen.
The Queen of Connaught.

Jefferies.—Nature near London. By RICHARD JEFFERIES, Author of "The Gamekeeper at Home." Crown 8vo, cloth extra, 6s.

Jennings (H. J.).—Curiosities of Criticism. By HENRY J. JENNINGS. Post 8vo, cloth limp, 2s. 6d.

Jennings (Hargrave). — The Rosicrucians: Their Rites and Mysteries. With Chapters on the Ancient Fire and Serpent Worshippers. By HARGRAVE JENNINGS. With Five full-page Plates and upwards of 300 Illustrations. A New Edition, crown 8vo, cloth extra, 7s. 6d.

Jerrold (Tom), Works by:

The Garden that Paid the Rent. By TOM JERROLD. Fcap. 8vo, illustrated cover, 1s.; cloth limp, 1s. 6d.

Household Horticulture: A Gossip about Flowers. By TOM and JANE JERROLD. Illustrated. Post 8vo, cloth limp, 2s. 6d.

Our Kitchen Garden: The Plants we Grow, and How we Cook Them. By TOM JERROLD. Post 8vo, cloth limp, 2s. 6d.

Jesse.—Scenes and Occupations of a Country Life. By EDWARD JESSE. Post 8vo, cloth limp, 2s.

Jones (William, F.S.A.), Works by:

Finger-Ring Lore: Historical, Legendary, and Anecdotal. With over 200 Illustrations. Crown 8vo, cloth extra, 7s. 6d.

Credulities, Past and Present; including the Sea and Seamen, Miners, Talismans, Word and Letter Divination, Exorcising and Blessing of Animals, Birds, Eggs, Luck, &c. With an Etched Frontispiece. Crown 8vo, cloth extra, 7s. 6d.

Crowns and Coronations: A History of Regalia in all Times and Countries. With One Hundre Illustrations. Crown 8vo, cloth extra, 7s. 6d.

Jonson's (Ben) Works. With Notes Critical and Explanatory, and a Biographical Memoir by WILLIAM GIFFORD. Edited by Colonel CUNNINGHAM. Three Vols., crown 8vo, cloth extra, 18s.; or separately, 6s. per Volume.

Josephus,The Complete Works of. Translated by WHISTON. Containing both "The Antiquities of the Jews" and "The Wars of the Jews." Two Vols., 8vo, with 52 Illustrations and Maps, cloth extra, gilt, 14s.

Kavanagh.—The Pearl Foun-tain, and other Fairy Stories. By BRIDGET and JULIA KAVANAGH. With Thirty Illustrations by J. MOYR SMITH. Small 8vo, cloth gilt, 6s.

Kempt.—Pencil and Palette: Chapters on Art and Artists. By ROBERT KEMPT. Post 8vo, cloth limp, 2s. 6d.

Kingsley (Henry), Novels by: Each crown 8vo, cloth extra, 3s. 6d.; or post 8vo, illustrated boards, 2s.

    Oakshott Castle.
    Number Seventeen.

Lamb (Charles):

Mary and Charles Lamb: Their Poems, Letters, and Remains. With Reminiscences and Notes by W. CAREW HAZLITT. With HANCOCK'S Portrait of the Essayist, Facsimiles of the Title-pages of the rare First Editions of Lamb's and Coleridge's Works, and numerous Illustrations. Crown 8vo, cloth extra, 10s. 6d.

Lamb's Complete Works, in Prose and Verse, reprinted from the Original Editions, with many Pieces hitherto unpublished. Edited, with Notes and Introduction, by R. H. SHEPHERD. With Two Portraits and Facsimile of a Page of the "Essay on Roast Pig." Crown 8vo, cloth extra, 7s. 6d.

The Essays of Elia. Complete Edition. Post 8vo, cloth extra, 2s.

Poetry for Children, and Prince Dorus. By CHARLES LAMB. Carefully Reprinted from unique copies. Small 8vo, cloth extra, 5s.

Lares and Penates; or, The Background of Life. By FLORENCE CADDY. Crown 8vo, cloth extra, 6s.

Lane's Arabian Nights, &c.:

The Thousand and One Nights: commonly called, in England, "THE ARABIAN NIGHTS' ENTERTAINMENTS." A New Translation from the Arabic, with copious Notes, by EDWARD WILLIAM LANE. Illustrated by many hundred Engravings on Wood, from Original Designs by WM. HARVEY. A New Edition, from a Copy annotated by the Translator, edited by his Nephew, EDWARD STANLEY POOLE. With a Preface by STANLEY LANE-POOLE. Three Vols., demy 8vo, cloth extra, 7s. 6d. each.

Lane's Arabian Nights, &c.:

Arabian Society in the Middle Ages: Studies from "The Thousand and One Nights." By EDWARD WILLIAM LANE, Author of "The Modern Egyptians," &c. Edited by STANLEY LANE-POOLE. Crown 8vo, cloth extra, 6s.

Larwood (Jacob), Works by:

The Story of the London Parks With Illustrations. Crown 8vo, cloth extra, 3s. 6d.

Clerical Anecdotes. Post 8vo, cloth limp, 2s. 6d.

Forensic Anecdotes Post 8vo, cloth limp, 2s. 6d.

Theatrical Anecdotes. Post 8vo, cloth limp, 2s. 6d.

Leigh (Henry S.), Works by:

Carols of Cockayne. With numerous Illustrations. Post 8vo, cloth limp, 2s. 6d.

Jeux d'Esprit. Collected and Edited by HENRY S. LEIGH. Post 8vo, cloth limp 2s. 6d.

Life in London; or, The History of Jerry Hawthorn and Corinthian Tom. With the whole of CRUIKSHANK'S Illustrations, in Colours, after the Originals. Crown 8vo, cloth extra, 7s. 6d.

Linton (E. Lynn), Works by:

Witch Stories. Post 8vo, cloth limp, 2s. 6d.

The True Story of Joshua Davidson Post 8vo, cloth limp, 2s. 6d.

Crown 8vo, cloth extra, 3s. 6d. each; post 8vo, illustrated boards, 2s.

Patricia Kemball.
The Atonement of Leam Dundas.
The World Well Lost.
Under which Lord?
With a Silken Thread.
The Rebel of the Family.
"My Love!"

Ione. Three Vols., crown 8vo, 31s. 6d.
    [Shortly.

Locks and Keys.—On the De-velopment and Distribution of Primitive Locks and Keys. By Lieut.-Gen. PITT-RIVERS, F.R.S. With numerous Illustrations. Demy 4to, half Roxburghe, 16s.

Longfellow:

Longfellow's Complete Prose Works. Including "Outre Mer," "Hyperion," "Kavanagh," "The Poets and Poetry of Europe," and "Driftwood." With Portrait and Illustrations by VALENTINE BROMLEY. Crown 8vo, cloth extra, 7s. 6d.

Longfellow's Poetical Works. Carefully Reprinted from the Original Editions. With numerous fine Illustrations on Steel and Wood. Crown 8vo, cloth extra, 7s. 6d.

Lucy.—Gideon Fleyce: A Novel. By HENRY W. LUCY. Crown 8vo, cloth extra, 3s. 6d.

Lunatic Asylum, My Experiences in a. By A SANE PATIENT. Crown 8vo, cloth extra, 5s.

Lusiad (The) of Camoens. Translated into English Spenserian Verse by ROBERT FFRENCH DUFF. Demy 8vo, with Fourteen full-page Plates, cloth boards, 18s.

McCarthy (Justin, M.P.), Works by:

A History of Our Own Times, from the Accession of Queen Victoria to the General Election of 1880. Four Vols. demy 8vo, cloth extra, 12s. each.—Also a POPULAR EDITION, in Four Vols. crown 8vo, cloth extra, 6s each.

A Short History of Our Own Times. One Volume, crown 8vo, cloth extra, 6s. *[Shortly.*

History of the Four Georges. Four Vols. demy 8vo, cloth extra, 12s. each. *[In preparation.*

Crown 8vo, cloth extra, 3s. 6d. each post 8vo, illustrated boards, 2s. each.

Dear Lady Disdain.
The Waterdale Neighbours.
My Enemy's Daughter.
A Fair Saxon.
Linley Rochford
Miss Misanthrope.
Donna Quixote.

The Comet of a Season. Crown 8vo, cloth extra, 3s. 6d.

Maid of Athens. With 12 Illustrations by F. BARNARD. 3 vols., crown 8vo, 31s. 6d. *[Shortly.*

McCarthy (Justin H.), Works by:

Serapion, and other Poems. Crown 8vo, cloth extra, 6s.

An Outline of the History of Ireland, from the Earliest Times to the Present Day. Cr. 8vo, 1s.; cloth, 1s. 6d.

MacDonald (George, LL.D.), Works by:

The Princess and Curdie. With 11 Illustrations by JAMES ALLEN. Small crown 8vo, cloth extra, 5s.

Gutta-Percha Willie, the Working Genius. With 9 Illustrations by ARTHUR HUGHES. Square 8vo, cloth extra, 3s. 6d.

Paul Faber, Surgeon. With a Frontispiece by J. E. MILLAIS. Crown 8vo, cloth extra, 3s. 6d.; post 8vo, illustrated boards, 2s.

Thomas Wingfold, Curate. With a Frontispiece by C. J. STANILAND. Crown 8vo, cloth extra, 3s. 6d.; post 8vo, illustrated boards, 2s.

Macdonell.—Quaker Cousins: A Novel. By AGNES MACDONELL. Crown 8vo, cloth extra, 3s. 6d.; post 8vo, illustrated boards, 2s.

Macgregor. — Pastimes and Players. Notes on Popular Games. By ROBERT MACGREGOR. Post 8vo, cloth limp, 2s. 6d.

Maclise Portrait-Gallery (The) of Illustrious Literary Characters; with Memoirs—Biographical, Critical, Bibliographical, and Anecdotal—illustrative of the Literature of the former half of the Present Century. By WILLIAM BATES, B.A. With 85 Portraits printed on an India Tint. Crown 8vo, cloth extra, 7s. 6d.

Macquoid (Mrs.), Works by:

In the Ardennes. With 50 fine Illustrations by THOMAS R. MACQUOID. Square 8vo, cloth extra, 10s. 6d.

Pictures and Legends from Normandy and Brittany. With numerous Illustrations by THOMAS R. MACQUOID. Square 8vo, cloth gilt, 10s. 6d.

Through Normandy. With 90 Illustrations by T. R. MACQUOID. Square 8vo, cloth extra, 7s. 6d

Through Brittany. With numerous Illustrations by T. R. MACQUOID. Square 8vo, cloth extra, 7s. 6d.

About Yorkshire. With 67 Illustrations by T. R. MACQUOID, Engraved by SWAIN. Square 8vo, cloth extra, 10s. 6d.

The Evil Eye, and other Stories. Crown 8vo, cloth extra, 3s. 6d.; post 8vo, illustrated boards, 2s.

Lost Rose, and other Stories. Crown 8vo, cloth extra, 3s. 6d.; post 8vo, illustrated boards, 2s.

Mackay.—Interludes and Undertones: Poems of the End of Life. By CHARLES MACKAY, LL.D. Crown 8vo, cloth extra, 6s.   [*In the press.*

Magician's Own Book (The): Performances with Cups and Balls, Eggs, Hats, Handkerchiefs, &c. All from actual Experience. Edited by W. H. CREMER. With 200 Illustrations. Crown 8vo, cloth extra, 4s. 6d.

Magic No Mystery: Tricks with Cards, Dice, Balls, &c., with fully descriptive Directions; the Art of Secret Writing; Training of Performing Animals, &c. With Coloured Frontispiece and many Illustrations. Crown 8vo, cloth extra, 4s. 6d.

Magna Charta. An exact Facsimile of the Original in the British Museum, printed on fine plate paper, 3 feet by 2 feet, with Arms and Seals emblazoned in Gold and Colours. Price 5s.

Mallock (W. H.), Works by:

The New Republic; or, Culture, Faith and Philosophy in an English Country House. Post 8vo, cloth limp, 2s. 6d.; Cheap Edition, illustrated boards, 2s.

The New Paul and Virginia; or, Positivism on an Island. Post 8vo, cloth limp, 2s. 6d.

Poems. Small 4to, bound in parchment, 8s.

Is Life worth Living? Crown 8vo, cloth extra, 6s.

Mallory's (Sir Thomas) Mort d'Arthur: The Stories of King Arthur and of the Knights of the Round Table. Edited by B. MONTGOMERIE RANKING. Post 8vo, cloth limp, 2s.

Marlowe's Works. Including his Translations. Edited, with Notes and Introduction, by Col. CUNNINGHAM. Crown 8vo, cloth extra, 6s.

Marryat (Florence), Novels by:

Crown 8vo, cloth extra, 3s. 6d. each; or, post 8vo, illustrated boards, 2s.

Open! Sesame!
Written In Fire.

Post 8vo, illustrated boards, 2s. each.
A Harvest of Wild Oats.
A Little Stepson.
Fighting the Air.

Mark Twain, Works by:

The Choice Works of Mark Twain. Revised and Corrected throughout by the Author. With Life, Portrait, and numerous Illustrations. Crown 8vo, cloth extra, 7s. 6d.

The Adventures of Tom Sawyer. With 100 Illustrations. Small 8vo, cloth extra, 7s. 6d. CHEAP EDITION, illustrated boards, 2s.

An Idle Excursion, and other Sketches. Post 8vo, illustrated boards, 2s.

The Prince and the Pauper. With nearly 200 Illustrations. Crown 8vo, cloth extra, 7s. 6d.

The Innocents Abroad; or, The New Pilgrim's Progress: Being some Account of the Steamship "Quaker City's" Pleasure Excursion to Europe and the Holy Land. With 234 Illustrations. Crown 8vo, cloth extra, 7s. 6d. CHEAP EDITION (under the title of "MARK TWAIN'S PLEASURE TRIP"), post 8vo, illust. boards, 2s.

A Tramp Abroad. With 314 Illustrations. Crown 8vo, cloth extra, 7s. 6d.

The Stolen White Elephant, &c. Crown 8vo, cloth extra, 6s.

Life on the Mississippi. With about 300 Original Illustrations. Crown 8vo, cloth extra, 7s. 6d.

Massinger's Plays. From the Text of WILLIAM GIFFORD. Edited by Col. CUNNINGHAM. Crown 8vo, cloth extra, 6s.

Mayhew.—London Characters and the Humorous Side of London Life. By HENRY MAYHEW. With numerous Illustrations. Crown 8vo, cloth extra, 3s. 6d.

Mayfair Library, The:

Post 8vo, cloth limp, 2s. 6d. per Volume.

A Journey Round My Room. By XAVIER DE MAISTRE. Translated by HENRY ATTWELL.

Latter-Day Lyrics. Edited by W. DAVENPORT ADAMS.

Quips and Quiddities. Selected by W. DAVENPORT ADAMS.

The Agony Column of "The Times," from 1800 to 1870. Edited, with an Introduction, by ALICE CLAY.

Balzac's "Comedie Humaine" and its Author. With Translations by H. H. WALKER.

Melancholy Anatomised: A Popular Abridgment of "Burton's Anatomy of Melancholy."

Gastronomy as a Fine Art. By BRILLAT-SAVARIN.

MAYFAIR LIBRARY, *continued*—

The Speeches of Charles Dickens.

Literary Frivolities, Fancies, Follies, and Frolics. By W. T. DOBSON.

Poetical Ingenuities and Eccentricities. Selected and Edited by W. T. DOBSON.

The Cupboard Papers. By FIN-BEC.

Original Plays by W. S. GILBERT. FIRST SERIES. Containing: The Wicked World — Pygmalion and Galatea—Charity — The Princess—The Palace of Truth—Trial by Jury.

Original Plays by W. S. GILBERT. SECOND SERIES. Containing: Broken Hearts — Engaged — Sweethearts—Gretchen—Dan'l Druce—Tom Cobb—H.M.S. Pinafore — The Sorcerer—The Pirates of Penzance.

Animals and their Masters. By Sir ARTHUR HELPS.

Social Pressure. By Sir ARTHUR HELPS.

Curiosities of Criticism. By HENRY J. JENNINGS.

The Autocrat of the Breakfast-Table. By OLIVER WENDELL HOLMES. Illustrated by J. GORDON THOMSON.

Pencil and Palette. By ROBERT KEMPT.

Clerical Anecdotes. By JACOB LARWOOD.

Forensic Anecdotes; or, Humour and Curiosities of the Law and Men of Law. By JACOB LARWOOD.

Theatrical Anecdotes. By JACOB LARWOOD.

Carols of Cockayne. By HENRY S. LEIGH.

Jeux d'Esprit. Edited by HENRY S. LEIGH.

True History of Joshua Davidson. By E. LYNN LINTON.

Witch Stories. By E. LYNN LINTON.

Pastimes and Players. By ROBERT MACGREGOR.

The New Paul and Virginia. By W. H. MALLOCK.

The New Republic. By W. H. MALLOCK.

Muses of Mayfair. Edited by H. CHOLMONDELEY-PENNELL.

Thoreau: His Life and Aims. By H. A. PAGE.

Puck on Pegasus. By H. CHOLMONDELEY-PENNELL.

Puniana. By the Hon. HUGH ROWLEY.

More Puniana. By the Hon. HUGH ROWLEY.

The Philosophy of Handwriting. By DON FELIX DE SALAMANCA.

MAYFAIR LIBRARY, *continued*—

By Stream and Sea. By WILLIAM SENIOR.

Old Stories Re-told. By WALTER THORNBURY.

Leaves from a Naturalist's Note-Book. By Dr. ANDREW WILSON.

Medicine, Family.—One Thousand Medical Maxims and Surgical Hints, for Infancy, Adult Life, Middle Age, and Old Age. By N. E. DAVIES, Licentiate of the Royal College of Physicians of London. Crown 8vo, 1s. ; cloth, 1s. 6d.

Merry Circle (The): A Book of New Intellectual Games and Amusements. By CLARA BELLEW. With numerous Illustrations. Crown 8vo, cloth extra, 4s. 6d.

Middlemass (Jean), Novels by:

Touch and Go. Crown 8vo, cloth extra, 3s. 6d.; post 8vo, illustrated boards, 2s.

Mr. Dorillion. Post 8vo, illustrated boards, 2s.

Miller.—Physiology for the Young; or, The House of Life: Human Physiology, with its application to the Preservation of Health. For use in Classes and Popular Reading. With numerous Illustrations By Mrs. F. FENWICK MILLER. Small 8vo, cloth limp, 2s. 6d.

Milton (J. L.), Works by:

The Hygiene of the Skin. A Concise Set of Rules for the Management of the Skin; with Directions for Diet, Wines, Soaps, Baths, &c. Small 8vo, 1s. ; cloth extra, 1s. 6d.

The Bath in Diseases of the Skin. Small 8vo, 1s.; cloth extra, 1s. 6d.

The Laws of Life, and their Relation to Diseases of the Skin. Small 8vo, 1s. ; cloth extra, 1s. 6d.

Moncrieff. — The Abdication; or, Time Tries All. An Historical Drama. By W. D. SCOTT-MONCRIEFF. With Seven Etchings by JOHN PETTIE, R.A., W. Q. ORCHARDSON, R.A., J. MACWHIRTER, A.R.A., COLIN HUNTER, R. MACBETH, and TOM GRAHAM. Large 4to, bound in buckram, 21s.

Murray (D. Christie), Novels by:

A Life's Atonement. Crown 8vo, cloth extra. 3s. 6d.; post 8vo, illustrated boards, 2s.

Joseph's Coat. With Illustrations by F. BARNARD. Crown 8vo, cloth extra, 3s. 6d.

D. C Murray's Novels, *continued—*

Coals of Fire. With Illustrations by Arthur Hopkins and others. Crown 8vo, cloth extra, 3s. 6d.

A Model Father, and other Stories. Crown 8vo, cloth extra, 3s. 6d.; post 8vo, illustrated boards, 2s.

Val Strange: A Story of the Primrose Way. Crown 8vo, cloth extra, 3s. 6d.

Hearts. New and Cheaper Edition. Cr. 8vo, cloth extra, 3s. 6d. [*Shortly.*

By the Gate of the Sea. Two Vols., post 8vo, 12s.

The Way of the World. Three Vols., crown 8vo, 31s. 6d. [*Shortly.*

North Italian Folk. By Mrs. Comyns Carr. Illust. by Randolph Caldecott. Sq. 8vo, cloth extra, 7s. 6d.

Number Nip (Stories about), the Spirit of the Giant Mountains. Retold for Children by Walter Grahame. With Illustrations by J. Moyr Smith. Post 8vo, cloth extra, 5s.

Oliphant. — Whiteladies: A Novel. With Illustrations by Arthur Hopkins and Henry Woods. Crown 8vo, cloth extra, 3s. 6d.; post 8vo, illustrated boards, 2s.

O'Reilly.—Phœbe's Fortunes: A Novel. With Illustrations by Henry Tuck. Post 8vo, illustrated boards, 2s.

O'Shaughnessy (Arth.), Works by:

Songs of a Worker. Fcap. 8vo, cloth extra, 7s. 6d.

Music and Moonlight. Fcap. 8vo, cloth extra, 7s. 6d.

Lays of France. Crown 8vo, cloth extra, 10s. 6d.

Ouida, Novels by. Crown 8vo, cloth extra, 5s. each; post 8vo, illustrated boards, 2s. each.

Held in Bondage.
Strathmore.
Chandos.
Under Two Flags.
Idalia.
Cecil Castlemaine's Gage.
Tricotrin.
Puck.
Folle Farine.
A Dog of Flanders.
Pascarel.
Two Little Wooden Shoes.

Ouida's Novels, *continued—*

Signa.
In a Winter City
Ariadne.
Friendship.
Moths
Pipistrello.
A Village Commune.

In Maremma. Crown 8vo, cloth extra, 5s.

Bimbi: Stories for Children. Square 8vo, cloth gilt, cinnamon edges, 7s. 6d.

Wanda: A Novel. Crown 8vo, cloth extra, 5s. [*Shortly.*

Wisdom, Wit, and Pathos. Selected from the Works of Ouida, by F. Sydney Morris. Small crown 8vo, cloth extra, 5s. [*In the press.*

Page (H. A.), Works by:

Thoreau: His Life and Aims: A Study. With a Portrait. Post 8vo, cloth limp, 2s 6d.

Lights on the Way: Some Tales within a Tale. By the late J. H. Alexander, B.A. Edited by H. A. Page. Crown 8vo, cloth extra, 6s.

Pascal's Provincial Letters. A New Translation, with Historical Introduction and Notes, by T. M'Crie, D.D. Post 8vo cloth limp, 2s.

Paul Ferroll:

Post 8vo, illustrated boards, 2s. each.
Paul Ferroll: A Novel.
Why Paul Ferroll Killed His Wife.

Payn (James), Novels by:

Each crown 8vo, cloth extra, 3s. 6d.; or post 8vo, illustrated boards, 2s.

Lost Sir Massingberd.
The Best of Husbands.
Walter's Word.
Halves.
Fallen Fortunes.
What He Cost Her.
Less Black than We're Painted
By Proxy.
Under One Roof.
High Spirits.
Carlyon's Year.
A Confidential Agent
Some Private Views.
From Exile.

JAMES PAYN'S NOVELS, *continued—*
Post 8vo, illustrated boards, 2s. each.

A Perfect Treasure.
Bentinck's Tutor.
Murphy's Master.
A County Family.
At Her Mercy.
A Woman's Vengeance'
Cecil's Tryst
The Clyffards of Clyffe.
The Family Scapegrace.
The Foster Brothers.
Found Dead.
Gwendoline's Harvest.
Humorous Stories.
Like Father, Like Son.
A Marine Residence.
Married Beneath Him.
Mirk Abbey.
Not Wooed, but Won.
Two Hundred Pounds Reward.

Crown 8vo, cloth extra, 3s. 6d. each.
A Grape from a Thorn. With Illustrations by W. SMALL.
For Cash Only.   **Kit: A Memory.**

Pennell (H. Cholmondeley),
Works by: Post 8vo, cloth limp, 2s. 6d. each.

Puck on Pegasus. With Illustrations.
The Muses of Mayfair. Vers de Société, Selected and Edited by H. C. PENNELL.

Phelps.—Beyond the Gates.
By ELIZABETH STUART PHELPS, Author of "The Gates Ajar." Post 8vo, cloth limp, 2s 6d Published by special arrangement with the Author, and Copyright in England and its Dependencies.   [*Shortly.*

Planche (J. R.), Works by:
The Cyclopædia of Costume; or, A Dictionary of Dress—Regal, Ecclesiastical, Civil, and Military—from the Earliest Period in England to the Reign of George the Third. Including Notices of Contemporaneous Fashions on the Continent, and a General History of the Costumes of the Principal Countries of Europe. Two Vols., demy 4to, half morocco, profusely Illustrated with Coloured and Plain Plates and Woodcuts, £7 7s. The Vols may also be had *separately* (each complete in itself) at £3 13s. 6d. each: Vol. I. THE DICTIONARY. Vol. II. A GENERAL HISTORY OF COSTUME IN EUROPE.

PLANCHE'S WORKS, *continued—*
The Pursuivant of Arms; or, Heraldry Founded upon Facts. With Coloured Frontispiece and 200 Illustrations. Cr. 8vo, cloth extra, 7s. 6d.
Songs and Poems, from 1819 to 1879. Edited, with an Introduction, by his Daughter, Mrs. MACKARNESS. Crown 8vo, cloth extra, 6s.

Pirkis.—Trooping with Crows:
A Story. By CATHERINE PIRKIS. Fcap 8vo, picture cover, 1s

Play-time: Sayings and Doings of Babyland. By EDWARD STANFORD. Large 4to, handsomely printed in Colours, 5s.

Plutarch's Lives of Illustrious
Men. Translated from the Greek, with Notes Critical and Historical, and a Life of Plutarch, by JOHN and WILLIAM LANGHORNE. Two Vols., 8vo, cloth extra, with Portraits, 10s. 6d.

Poe (Edgar Allan):—
The Choice Works, in Prose and Poetry, of EDGAR ALLAN POE. With an Introductory Essay by CHARLES BAUDELAIRE, Portrait and Facsimiles. Cr. 8vo, cloth extra, 7s 6d.
The Mystery of Marie Roget, and other Stories. Post 8vo, illustrated boards, 2s.

Pope's Poetical Works. Complete in One Volume. Post 8vo, cloth limp, 2s.

Price (E. C.), Novels by:
Valentina: A Sketch. With a Frontispiece by HAL LUDLOW. Crown 8vo, cloth extra, 3s. 6d.; post 8vo, illustrated boards, 2s.
The Foreigners. Three Vols., crown 8vo, 31s. 6d.   [*Shortly.*

Proctor (Richd. A.), Works by:
Flowers of the Sky. With 55 Illustrations. Small crown 8vo, cloth extra, 4s. 6d.
Easy Star Lessons. With Star Maps for Every Night in the Year, Drawings of the Constellations, &c. Crown 8vo, cloth extra, 6s.
Familiar Science Studies. Crown 8vo, cloth extra, 7s. 6d.
Myths and Marvels of Astronomy. Crown 8vo, cloth extra, 6s.
Pleasant Ways in Science. Crown 8vo, cloth extra, 6s.
Rough Ways made Smooth: A Series of Familiar Essays on Scientific Subjects. Cr. 8vo, cloth extra, 6s.

R. A. PROCTOR'S WORKS, *continued*—

Our Place among Infinities: A Series of Essays contrasting our Little Abode in Space and Time with the Infinities Around us. Crown 8vo, cloth extra, 6s.

The Expanse of Heaven: A Series of Essays on the Wonders of the Firmament. Cr. 8vo, cloth extra, 6s.

Saturn and Its System. New and Revised Edition, with 13 Steel Plates. Demy 8vo, cloth extra, 10s. 6d.

The Great Pyramid: Observatory, Tomb, and Temple. With Illustrations. Crown 8vo, cloth extra, 6s.

Mysteries of Time and Space. With Illustrations. Crown 8vo, cloth extra, 7s. 6d.

Wages and Wants of Science Workers. Crown 8vo, 1s. 6d.

Pyrotechnist's Treasury (The); or, Complete Art of Making Fireworks. By THOMAS KENTISH. With numerous Illustrations. Crown 8vo, cloth extra, 4s. 6d.

Rabelais' Works. Faithfully Translated from the French, with variorum Notes, and numerous characteristic Illustrations by GUSTAVE DORE. Crown 8vo, cloth extra, 7s. 6d.

Rambosson.—Popular Astronomy. By J. RAMBOSSON, Laureate of the Institute of France. Translated by C. B. PITMAN. Crown 8vo, cloth gilt, with numerous Illustrations, and a beautifully executed Chart of Spectra, 7s. 6d.

Reader's Handbook (The) of Allusions, References, Plots, and Stories. By the Rev. Dr. BREWER. Third Edition, revised throughout, with a New Appendix, containing a COMPLETE ENGLISH BIBLIOGRAPHY. Crown 8vo, 1,400 pages, cloth extra, 7s. 6d.

Reade (Charles, D.C.L.), Novels by. Each post 8vo, illustrated boards, 2s.; or crown 8vo, cloth extra, Illustrated, 3s. 6d.

Peg Woffington. Illustrated by S. L. FILDES, A.R.A.

Christie Johnstone. Illustrated by WILLIAM SMALL.

It Is Never Too Late to Mend. Illustrated by G. J. PINWELL.

The Course of True Love Never did run Smooth. Illustrated by HELEN PATERSON.

CHARLES READE'S NOVELS, *continued*—

The Autobiography of a Thief; Jack of all Trades; and James Lambert. Illustrated by MATT STRETCH.

Love me Little, Love me Long. Illustrated by M. ELLEN EDWARDS.

The Double Marriage. Illustrated by Sir JOHN GILBERT, R.A., and CHARLES KEENE.

The Cloister and the Hearth. Illustrated by CHARLES KEENE.

Hard Cash. Illustrated by F. W. LAWSON.

Griffith Gaunt. Illustrated by S. L. FILDES, A.R.A., and WM. SMALL.

Foul Play. Illustrated by GEORGE DU MAURIER.

Put Yourself in His Place. Illustrated by ROBERT BARNES.

A Terrible Temptation. Illustrated by EDWARD HUGHES and A. W. COOPER.

The Wandering Heir. Illustrated by HELEN PATERSON, S. L. FILDES, A.R.A., CHARLES GREEN, and HENRY WOODS, A.R.A.

A Simpleton. Illustrated by KATE CRAUFORD.

A Woman-Hater. Illustrated by THOS. COULDERY.

Readiana. With a Steel Plate Portrait of CHARLES READE.

A New Collection of Stories. In Three Vols., crown 8vo. [*Preparing.*

Richardson. — A Ministry of Health, and other Papers. By BENJAMIN WARD RICHARDSON, M.D., &c. Crown 8vo, cloth extra, 6s.

Riddell (Mrs. J. H.), Novels by:

Her Mother's Darling. Crown 8vo, cloth extra, 3s. 6d.; post 8vo, illustrated boards, 2s.

The Prince of Wales's Garden Party, and other Stories. With a Frontispiece by M. ELLEN EDWARDS. Crown 8vo, cloth extra, 3s. 6d.

Rimmer (Alfred), Works by:

Our Old Country Towns. By ALFRED RIMMER. With over 50 Illustrations by the Author. Square 8vo, cloth extra, gilt, 10s. 6d.

Rambles Round Eton and Harrow. By ALFRED RIMMER. With 50 Illustrations by the Author. Square 8vo, cloth gilt, 10s. 6d.

About England with Dickens. With 58 Illustrations by ALFRED RIMMER and C. A. VANDERHOOF. Square 8vo, cloth gilt, 10s. 6d.

Robinson (F. W.), Novels by:

Women are Strange. Crown 8vo, cloth extra, 3s. 6d.

The Hands of Justice. Crown 8vo, cloth extra, 3s. 6d.

Robinson (Phil), Works by:

The Poets' Birds. Crown 8vo, cloth extra, 7s. 6d.

The Poets' Beasts. Crown 8vo, cloth extra, 7s. 6d. [*In preparation.*

Robinson Crusoe A beautiful reproduction of Major's Edition, with 37 Wood cuts and Two Steel Plates by GEORGE CRUIKSHANK, choicely printed. Crown 8vo, cloth extra, 7s. 6d. 100 Large-Paper copies, printed on hand-made paper, with India proofs of the Illustrations, price 36s.

Rochefoucauld's Maxims and Moral Reflections. With Notes, and an Introductory Essay by SAINTE-BEUVE. Post 8vo, cloth limp, 2s.

Roll of Battle Abbey, The; or, A List of the Principal Warriors who came over from Normandy with William the Conqueror, and Settled in this Country, A.D. 1066-7. With the principal Arms emblazoned in Gold and Colours. Handsomely printed, price 5s.

Rowley (Hon. Hugh), Works by:
Post 8vo, cloth limp, 2s. 6d. each.

Puniana: Riddles and Jokes. With numerous Illustrations.

More Puniana. Profusely Illustrated.

Russell (Clark).—Round the Galley-Fire. By W. CLARK RUSSELL, Author of "The Wreck of the *Grosvenor.*" Cr. 8vo, cloth extra, 6s.

Sala.—Gaslight and Daylight. By GEORGE AUGUSTUS SALA. Pos 8vo, illustrated boards, 2s.

Sanson.—Seven Generations of Executioners: Memoirs of the Sanson Family (1688 to 1847). Edited by HENRY SANSON. Crown 8vo, cloth extra, 3s. 6d.

Saunders (John), Novels by:
Crown 8vo, cloth extra, 3s. 6d. each; or post 8vo, illustrated boards, 2s. each.

Bound to the Wheel.

One Against the World.

Guy Waterman

The Lion in the Path.

The Two Dreamers,

Science Gossip: An Illustrated Medium of Interchange and Gossip for Students and Lovers of Nature. Edited by J. E. TAYLOR, Ph.D., F.L.S., F.G.S. Monthly, price 4d; Annual Subscription 5s. (including Postage). Vols. I. to XIV. may be had at 7s. 6d. each; and Vols. XV. to XVIII. (1882), at 5s. each. Among the subjects included in its pages will be found: Aquaria, Bees, Beetles, Birds, Butterflies, Ferns, Fish, Flies, Fossils, Fungi, Geology, Lichens, Microscopes, Mosses, Moths, Reptiles, Seaweeds, Spiders, Telescopes, Wild Flowers, Worms, &c.

"Secret Out" Series, The:
Crown 8vo, cloth extra, profusely Illustrated, 4s. 6d. each.

The Secret Out: One Thousand Tricks with Cards, and other Re-creations; with Entertaining Experiments in Drawing-room or "White Magic." By W. H. CREMER. 300 Engravings.

The Pyrotechnist's Treasury; or, Complete Art of Making Fireworks By THOMAS KENTISH. With numerous Illustrations.

The Art of Amusing: A Collection of Graceful Arts, Games, Tricks, Puzzles, and Charades. By FRANK BELLEW. With 300 Illustrations.

Hanky-Panky: Very Easy Tricks, Very Difficult Tricks, White Magic, Sleight of Hand. Edited by W. H. CREMER. With 200 Illustrations.

The Merry Circle: A Book of New Intellectual Games and Amusements By CLARA BELLEW. With many Illustrations.

Magician's Own Book: Performances with Cups and Balls, Eggs, Hats, Handkerchiefs, &c. All from actual Experience. Edited by W. H. CRE-MER. 200 Illustrations.

Magic No Mystery: Tricks with Cards, Dice, Balls, &c., with fully descriptive Directions; the Art of Secret Writing; Training of Per-forming Animals, &c. With Co-loured Frontispiece and many Illus-trations.

Senior (William), Works by:

Travel and Trout in the Antipodes. Crown 8vo, cloth extra, 6s.

By Stream and Sea. Post 8vo, cloth limp, 2s. 6d.

Shakespeare :

The First Folio Shakespeare.—Mr. WILLIAM SHAKESPEARE'S Comedies, Histories, and Tragedies. Published according to the true Originall Copies. London, Printed by ISAAC IAGGARD and ED. BLOUNT. 1623.—A Reproduction of the extremely rare original, in reduced facsimile, by a photographic process—ensuring the strictest accuracy in every detail. Small 8vo, half-Roxburghe, 7s. 6d.

The Lansdowne Shakespeare. Beautifully printed in red and black, in small but very clear type. With engraved facsimile of DROESHOUT'S Portrait. Post 8vo, cloth extra, 7s. 6d.

Shakespeare for Children: Tales from Shakespeare. By CHARLES and MARY LAMB. With numerous Illustrations, coloured and plain, by J. MOYR SMITH. Crown 4to, cloth gilt, 6s.

The Handbook of Shakespeare Music. Being an Account of 350 Pieces of Music, set to Words taken from the Plays and Poems of Shakespeare, the compositions ranging from the Elizabethan Age to the Present Time. By ALFRED ROFFE. 4to, half-Roxburghe, 7s.

A Study of Shakespeare. By ALGERNON CHARLES SWINBURNE. Crown 8vo, cloth extra, 8s.

Shelley's Complete Works, in Four Vols., post 8vo, cloth limp, 8s. ; or separately, 2s. each. Vol. I. contains his Early Poems, Queen Mab, &c., with an Introduction by LEIGH HUNT; Vol. II., his Later Poems, Laon and Cythna, &c. ; Vol. III., Posthumous Poems, the Shelley Papers, &c. ; Vol. IV., his Prose Works, including A Refutation of Deism, Zastrozzi, St. Irvyne, &c.

Sheridan's Complete Works, with Life and Anecdotes. Including his Dramatic Writings, printed from the Original Editions, his Works in Prose and Poetry, Translations, Speeches, Jokes, Puns, &c. With a Collection of Sheridaniana. Crown 8vo, cloth extra, gilt, with 10 full-page Tinted Illustrations, 7s. 6d.

Short Sayings of Great Men. With Historical and Explanatory Notes by SAMUEL A. BENT, M.A. Demy 8vo, cloth extra, 7s. 6d.

Sidney's (Sir Philip) Complete Poetical Works, including all those in "Arcadia." With Portrait, Memorial-Introduction, Essay on the Poetry of Sidney, and Notes, by the Rev. A. B. GROSART, D.D. Three Vols., crown 8vo, cloth boards, 18s.

Signboards: Their History. With Anecdotes of Famous Taverns and Remarkable Characters. By JACOB LARWOOD and JOHN CAMDEN HOTTEN. Crown 8vo, cloth extra, with 100 Illustrations, 7s. 6d.

Sketchley.—A Match in the Dark. By ARTHUR SKETCHLEY. Post 8vo, illustrated boards, 2s.

Slang Dictionary, The : Etymological, Historical, and Anecdotal. Crown 8vo, cloth extra, gilt, 6s. 6d.

Smith (J. Moyr), Works by :

The Prince of Argolis : A Story of the Old Greek Fairy Time. By J. MOYR SMITH. Small 8vo, cloth extra, with 130 Illustrations, 3s. 6d.

Tales of Old Thule. Collected and Illustrated by J. MOYR SMITH. Crown 8vo, cloth gilt, profusely Illustrated, 6s.

The Wooing of the Water Witch: A Northern Oddity. By EVAN DALDORNE. Illustrated by J. MOYR SMITH. Small 8vo, cloth extra, 6s.

South-West, The New : Travelling Sketches from Kansas, New Mexico, Arizona, and Northern Mexico. By ERNST VON HESSE-WARTEGG. With 100 fine Illustrations and 3 Maps. 8vo, cloth extra, 14s. [*In preparation.*

Spalding.–Elizabethan Demonology: An Essay in Illustration of the Belief in the Existence of Devils, and the Powers possessed by Them. By T. ALFRED SPALDING, LL.B. Crown 8vo, cloth extra, 5s.

Speight. — The Mysteries of Heron Dyke. By T. W. SPEIGHT. With a Frontispiece by M. ELLEN EDWARDS. Crown 8vo, cloth extra, 3s. 6d. ; post 8vo, illustrated boards, 2s.

Spenser for Children. By M. H. TOWRY. With Illustrations by WALTER J. MORGAN. Crown 4to, with Coloured Illustrations, cloth gilt, 6s.

Staunton.—Laws and Practice of Chess; Together with an Analysis of the Openings, and a Treatise on End Games. By HOWARD STAUNTON. Edited by ROBERT B. WORMALD. A New Edition, small crown 8vo, cloth extra, 5s.

Stedman. — Victorian Poets: Critical Essays. By EDMUND CLARENCE STEDMAN. Crown 8vo, cloth extra, 9s.

Sterndale.—The Afghan Knife: A Novel. By ROBERT ARMITAGE STERNDALE, F.R.G.S. Cr. 8vo, cloth extra, 3s. 6d.; post 8vo, illustrated boards, 2s.

Stevenson (R. Louis), Works by:

Familiar Studies of Men and Books. Crown 8vo, cloth extra, 6s.

New Arabian Nights. New and Cheaper Edit. Cr. 8vo, cloth extra, 6s.

The Silverado Squatters. Crown 8vo, cloth extra, 6s.   [*In the press.*

St. John.—A Levantine Family By BAYLE ST. JOHN. Post 8vo, illustrated boards, 2s.

Stoddard.—Summer Cruising in the South Seas. By CHARLES WARREN STODDARD. Illustrated by WALLIS MACKAY. Crown 8vo, cloth extra, 3s. 6d.

St. Pierre.—Paul and Virginia, and The Indian Cottage. By BERNARDIN DE ST. PIERRE. Edited, with Life, by the Rev. E. CLARKE. Post 8vo, cloth limp, 2s.

Strahan.—Twenty Years of a Publisher's Life. By ALEXANDER STRAHAN. Two Vols., crown 8vo, with numerous Portraits and Illustrations, 24s.   [*In preparation.*

Strutt's Sports and Pastimes of the People of England; including the Rural and Domestic Recreations, May Games, Mummeries, Shows, Processions, Pageants, and Pompous Spectacles, from the Earliest Period to the Present Time. With 140 Illustrations. Edited by WILLIAM HONE. Crown 8vo, cloth extra, 7s. 6d.

Suburban Homes (The) of London: A Residential Guide to Favourite London Localities, their Society, Celebrities, and Associations. With Notes on their Rental, Rates, and House Accommodation. With a Map of Suburban London. Crown 8vo, cloth extra, 7s. 6d.

Swift's Choice Works, in Prose and Verse. With Memoir, Portrait, and Facsimiles of the Maps in the Original Edition of " Gulliver's Travels." Cr. 8vo, cloth extra, 7s. 6d.

Swinburne (Algernon C.), Works by:

The Queen Mother and Rosamond. Fcap. 8vo, 5s.

Atalanta in Calydon. Crown 8vo, 6s.

Chastelard. A Tragedy. Crown 8vo, 7s.

Poems and Ballads. FIRST SERIES. Fcap. 8vo, 9s. Also in crown 8vo, at same price.

Poems and Ballads. SECOND SERIES. Fcap. 8vo, 9s. Also in crown 8vo, at same price.

Notes on Poems and Reviews. 8vo, 1s.

William Blake: A Critical Essay. With Facsimile Paintings. Demy 8vo, 16s.

Songs before Sunrise. Crown 8vo, 10s. 6d.

Bothwell: A Tragedy. Crown 8vo, 12s. 6d.

George Chapman: An Essay. Crown 8vo, 7s.

Songs of Two Nations. Crown 8vo, 6s.

Essays and Studies. Crown 8vo, 12s.

Erechtheus: A Tragedy. Crown 8vo, 6s.

Note of an English Republican on the Muscovite Crusade. 8vo, 1s.

A Note on Charlotte Brontë. Crown 8vo, 6s.

A Study of Shakespeare. Crown 8vo, 8s.

Songs of the Springtides. Crown 8vo, 6s.

Studies in Song. Crown 8vo, 7s.

Mary Stuart: A Tragedy. Crown 8vo, 8s.

Tristram of Lyonesse, and other Poems. Crown 8vo, 9s.

A Century of Roundels. Small 4to, cloth extra, 8s.

Syntax's (Dr.) Three Tours: In Search of the Picturesque, in Search of Consolation, and in Search of a Wife. With the whole of ROWLANDSON's droll page Illustrations in Colours and a Life of the Author by J. C. HOTTEN. Medium 8vo, cloth extra, 7s. 6d.

Taine's History of English Literature. Translated by HENRY VAN LAUN. Four Vols., small 8vo, cloth boards, 30s.—POPULAR EDITION, in Two Vols., crown 8vo, cloth extra, 15s.

Taylor's (Bayard) Diversions of the Echo Club: Burlesques of Modern Writers Post 8vo, cloth limp, 2s.

Taylor's (Tom) Historical Dramas: "Clancarty," "Jeanne Darc," "'Twixt Axe and Crown," "The Fool's Revenge," "Arkwright's Wife," "Anne Boleyn," "Plot and Passion." One Vol., crown 8vo, cloth extra, 7s. 6d.

„ The Plays may also be had separately, at 1s. each.

Thackerayana: Notes and Anecdotes. Illustrated by Hundreds of Sketches by WILLIAM MAKEPEACE THACKERAY, depicting Humorous Incidents in his School-life, and Favourite Characters in the books of his every-day reading. With Coloured Frontispiece. Crown 8vo, cloth extra, 7s. 6d.

Thomas (Bertha), Novels by :
Each crown 8vo, cloth extra, 3s. 6d. ; or post 8vo, illustrated boards, 2s.
   Cressida.
   Proud Maisie.
   The Violin-Player.

Thomson's Seasons and Castle of Indolence. With a Biographical and Critical Introduction by ALLAN CUNNINGHAM, and over 50 fine Illustrations on Steel and Wood. Crown 8vo, cloth extra, gilt edges, 7s. 6d.

Thornbury (Walter), Works by :
Haunted London. Edited by EDWARD WALFORD, M.A. With Illustrations by F. W. FAIRHOLT, F.S.A. Crown 8vo, cloth extra, 7s. 6d.

The Life and Correspondence of J. M. W. Turner. Founded upon Letters and Papers furnished by his Friends and fellow Academicians. With numerous Illustrations in Colours, facsimiled from Turner's Original Drawings. Crown 8vo, cloth extra, 7s. 6d.

Old Stories Re-told. Post 8vo, cloth limp, 2s. 6d.

Tales for the Marines. Post 8vo, illustrated boards, 2s.

Timbs (John), Works by :
The History of Clubs and Club Life in London. With Anecdotes of its Famous Coffee-houses, Hostelries, and Taverns. With numerous Illustrations. Cr. 8vo, cloth extra, 7s. 6d.

English Eccentrics and Eccentricities: Stories of Wealth and Fashion, Delusions, Impostures, and Fanatic Missions, Strange Sights and Sporting Scenes, Eccentric Artists, Theatrical Folks, Men of Letters, &c. With nearly 50 Illusts. Crown 8vo, cloth extra, 7s. 6d.

Torrens. — The Marquess Wellesley, Architect of Empire. An Historic Portrait. By W. M. TORRENS, M.P. Demy 8vo, cloth extra, 14s.

Trollope (Anthony), Novels by :
The Way We Live Now. With Illustrations. Crown 8vo, cloth extra, 3s. 6d. post 8vo, illust. boards, 2s.

The American Senator. Cr 8vo, cl. extra, 3s. 6d ; post 8vo, illust. bds., 2s.

Kept in the Dark. With a Frontispiece by J. E. MILLAIS, R.A. Crown 8vo, cloth extra, 3s. 6d.

Frau Frohmann, &c. With Frontispiece. Crown 8vo, cloth extra, 3s. 6d.

Marion Fay. Cr. 8vo, cl. extra, 3s. 6d.

Mr. Scarborough's Family. Crown 8vo, cloth extra, 3s. 6d.

The Land-Leaguers. Three Vols., crown 8vo, 31s. 6d.   [*Shortly.*

Trollope (Frances E.), Works by :
Crown 8vo, cloth extra, 3s. 6d. each.
Like Ships upon the Sea.
Mabel's Progress.
Anne Furness.

Trollope (T. A.).—Diamond Cut Diamond, and other Stories. By THOMAS ADOLPHUS TROLLOPE. Crown 8vo, cloth extra, 3s. 6d.; post 8vo, illustrated boards, 2s.

Tytler (Sarah), Novels by :
What She Came Through. Crown 8vo, cloth extra, 3s. 6d. ; post 8vo, illustrated boards, 2s.

The Bride's Pass. With a Frontispiece by P. MACNAB. Crown 8vo, cloth extra, 3s. 6d.

Van Laun.—History of French Literature. By HENRY VAN LAUN. Complete in Three Vols., demy 8vo, cloth boards, 7s. 6d. each.

Villari. — A Double Bond : A Story. By LINDA VILLA Fcap. 8vo, picture cover, 1s.

Walcott.— Church Work and

Life in English Minsters; and the English Student's Monasticon. By the Rev. MACKENZIE E. C. WALCOTT, B.D. Two Vols., crown 8vo, cloth extra, with Map and Ground-Plans, 14s.

Walford (Edw., M.A.),Works by:

The County Families of the United Kingdom. Containing Notices of the Descent, Birth, Marriage, Education, &c., of more than 12,000 disnguished Heads of Families, their Heirs Apparent or Presumptive, the Offices they hold or have held, their Town and Country Addresses, Clubs, &c. The Twenty-third Annual Edition, for 1883, cloth, full gilt, 50s.

The Shilling Peerage (1883). Containing an Alphabetical List of the House of Lords, Dates of Creation, Lists of Scotch and Irish Peers, Addresses, &c. 32mo, cloth, 1s. Published annually.

The Shilling Baronetage (1883). Containing an Alphabetical List of the Baronets of the United Kingdom, Short Biographical Notices, Dates of Creation, Addresses, &c. 32mo, cloth, 1s. Published annually.

The Shilling Knightage (1883). Containing an Alphabetical List of the Knights of the United Kingdom, short Biographical Notices, Dates of Creation, Addresses, &c. 32mo, cloth, 1s. Published annually.

The Shilling House of Commons (1883). Containing a List of all the Members of the British Parliament, their Town and Country Addresses, &c. 32mo, cloth, 1s. Published annually.

The Complete Peerage, Baronetage, Knightage, and House of Commons (1883). In One Volume, royal 32mo, cloth extra, gilt edges, 5s. Published annually.

Haunted London. By WALTER THORNBURY. Edited by EDWARD WALFORD, M.A. With Illustrations by F. W. FAIRHOLT, F.S.A. Crown 8vo, cloth extra, 7s. 6d.

Walton and Cotton's Complete

Angler; or, The Contemplative Man's Recreation; being a Discourse of Rivers, Fishponds, Fish and Fishing, written by IZAAK WALTON; and Instructions how to Angle for a Trout or Grayling in a clear Stream, by CHARLES COTTON. With Original Memoirs and Notes by Sir HARRIS NICOLAS, and 61 Copperplate Illustrations. Large crown 8vo, cloth antique, 7s. 6d.

Wanderer's Library, The:

Crown 8vo, cloth extra, 3s. 6d. each.

Wanderings in Patagonia; or, Life among the Ostrich Hunters. By JULIUS BEERBOHM. Illustrated.

Camp Notes: Stories of Sport and Adventure in Asia, Africa, and America. By FREDERICK BOYLE.

Savage Life. By FREDERICK BOYLE.

Merrie England in the Olden Time. By GEORGE DANIEL. With Illustrations by ROBT. CRUIKSHANK.

Circus Life and Circus Celebrities. By THOMAS FROST.

The Lives of the Conjurers. By THOMAS FROST.

The Old Showmen and the Old London Fairs. By THOMAS FROST.

Low-Life Deeps. An Account of the Strange Fish to be found there. By JAMES GREENWOOD.

The Wilds of London. By JAMES GREENWOOD.

Tunis: The Land and the People. By the Chevalier de HESSE-WARTEGG. With 22 Illustrations.

The Life and Adventures of a Cheap Jack. By One of the Fraternity. Edited by CHARLES HINDLEY.

The World Behind the Scenes. By PERCY FITZGERALD.

Tavern Anecdotes and Sayings Including the Origin of Signs, and Reminiscences connected with Taverns, Coffee Houses, Clubs, &c. By CHARLES HINDLEY. With Illusts.

The Genial Showman: Life and Adventures of Artemus Ward. By E. P. HINGSTON. With a Frontispiece.

The Story of the London Parks. By JACOB LARWOOD. With Illusts.

London Characters. By HENRY MAYHEW. Illustrated.

Seven Generations of Executioners: Memoirs of the Sanson Family (1688 to 1847). Edited by HENRY SANSON.

Summer Cruising in the South Seas. By CHARLES WARREN STODDARD. Illust. by WALLIS MACKAY.

Warner.—A Roundabout Jour-

ney. By CHARLES DUDLEY WARNER, Author of "My Summer in a Garden," Cr. 8vo, cloth extra, 6s. [*In preparation.*

Warrants, &c. :—

Warrant to Execute Charles I. An exact Facsimile, with the Fifty-nine Signatures, and corresponding Seals. Carefully printed on paper to imitate the Original, 22 in. by 14 in. Price 2s.

WARRANTS, &c., *continued—*

Warrant to Execute Mary Queen of Scots. An exact Facsimile, including the Signature of Queen Elizabeth, and a Facsimile of the Great Seal. Beautifully printed on paper to imitate the Original MS. Price 2s.

Magna Charta. An Exact Facsimile of the Original Document in the British Museum, printed on fine plate paper, nearly 3 feet long by 2 feet wide, with the Arms and Seals emblazoned in Gold and Colours. Price 5s.

The Roll of Battle Abbey; or, A List of the Principal Warriors who came over from Normandy with William the Conqueror, and Settled in this Country, A.D. 1066-7. With the principal Arms emblazoned in Gold and Colours. Price 5s.

Westropp.—Handbook of Pottery and Porcelain; or, History of those Arts from the Earliest Period. By HODDER M. WESTROPP. With numerous Illustrations, and a List of Marks. Crown 8vo, cloth limp, 4s. 6d.

Whistler v. Ruskin: Art and Art Critics. By J. A. MACNEILL WHISTLER. Seventh Edition, square 8vo, 1s.

White's Natural History of Selborne. Edited, with Additions, by THOMAS BROWN, F.L.S. Post 8vo, cloth limp, 2s.

Wilson (Dr. Andrew, F.R.S.E.), Works by:

Chapters on Evolution: A Popular History of the Darwinian and Allied Theories of Development. Second Edition. Crown 8vo, cloth extra, with 259 Illustrations, 7s. 6d.

Leaves from a Naturalist's Notebook. Post 8vo, cloth limp, 2s. 6d.

Leisure-Time Studies, chiefly Biological. Second Edition. Crown 8vo, cloth extra, with Illustrations, 6s.

Williams (W. Mattieu, F.R.A.S.), Works by:

Science in Short Chapters. Crown 8vo, cloth extra, 7s. 6d.

A Simple Treatise on Heat. Crown 8vo, cloth limp, with Illustrations, 2s. 6d.

Wilson (C.E.).—Persian Wit and Humour: Being the Sixth Book of the Baharistan of Jami, Translated for the first time from the Original Persian into English Prose and Verse. With Notes by C. E. WILSON, M.R.A.S., Assistant Librarian Royal Academy of Arts. Crown 8vo, parchment binding, 4s.

Winter (J. S.), Stories by:

Cavalry Life. Crown 8vo, cloth extra, 3s. 6d.

Regimental Legends. Crown 8vo, cloth extra, 3s. 6d.

Wood.—Sabina: A Novel. By Lady WOOD. Post 8vo, illustrated boards, 2s.

Words, Facts, and Phrases: A Dictionary of Curious, Quaint, and Out-of-the-Way Matters. By ELIEZER EDWARDS. Crown 8vo, half-bound, 12s. 6d.

Wright (Thomas), Works by:

Caricature History of the Georges. (The House of Hanover.) With 400 Pictures, Caricatures, Squibs, Broadsides, Window Pictures, &c. Crown 8vo, cloth extra, 7s. 6d.

History of Caricature and of the Grotesque in Art, Literature, Sculpture, and Painting. Profusely Illustrated by F. W. FAIRHOLT, F.S.A. Large post 8vo, cloth extra, 7s. 6d.

Yates (Edmund), Novels by:

Post 8vo, illustrated boards, 2s. each.
Castaway.
The Forlorn Hope.
Land at Last.

NOVELS BY THE BEST AUTHORS.

NEW NOVELS at every Library.

All In a Garden Fair. By WALTER BESANT. Three Vols. [*Shortly.*

Annan Water. By ROBERT BUCHANAN. Three Vols. [*Shortly.*

Fancy-Free, &c. By CHARLES GIBBON. Three Vols. [*Shortly.*

Fortune's Fool. By JULIAN HAWTHORNE. Three Vols.

Ione. By E. LYNN LINTON. Three Vols. [*Shortly.*

The Way of the World. By D. CHRISTIE MURRAY. Three Vols. [*Shortly.*

The Foreigners. By E. C. PRICE. Three Vols. [*Shortly.*

Maid of Athens. By JUSTIN MCCARTHY, M.P. With 12 Illustrations by FRED. BARNARD. Three Vols. [*Shortly.*

By the Gate of the Sea. By DAVID CHRISTIE MURRAY. Two Vols., post 8vo, 12s.

The Canon's Ward. By JAMES PAYN. Three Vols. [*Jan.*, 1884.

A New Collection of Stories by CHARLES READE is now in preparation, in Three Vols.

The Land-Leaguers. By ANTHONY TROLLOPE. Three Vols. [*Shortly.*

THE PICCADILLY NOVELS.

Popular Stories by the Best Authors. LIBRARY EDITIONS, many Illustrated, crown 8vo, cloth extra, 3s. 6d. each.

BY MRS. ALEXANDER.
Maid, Wife, or Widow?

BY W. BESANT & JAMES RICE.
Ready-Money Mortiboy.
My Little Girl.
The Case of Mr. Lucraft.
This Son of Vulcan.
With Harp and Crown.
The Golden Butterfly.
By Celia's Arbour.
The Monks of Thelema.
'Twas In Trafalgar's Bay.
The Seamy Side.
The Ten Years' Tenant.
The Chaplain of the Fleet.

BY WALTER BESANT.
All Sorts and Conditions of Men.
The Captains' Room.

BY ROBERT BUCHANAN.
A Child of Nature.
God and the Man.
The Shadow of the Sword.
The Martyrdom of Madeline.
Love Me for Ever.

BY MRS. H. LOVETT CAMERON.
Deceivers Ever.
Juliet's Guardian.

BY MORTIMER COLLINS.
Sweet Anne Page.
Transmigration.
From Midnight to Midnight.

MORTIMER & FRANCES COLLINS.
Blacksmith and Scholar.
The Village Comedy.
You Play me False.

BY WILKIE COLLINS.
Antonina.
Basil.
Hide and Seek.
The Dead Secret.
Queen of Hearts.
My Miscellanies.
Woman In White.
The Moonstone.
Man and Wife.
Poor Miss Finch.
Miss or Mrs?
New Magdalen.
The Frozen Deep.
The Law and the Lady.
The Two Destinies
Haunted Hotel.
The Fallen Leaves
Jezebel's Daughter
The Black Robe.
Heart and Science

BY DUTTON COOK.
Paul Foster's Daughter.

BY WILLIAM CYPLES.
Hearts of Gold.

BY J. LEITH DERWENT.
Our Lady of Tears.
Circe's Lovers.

PICCADILLY NOVELS, *continued—*

BY M. BETHAM-EDWARDS.
Felicia

BY MRS. ANNIE EDWARDES.
Archie Lovell.

BY R. E. FRANCILLON.
Olympia. | Queen Cophetua.
One by One.

BY EDWARD GARRETT.
The Capel Girls.

BY CHARLES GIBBON.
Robin Gray.
For Lack of Gold.
In Love and War.
What will the World Say?
For the King.
In Honour Bound.
Queen of the Meadow.
In Pastures Green.
The Flower of the Forest.
A Heart's Problem.
The Braes of Yarrow.
The Golden Shaft.
Of High Degree.

BY THOMAS HARDY.
Under the Greenwood Tree

BY JULIAN HAWTHORNE.
Garth.
Ellice Quentin.
Sebastian Strome.
Prince Saroni's Wife.
Dust.

BY SIR A. HELIS.
Ivan de Biron.

BY MRS. ALFRED HUNT.
Thornicroft's Model.
The Leaden Casket.
Self-Condemned.

BY JEAN INGELOW.
Fated to be Free.

BY HENRY JAMES, Jun.
Confidence.

BY HARRIETT JAY.
The Queen of Connaught.
The Dark Colleen.

BY HENRY KINGSLEY.
Number Seventeen.
Oakshott Castle.

PICCADILLY NOVELS, *continued—*

BY E. LYNN LINTON.
Patricia Kemball.
Atonement of Leam Dundas.
The World Well Lost.
Under which Lord?
With a Silken Thread.
The Rebel of the Family.
"My Love!"

BY HENRY W. LUCY.
Gideon Fleyce.

BY JUSTIN McCARTHY, M.P.
The Waterdale Neighbours.
My Enemy's Daughter.
Linley Rochford. | A Fair Saxon.
Dear Lady Disdain.
Miss Misanthrope.
Donna Quixote.
The Comet of a Season.

BY GEORGE MACDONALD, LL.D.
Pau Faber, Surgeon.
Thomas Wingfold, Curate.

BY MRS. MACDONELL.
Quaker Cousins.

BY KATHARINE S. MACQUOID.
Lost Rose. | The Evil Eye.

BY FLORENCE MARRYAT.
Open! Sesame! | Written in Fire.

BY JEAN MIDDLEMASS.
Touch and Go.

BY D. CHRISTIE MURRAY.
Life's Atonement. | Coals of Fire.
Joseph's Coat. | Val Strange.
A Model Father. | Hearts.

BY MRS. OLIPHANT.
Whiteladies.

BY JAMES PAYN.
Lost Sir Massing-   High Spirits.
  berd.   Under One Roof.
Best of Husbands   Carlyon's Year.
Fallen Fortunes.   A Confidential
Halves.   Agent.
Walter's Word.   From Exile.
What He Cost Her   A Grape from a
Less Black than   Thorn.
  We're Painted.   For Cash Only.
By Proxy.   Kit: A Memory.

PICCADILLY NOVELS, *continued—*

BY E. C. PRICE.
Valentina.

BY CHARLES READE, D.C.L.
It Is Never Too Late to Mend.
Hard Cash. | Peg Woffington.
Christie Johnstone.
Griffith Gaunt.
The Double Marriage.
Love Me Little, Love Me Long.
Foul Play.
The Cloister and the Hearth.
The Course of True Love.
The Autobiography of a Thief.
Put Yourself In His Place.
A Terrible Temptation.
The Wandering Heir. | A Simpleton.
A Woman-Hater. | Readiana.

BY MRS. J. H. RIDDELL.
Her Mother's Darling.
Prince of Wales's Garden-Party.

BY F. W. ROBINSON.
Women are Strange.
The Hands of Justice.

BY JOHN SAUNDERS.
Bound to the Wheel.
Guy Waterman.
One Against the World.
The Lion In the Path.
The Two Dreamers.

PICCADILLY NOVELS, *continued—*

BY T. W. SPEIGHT.
The Mysteries of Heron Dyke.

BY R. A. STERNDALE.
The Afghan Knife.

BY BERTHA THOMAS.
Proud Maisie. | Cressida.
The Violin-Player.

BY ANTHONY TROLLOPE.
The Way we Live Now.
The American Senator.
Frau Frohmann.
Marion Fay.
Kept in the Dark.
Mr. Scarborough's Family.

BY FRANCES E. TROLLOPE.
Like Ships upon the Sea.
Anne Furness.
Mabel's Progress.

BY T. A. TROLLOPE.
Diamond Cut Diamond.

BY SARAH TYTLER
What She Came Through.
The Bride's Pass.

BY J. S. WINTER.
Cavalry Life.
Regimental Legends.

CHEAP EDITIONS OF POPULAR NOVELS.
Post 8vo, illustrated boards, 2s. each.

[WILKIE COLLINS'S NOVELS and BESANT and RICE'S NOVELS may also be had in cloth limp at 2s. 6d. *See, too, the* PICCADILLY NOVELS, *for Library Editions.*]

BY EDMOND ABOUT.
The Fellah.

BY HAMILTON AÏDÉ.
Carr of Carrlyon. | Confidences.

BY MRS. ALEXANDER.
Maid, Wife, or Widow?

BY SHELSLEY BEAUCHAMP.
Grantley Grange.

BY W. BESANT & JAMES RICE.
Ready-Money Mortiboy.
With Harp and Crown.
This Son of Vulcan.
My Little Girl.
The Case of Mr. Lucraft.

BY BESANT AND RICE—*continued.*
The Golden Butterfly.
By Celia's Arbour.
The Monks of Thelema.
'Twas In Trafalgar's Bay.
The Seamy Side.
The Ten Years' Tenant.
The Chaplain of the Fleet.

BY FREDERICK BOYLE.
Camp Notes. | Savage Life.

BY BRET HARTE.
An Heiress of Red Dog.
Gabriel Conroy.
The Luck of Roaring Camp.
Flip.

CHEAP POPULAR NOVELS, *continued—*

BY ROBERT BUCHANAN.
The Shadow of the Sword.
A Child of Nature.

BY MRS. BURNETT.
Surly Tim.

BY MRS. LOVETT CAMERON.
Deceivers Ever.
Juliet's Guardian.

BY MACLAREN COBBAN.
The Cure of Souls.

BY C. ALLSTON COLLINS.
The Bar Sinister.

BY WILKIE COLLINS.
Antonina.
Basil.
Hide and Seek.
The Dead Secret.
Queen of Hearts.
My Miscellanies.
The Woman in White.
The Moonstone.
Man and Wife.
Poor Miss Finch.
Miss or Mrs. ?
The New Magdalen.
The Frozen Deep.
The Law and the Lady.
The Two Destinies.
The Haunted Hotel.
The Fallen Leaves.
Jezebel's Daughter.
The Black Robe.

BY MORTIMER COLLINS.
Sweet Anne Page.
Transmigration.
From Midnight to Midnight.
A Fight with Fortune.

MORTIMER & FRANCES COLLINS.
Sweet and Twenty.
Frances.
Blacksmith and Scholar.
The Village Comedy.
You Play me False.

BY DUTTON COOK.
Leo.
Paul Foster's Daughter.

BY J. LEITH DERWENT.
Our Lady of Tears.

CHEAP POPULAR NOVELS, *continued—*

BY CHARLES DICKENS.
Sketches by Boz.
The Pickwick Papers.
Oliver Twist.
Nicholas Nickleby.

BY MRS. ANNIE EDWARDES.
A Point of Honour.
Archie Lovell.

BY M. BETHAM-EDWARDS.
Felicia.

BY EDWARD EGGLESTON.
Roxy.

BY PERCY FITZGERALD.
Bella Donna.
Never Forgotten.
The Second Mrs. Tillotson.
Polly.
Seventy-five Brooke Street.

BY ALBANY DE FONBLANQUE.
Filthy Lucre.

BY R. E. FRANCILLON.
Olympia.
Queen Cophetua.
One by One.

BY EDWARD GARRETT.
The Capel Girls.

BY CHARLES GIBBON.
Robin Gray.
For Lack of Gold.
What will the World Say ?
In Honour Bound.
The Dead Heart.
In Love and War.
For the King.
Queen of the Meadow.
In Pastures Green.

BY WILLIAM GILBERT.
Dr. Austin's Guests.
The Wizard of the Mountain.
James Duke.

BY JAMES GREENWOOD.
Dick Temple.

BY ANDREW HALLIDAY.
Every-Day Papers.

BY LADY DUFFUS HARDY.
Paul Wynter's Sacrifice.

BY THOMAS HARDY.
Under the Greenwood Tree.

CHEAP POPULAR NOVELS, *continued—*
BY JULIAN HAWTHORNE.
Garth.
Ellice Quentin.
Sebastian Strome.
BY SIR ARTHUR HELPS.
Ivan de Biron.

BY TOM HOOD.
A Golden Heart.

BY VICTOR HUGO.
The Hunchback of Notre Dame.

BY MRS. ALFRED HUNT.
Thornicroft's Model.
The Leaden Casket.

BY JEAN INGELOW.
Fated to be Free.

BY HENRY JAMES, Jun.
Confidence.

BY HARRIETT JAY.
The Dark Colleen.
The Queen of Connaught.

BY HENRY KINGSLEY.
Oakshott Castle.
Number Seventeen.

BY E. LYNN LINTON.
Patricia Kemball.
The Atonement of Leam Dundas.
The World Well Lost.
Under which Lord?
With a Silken Thread.
The Rebel of the Family.
"My Love!"

BY JUSTIN McCARTHY, M.P.
Dear Lady Disdain.
The Waterdale Neighbours.
My Enemy's Daughter.
A Fair Saxon.
Linley Rochford.
Miss Misanthrope.
Donna Quixote.

BY GEORGE MACDONALD.
Paul Faber, Surgeon.
Thomas Wingfold, Curate.

BY MRS. MACDONELL.
Quaker Cousins.

BY KATHARINE S. MACQUOID.
The Evil Eye. | Lost Rose.

BY W. H. MALLOCK.
The New Republic.

CHEAP POPULAR NOVELS, *continued—*
BY FLORENCE MARRYAT.
Open! Sesame!
A Harvest of Wild Oats.
A Little Stepson.
Fighting the Air.
Written in Fire.

BY JEAN MIDDLEMASS.
Touch and Go. | Mr. Dorillion.

BY D. CHRISTIE MURRAY.
A Life's Atonement.
A Model Father.

BY MRS. OLIPHANT.
Whiteladies.

BY MRS. ROBERT O'REILLY.
Phœbe's Fortunes.

BY OUIDA.
LIBRARY EDITIONS of OUIDA's NOVELS may be had in crown 8vo, cloth extra, at 5s. each.

Held in Bondage.
Strathmore.
Chandos.
Under Two Flags.
Idalia.
Cecil Castlemaine.
Tricotrin.
Puck.
Folle Farine.
A Dog of Flanders.
Pascarel.
Two Little Wooden Shoes.
Signa.
In a Winter City.
Ariadne.
Friendship.
Moths.
Pipistrello.
A Village Commune.

BY JAMES PAYN.
Lost Sir Massingberd.
A Perfect Treasure.
Bentinck's Tutor.
Murphy's Master.
A County Family.
At Her Mercy.
A Woman's Vengeance.
Cecil's Tryst.
Clyffards of Clyffe
The Family Scapegrace.
Foster Brothers.
Found Dead.
Best of Husbands
Walter's Word.
Halves.
Fallen Fortunes.
What He Cost Her
Humorous Stories
Gwendoline's Harvest.
Like Father, Like Son.
A Marine Residence.
Married Beneath Him.
Mirk Abbey.
Not Wooed, but Won.
£200 Reward.
Less Black than We're Painted.
By Proxy.
Under One Roof.
High Spirits.
Carlyon's Year.
A Confidential Agent.
Some Private Views.
From Exile.

CHEAP POPULAR NOVELS, *continued—*

BY EDGAR A. POE.
The Mystery of Marie Roget.

BY E. C. PRICE.
Valentina.

BY CHARLES READE.
It Is Never Too Late to Mend.
Hard Cash.
Peg Woffington.
Christie Johnstone.
Griffith Gaunt.
Put Yourself In His Place.
The Double Marriage.
Love Me Little, Love Me Long.
Foul Play.
The Cloister and the Hearth
The Course of True Love.
Autobiography of a Thief.
A Terrible Temptation.
The Wandering Heir.
A Simpleton.
A Woman-Hater.
Readiana.

BY MRS. RIDDELL.
Her Mother's Darling.

BY BAYLE ST. JOHN.
A Levantine Family.

BY GEORGE AUGUSTUS SALA.
Gaslight and Daylight.

BY JOHN SAUNDERS.
Bound to the Wheel.
One Against the World.
Guy Waterman.
The Lion in the Path.
The Two Dreamers.

BY ARTHUR SKETCHLEY.
A Match in the Dark.

BY T. W. SPEIGHT.
The Mysteries of Heron Dyke.

BY R. A. STERNDALE.
The Afghan Knife.

BY BERTHA THOMAS.
Cressida. | Proud Maisie.
The Violin-Player.

CHEAP POPULAR NOVELS, *continued—*

BY WALTER THORNBURY.
Tales for the Marines.

BY T. ADOLPHUS TROLLOPE.
Diamond Cut Diamond.

BY ANTHONY TROLLOPE.
The Way We Live Now.
The American Senator.

BY MARK TWAIN.
Tom Sawyer.
An Idle Excursion.
A Pleasure Trip on the Continent
of Europe.

BY SARAH TYTLER.
What She Came Through.

BY LADY WOOD.
Sabina.

BY EDMUND YATES.
Castaway.
The Forlorn Hope.
Land at Last.

ANONYMOUS
Paul Ferroll.
Why Paul Ferroll Killed his Wife.

Fcap. 8vo, picture covers, 1s. each.
Jeff Briggs's Love Story. By BRET
HARTE.
The Twins of Table Mountain. By
BRET HARTE.
Mrs. Gainsborough's Diamonds. By
JULIAN HAWTHORNE.
Kathleen Mavourneen. By Author
of "That Lass o' Lowrie's."
Lindsay's Luck. By the Author of
"That Lass o' Lowrie's."
Pretty Polly Pemberton. By the
Author of "That Lass o' Lowrie's."
Trooping with Crows. By Mrs.
PIRKIS.
The Professor's Wife. By LEONARD
GRAHAM.
A Double Bond. By LINDA VILLARI.
Esther's Glove. By R. E. FRANCILLON.
The Garden that Paid the Rent.
By TOM JERROLD.